A gift

neigh...

£4.5

14 4 23

A TINY FEELING OF FEAR

ALSO BY THIS AUTHOR

THE RADIO

THE PAGE

BROKEN BRANCHES

A TINY FEELING OF FEAR

M. JONATHAN LEE

This paperback edition published | 2017

First published | 2015
2 3 4 5 6 7 8 9

Hideaway Fall publishing
BBIC S75 1JL UK
www.hideawayfall.com

ISBN | 978-0-9954923-2-5
Copyright © M Jonathan Lee 2015

A catalogue copy of this book is available from the British Library.

Set in Century Schoolbook MT

Lyrics reproduced by kind permission of Jimmy Stadt courtesy of Polar Bear Club © Bridge Nine Records 2009 and © Rise Records 2013. Lyrics by Conor Oberst courtesy of Bright Eyes © Saddle Creek Records / Sony Publishing 2002 Original art by Terry Brookes | 2015

Printed and bound by Charlesworth Press | 2017
Visit www.jonathanleeauthor.com | www.hideawayfall.com

For Annabel

Who gave me the courage to write this novel

"And you won't know if you believe
In something more than the belief.
There's no belief in simply being.

Been killing me for weeks
A garden weed that cracks concrete.
It hasn't been fair for so long
Growing up isn't moving on."

- Jimmy Stadt

"The future's got me worried such awful thoughts
My head's a carousel of pictures.
The spinning never stops
I just want someone to walk in front
And I'll follow the leader."

- Conor Oberst

chapter one

Firstly, I'd just like to thank each and every one of you for attending today. It is much appreciated.

Before we begin, I'd like to introduce myself.

Or at least one of myself.

My name is Andrew Walker.

So, why are we here? Actually, wait a minute. This isn't one of those questions about the earth or the sun or creation or humankind. I'm not asking the kind of question that our forefathers have struggled with century after century, the story of Christ or how many stars are in the galaxy or whether there is life on other planets. No, it's a little closer to home. Well, much closer, in fact. I'm talking about you and me. Me and you. Why are we here?

I can answer half of that question. The reason I am here. That's the easy bit. I'm here to tell you what it's like to be me.

I want to tell you everything because I've never told anyone my secrets before. I'm hoping that being honest with you may just save my life. And perhaps yours. Also, I can't think of anywhere else to turn.

My everyday experiences are mundane. I get up each morning and drive to work. I drive home each evening. I have my weekends off. I eat. I breathe. I sleep (sometimes). However, the other one of me is far more complicated. He follows me everywhere I go. He lives inside of me, you see. He causes feelings so strong that I truly feel they will burst out from within and devour me on the spot. His power is so, that I feel if you looked carefully you could see visible dents appearing in my chest from his continuous internal pounding.

So there you go. I've answered half of the question, the bit about why I am here. The other part is more difficult. The part about why you are here. I can't help you with this question. You are the only one who knows. For whatever reason, you've decided to open my story and have a look inside. And now you've found the opening page interesting enough to read to here.

And now to here.

And now to here.

And now to here.

(I realise that if the above pattern continues, it's unlikely we'll go on much further together, so I'll stop there.)

Anyway, our paths have now crossed. We are now intrinsically linked. And we have a journey to take together. I am so pleased that you've chosen to join me. I hope you will listen and promise, at least at this stage, to try not to judge me. Oh, and try to keep up. In return, I promise to be truthful throughout and tell you absolutely everything. I am hoping that by sharing this there is some salvation for me.

I hope that I live until I have finished my story.

That you don't find me dead a few chapters in (y'know, just as the story is getting going).

This is my story.

So come on, or you'll miss the start.

chapter two

A blackbird lives at the end of my garden. When I say the end of my garden, I expect you imagine a long, luscious green lawn expanding far and wide into the distance. I expect you imagine two rows of perfectly squared conifers protecting the flowerbeds around the perimeter of the lawn. A row of trees on either side. At the end of the garden, a secure wooden fence that stretches the width of the garden. Clematis and wisteria that weave their way along the fence, in and out of the wooden trellis that secures them, like a giant snakes and ladders board. There is perhaps a stone birdbath at the end of the garden, where the birds congregate and chatter excitedly as they tuck into the fat balls hanging sporadically from the various fruit trees.

The view from my window isn't like this at all. My kitchen window does look out onto a wooden fence; however, mine stretches for twelve feet, meeting two eight-foot high red-brick walls which line up in parallel on either side. The walls look tired and have long since spat out the cement that once kept the bricks together. I sometimes wonder how they are still standing. There is a path which leads to a small gate at the end. The path is pretty much useless now; it used to separate two neat rectangles of lawn, but I long since let the grass die. In all honesty, I couldn't be bothered to tend to it. Instead now on the right-hand side is a patch of mud which swallows up the numerous cigarette butts I flick onto it from the back door.

A few years ago (on a day when momentarily I felt inspired) I put pebbles down on the left side to tidy the place up. I even planted a few palm-like plants to add some colour and break up the numerous grey and copper-coloured stones. The plants didn't survive the winter. If you look carefully, you can see a couple of brown stalks still poking through. The garden is no more than twenty feet long. From here you get a good view of the blackbird.

It would be poetic to say that the blackbird were instead a raven and my life had striking similarities to Edgar Allan Poe's poem. That would in many ways be far more fitting, his presence an eerie reminder of the darkness that life brings. Evermore. For this to happen, the blackbird would have to put on a lot of weight. Also, he would have to do something about his brightly coloured beak. It's a real giveaway that would need a swift coat of black paint.

He visits me most days, sitting on the fence and staring directly at me. I am not sure of the purpose of his visits. It's certainly not food he is after. Nothing lives in my back garden. Even the worms would turn their noses up (this is probably anatomically incorrect) at this place. I am not sure what nutritional value discarded tobacco would have anyway. I think the bird arrives to taunt me. He looks into the window, reminding me of the life I lead within. His feathers are always glossy and sheen. Like he has somehow prepared himself in advance before he visits. He opens his wide orangey-yellow beak and sings to me. I get the impression he is happy; his

5

black beady eye shines as he chirps his melodies. His left eye is ringed in yellow, a halo that makes the marble-like beauty of his eye stand out further. His right eye, which he rarely shows, is different. No ring surrounds it, just more black feathers. I've not been able to see it up close, but I suspect this eye is blind. It is partially covered by a handful of feathers, its black gloss more charcoal. Not dissimilar to my pebbles. He sits in a way that ensures this eye is not on view.

He seems to speak directly to me. He ignores his disability and sings his perfect song as I stare back at him through the window. I am transfixed, listening to each note. I feel he is coaxing me to move on, to ignore my internal affliction. To overpower the feelings I suffer from and to never give up. Our eyes remain locked on one another for as long as the day allows before I have to get ready for work.

He only appears in the morning. Sometimes when I return home from work, exhausted from another day pretending to be someone else, I wish he were there to sing his song of hope. To coax me into believing that it is worth living through another evening.

chapter three

I have to tell you that today is not a good day. Not at all. Today is what I term a Car Day™.

In the life that I lead, there are only ever three types of days.

As I share my story with you, you will find that I don't like waking on any day of my life, but today is the worst by far. Perhaps it's better if I explain. Let me tell you about the three types of days. For ease, I've listed them below in order of the most preferable day to wake up to.

The Nothing Day™

The Nothing Day™ begins with nothing. It begins with waking prior to the alarm I have set on my phone chirping into life. My phone is the type that allows me to store numerous alarms for different days. It also allows me to name the alarms. I work unusual hours at the office. Some days I am required to be in very early, others I have to work very late. So, for early-morning starts around five thirty, my alarm is called: 'Okay, so it's early – now get on with it.' Conversely, on my later days when I can wake closer to eight, my alarm is called: 'A regular time to wake. You're just like everyone else now.' On weekends, my alarm is set for around eleven. This one is called: 'You've crawled your way through another week. Great.'

Each alarm has its own tone. I searched through all the available tones and set an appropriate one for each day. The early start has a painfully jaunty tune which demands that I switch it off immediately and get up. The weekend tone is more mournful. It's rare that I ever hear this one. I've been woken by the passenger that lives inside me long before eleven. Anyway, back to The Nothing Day™.

The Nothing Day™ begins with nothing.

The day begins with my eyes opening slowly, and a slight awareness of my surroundings. I wonder whether this is how everyone else feels when they wake. I lie for a second and listen. The next thing I do is carry out a full body scan. This may seem a strange thing to say. I don't know, perhaps you do it too. The best way to describe this is that it's almost like the scan you see in hospitals on TV, where a person is fed into a giant machine which develops a picture of their insides. This is what I do. Mentally, I scan every part of my body from my toes to the end of my fingers to ensure that everything feels alright. It's similar to when you take your car for a service. The only difference is that I check over every part of me.

If I am fortunate, I feel nothing. A feeling that nothing is obviously wrong and I am allowed to just lie for a while, listening to my own breathing. Feeling the warmth under the duvet. Feeling my head completely encapsulated by the cotton that surrounds the memory foam pillows which are moulded to the shape of my head.

That is not to say that The Nothing Day™ cannot change into either of the other days at any time. However, when it does arrive, for once I feel normal. If normal is feeling nothing.

The Panic Day™

In the interests of total honesty (which is, of course, the point of sharing this with you), I have to say that The Panic Day™ is the day that I experience most often. I've not yet recorded and mapped out the exact statistics, but I know that this day accounts for more than half – maybe two-thirds – of my waking moments.

The composition of The Panic Day™ is defined by three distinct experiences that occur concurrently. They are:

Paranoia: A feeling of total panic about what the entire world thinks of me. Who I am. How I look. Whether I am a good person. Whether anyone likes me. The mistakes I have made. The mistakes I am probably still making. The list is endless. The paranoia gets so strong that I panic about everything I have ever done in my life.

Butterflies: An uncompromising feeling in my chest. This is not the type of excited flutter that you may get before a special occasion or nervousness before an interview. This is pure darkness. Massive grey steel wings thrashing. Enormous bodies covered in dark, coarse hair bombarding me from the inside. Desperate to escape. The force is such that at times my hands and arms physically shake.

Unrelenting heartbeat: Put simply, my heart beats at an alarming rate. It contracts and expands so violently that I fear it may become detached from the arteries and veins that feed it. Its pulsating speed sometimes physically hurts.

As soon as my eyes open on a Panic Day™, I am greeted by giant dark butterflies, an assiduous heart and utter paranoia. I have to leave my bed immediately and begin my day. Distraction is the only tonic. I do everything at lightning speed. Shower, teeth brushed, dressed, out. I cannot afford to stop or be alone with my thoughts for even a moment. If I do, it will overpower me.

This is how I live.

So as to avoid repetition, you must assume that unless I tell you differently this is how I feel.

At least half of the time.

The Car Day™

Instead of generically explaining this, I'll tell you about this morning.

After all, fundamentally all Car Days™ are the same.

The Car Day™ is the worst way that any human day could begin. (I have to clarify that I don't believe for a moment that nobody else has these days. In fact, I suspect that, sadly, numerous people scattered through any nation, any creed, open their eyes to find days like this grimly waiting for them.)

The Car Day™ is worse than bleak. Today begins with the usual feeling of dark foreboding. The alarm springs into life and cuts like a knife through the sleep which is protecting me. Indeed, the alarm slashes and rips into my sleep, frantically butchering the peace that I am at that moment feeling. Once awake, I immediately feel the weight. It feels like my duvet has been replaced by a heavy metallic sheet, its weight pushing me deeper into the mattress, which strains from the pressure exerted from above. My neck muscles have tightened and the air above me is being powerfully sucked toward the carpet, forcing my head into the hardness of the pillow. An invisible hand holds my forehead, stopping me moving. It is painful around my shoulders; in my chest; in my head. My brain expands and pushes outwards until it stops, trapped by my skull, which causes a deep, painful numbness all around my head.

I reach over, pushing away the weight of the duvet, and switch off the alarm. And then I lie breathlessly staring at the ceiling. The effort to move my covers has drained all my energy. Butterflies and heartbeats are amplified one hundred times more than at any other time. They beat the same rhythm.

I am useless.

I am useless.

I am useless.

I climb from my bed, a deep fog covering the area around me. The light switch is almost indistinguishable from the wall. It moves in the fuzziness; little silvery dots appear and then disappear before my eyes, giving the appearance that the switch is moving around the wall. I reach the switch by indiscriminately banging against the wall with the ball of my hand. The bathroom light comes on, momentarily blinding me.

Although crystal water falls from the shower, it doesn't feel like it's cleaning me. The opposite, in fact. The water falls heavily, hitting my shoulders, forcing me to hold up my hand to deflect it. The pressure seems too much. I clean myself, feeling that the water is a thick grey sludge which is simply coating me in darkness.

I leave the shower and collect my towel.

It is an effort to even dry myself.

It is pointless.

Just like my life.

I drag clothing from the wardrobe, sending the hangers clattering against the wooden frame at the back. Hangers holding freshly ironed clothes drop to the floor. I don't care. They are left there. I button my shirt around my hideous body and pull on my trousers. I need to get out of the house.

I get into my car, and drive the few miles through the streets and then countryside toward the motorway. It is busy on the motorway and I weave in and out of traffic toward work. The journey usually takes around an hour.

Such is the weight of my thoughts that the car itself seems to perform sluggishly. My reactions are slowed and I get too close to the cars in front and alongside me. On a number of occasions I don't see the parade of brake lights until it is almost too late. My car stops short of attaching itself to the one in front.

But I don't care.

Truly, I don't.

This is not a flippant statement. I do not care.

Today is a Car Day™.

And I hope that this is the final Car Day™. The one that I have imagined. When the traffic separates and we are all travelling around the seventy-mile-an-hour speed limit. When we can see the open road ahead of us, there will be a manoeuvre. A brief manoeuvre just ahead of me that causes me to swerve. And as I do, I will strategically lose control of my car. I will take my hands from the wheel and place them on my knees. My car will screech across the motorway, inexplicably missing all other traffic, and leave the road. It will cross the hard shoulder and hit the crash barrier at the very point that one crash barrier finishes and the next begins. In that tiny gap. Then I will unfasten my seatbelt and my body will be thrown around the car as it twists and spins in the air. And the last thing I will feel, ever, will be the impact.

I hope that today is that Car Day™.

The one I've been waiting for.

For so long.

chapter four

As usual the journey into work passes without incident. I pull into the vast car park outside my office and switch off the engine. The company I work for is called PaigeAlex and we provide 'financial solutions'. My office is situated on a business park. I think it was one of the first ever designed. In the middle sits the car park, surrounded by low-rise office blocks built in bland yellow or red brick. They are all built in varying heights and look like a graphic equaliser frozen in time. Whose bright idea it was to face half of the office windows directly onto parked cars, I will never know. I check the time. Seven minutes until work officially begins. I sit in silence, watching the digital clock change until there is one solitary minute left. I pull the door handle and leave the car and cross the car park to the entrance of my building.

As I reach the door, I pause and look down at my shoes. They really could do with a shine. They're not dirty, just...well, dusty looking. I punch the code into the keypad to allow the magnetic door lock to open. I push the heavy door frame and straighten my tie. Today, I am wearing my Mr Grumpy tie. It's dark blue, and features a rectangular cartoon character at the bottom where it meets my belt. He has an angry look on his face and above him a white speech bubble states "I hate Mondays!" I can't remember where I got it. Of course, I hate it but I wear it to be ironic. I don't think my colleagues share the joke which amuses me all the more. I take a deep breath and walk down the corridor and up the stairs. My department is situated in a part of the office building you wouldn't visit unless you had to. We are at the end of a long corridor that leads to nowhere except for us. Most of the other departments in the company I work for are wide open areas where staff sit facing one another in banks of six desks. There are generally two or three doors which lead to other parts of the building. Staff walk through en route to meetings in other parts of the building. Not my department.

I have no choice but to come here. Each day I resolve to make the best of it. After all, I have to spend a good proportion of my time here. I carefully control what I tell my colleagues about my life away from the office. They only need know what I tell them. I fix my smile and push open the door. Two of the staff look up from their computer monitors and smile.

"Morning, Andrew."

"Good morning!" I stretch out the first word, similar to a TV quiz show host.

"You okay?" says Jacob.

"Absolutely awesome," I sing.

"Nice one," he says, "see you've got your tie on."

"Certainly have," I say.

He smiles and shakes his head slowly.

I walk down the length of the small office, passing each member of staff. Their desks all face toward the centre of the room and create the walkway I have to travel down to get to my desk. The room is painted a drab grey colour. Pictures of whales leaving the ocean and eagles in full flight surround us mounted in clip frames. Beneath them are words such as 'BELIEVE' and 'MOTIVATION' and 'ACHIEVE'. I think their purpose is to get the best from the staff. By comparing us to animals. Their only achievement is to break the bland monotony of the walls. I repeat my greeting to the other staff members and receive a collection of disinterested grunts that are just on the cusp of hello. One doesn't even look up. I notice he's clutching a stapler tightly.

I reach my desk, sit down and push the silver button on my computer to bring it to life. "Good weekend, Clare?" I say to the girl who sits directly opposite me.

She cranes her neck around her computer monitor to see me. "Yeah, thanks." She immediately moves back out of sight.

I pull up my socks. "Anything of interest happen?"

"No, not really. You?"

Her body language suggests she wants this conversation over with. I can also tell that she isn't vaguely interested in my response. A deep crimson rash begins to appear on her neck.

"Really, really good, thanks. Excellent."

She nods and conceals her face behind her monitor again. "Right!" she says, stretching out her arms and wiggling her fingers. She then leans in a little too close to the screen. It is obvious that she wants to give me the impression that she has something important to deal with. My computer makes a whirring noise, sounding like it is using every part of its processing power to start up. As I wait for it to lurch into life, I look around the office. You have never seen such a collection of unusual people. I don't just mean physically either.

There are six of us in total. We form the Compliance Department. Our role is to ensure that the advice that the salespeople at our company give to clients is correct. We are there to ensure that our sales force stick to the industry rules and don't provide advice that is unsuitable. We are effectively the police of the company. We find and expose any rogue staff within the company. We check everything. We comment on everything. We are the eyes and ears of the industry regulator. We constantly tell our salespeople that their recommendations to clients are wrong. We are the most reviled staff in the company. It is no wonder that we are placed in a room with only one exit and entrance – the only room in the entire building in which should a fire break out we would all likely perish. I've been here nine years. My job is to investigate complaints made by clients.

You have to be a certain type of person to work in the Compliance Department. There is just something about us. I don't know what it is. I hate to use the word odd, but it is fitting. Looking around this room, I see there is no better word to describe the people. Even if one or two of them could get away with not looking quite so odd, as soon as they opened their mouths, you would agree. Let me tell you a little more about them. From where I am sitting, to my left is Elaine.

Elaine

Ah, Elaine. Where do I start? The best way to describe Elaine is to tell you to imagine a person made from Play-Doh. Imagine the type of person made by a three year old. A greedy three year old. Elaine is a huge oval, with an equally fat head and four short limbs stuck to the sides. Her face is permanently red; her forehead and cheeks damp from sweat. Her black hair sits on top unbrushed, like an old Russian fur hat. Her attitude differs daily, though it's locked in a position between irritable and rude. She is permanently dieting and it's fair to say that she has consistently lost the battle in all the time I have known her. She is about fifteen years older than me; the only one here who is. She has also been here the longest. I come a close second. She's married with no kids. From time to time she can be very nice. Perhaps twice a year. I suspect it's her self-esteem that makes her this way.

Martin

Martin sits to Elaine's left. Two seats down from me. Martin resembles in every way the final lump of Play-Doh cleared away at the end of the day. The huge greyish-brown lump made up of all the remnants of smaller, discarded pieces. His brown hair is unwashed and his beard untrimmed, both of which collect little white pieces which crumble from his scalp and gather on his shoulders. Due to the mass of hair, it is difficult to see where

Martin's head finishes and his body begins. He wears thick glasses and trousers that are too small for him. I know this because when he stands the material is concertinaed around his groin and creates two fan-like shapes, one on each leg. You could easily be convinced that Martin knows everything about every single subject. I have never known him accept that he is wrong. He has an amazing knack of answering a question incorrectly and when challenged skilfully suggesting he was saying the opposite all along. He has an annoying obsession with stationery and labels every single item with his initials in white correction fluid.

Clare

Clare is tall and thin with no discerning change of shape from her shoulders to her feet. A mess of ginger curls sits on top of her head, which she attempts to control with a varying selection of hair grips, slides and headbands. None seem to work. She is married with two children and everything in the world worries her to the point of tears. I cannot remember ever hearing her laugh. She resembles a breadstick. On fire.

Jess

Jess sits next to Clare and is the newest member of the 'team', having joined a few years ago. I firmly believe that the word androgynous was coined in direct consultation with her. Her

19

dark hair is cropped short and she wears rectangular gold glasses. Her right ear is pierced in eight places. There are no piercings in her left ear, which for some reason bothers me. Her expression rarely changes from a poisonous look that warns off anyone from speaking to her. She only ever speaks when a direct question is asked of her and appears to hate everyone. I once carried out a survey of the words she spoke in a week: twelve. That's fewer than three a day. Once, I saw the outline of a large tattoo on her back through her white and grey cotton shirt. It looked like the wings of a dragon or griffin or something similar. I suspect she is an entirely different person outside work. She wears a tie. Go figure.

Jacob

Jacob is perhaps the only person in the department I have anything at all in common with. He is the nicest, most boring person I have ever met. He is always friendly, always helpful and never unkind. Our commonalties are generally linked to work (though he does read true crime books) and I know little of his life outside work. I do know he is married and has a dog. Jacob is the one who suggests departmental meals and get-togethers outside work. The ones that nobody ever attends. He favours using twenty words where one will do. If you were to ask him how his Christmas was, he would begin the story in October. You know the type.

(And lastly, there's me. As you know, it's going to take more than a few paragraphs to describe me.)

There's a strange dynamic in the department. Regardless of whether we have absolutely nothing in common, from a working perspective we all pretty much get on. As far as is possible anyway. As a team we are fiercely loyal and defend one other against anybody else within the company. Due to the nature of our work, criticism from staff and clients is a regular occurrence. From time to time (Jess excluded) we may take a few minutes out and chat. Usually about work stuff.

I find it genuinely fascinating that this disparate bunch of people followed their own paths through life and they all somehow led to this room. Seven hours a day. Five days a week. Every week.

I know that I cannot pick whom I work with. But despite their unusual quirks, I suppose my colleagues could have been much worse. I sometimes wonder what they would say if they were describing me.

My phone rings and distracts me from my departmental analysis.

"Hello?" I say.

"Hi, Andrew. I've Mr Stickles on for you?"

Internally, I sigh. Then I let it out.

"Go on then."

"Thank you."

I pause.

"Good morning, Mr Stickles," I say, adopting a chirpy tone.

"Andrew, good morning."

"How are you?" I sound interested. "Good weekend?"

"Very nice, thank you."

"Good."

The pleasantries are out of the way. It is clear that neither of us really cares how good the other's weekend was. Mr Stickles then spends the next ten minutes explaining the reason for his call. I get the chance to interject with one- or two-word sentences every few minutes. He isn't happy and this is no surprise. By definition the people who ring this department, ring me, are unhappy. This is my job. I have no choice but to try to make the best of it. Appear happy, appear interested.

Mr Stickles would have expected more from a firm like PaigeAlex. The first disappointment, he explains, was that his postcode was incorrect on the recent letter he was sent. What should have been an 'R' was an 'E'. He continues to explain that his highly confidential post could have been read by a complete stranger. Imagine that. He tells me that he couldn't 'begin to think' what would have happened with his financial data should it have got 'in to the wrong hands'.

I want to tell him that it was unlikely the letter would have been delivered elsewhere due to the fact that every other part of the address was correct, as was his name.

I also want to tell him that if it had been delivered to a stranger, it was even more unlikely that the recipient would have been vaguely interested. Much less 'steal his identity', as Mr Stickles contends.

Instead, I apologise.

I spend most of my working life apologising.

"Very well," he says. "And the second thing, well, is a little more serious."

"Oh dear."

"This invoice your company has sent to me."

"Right. Okay. Er, sorry, Mr Stickles, but I can't help with that –"

"Excuse me?"

"You see, I don't actually raise the invoices. It'll have been raised by whoever gives you financial advice."

"I don't care about that."

"Pardo–"

"I don't care who raised it. You all work for the same company so I want you to help me."

"Right. Well, I can try, but I'm–"

He speaks over me and tells me that I will sort his problem. He speaks with the tone of an old schoolmaster. I take on the role of scolded pupil. I have no choice. It is my job. Although I have no knowledge or authority to deal with this matter, I decide it's more professional to hear him out and pass on any message to the relevant person. Whilst he tells me that he has been a client for more than thirty years, I'm clicking through folders on the screen in an attempt to get to a copy of the invoice.

"Yes, the invoice, Andrew. Dated twelfth of December 2014."

I'm still clicking. It's not in the folder it should be in.

"You do know the one I mean, don't you, Andrew? Or are you going to tell me that you can't access that information for me either?"

"No, it's not a problem. I have the invoice here."

"Thank God," he says sarcastically.

I've found it. The computer seems to purposefully slow down whilst opening the file. The green hard-drive light winks at me. I can see a ghost of the invoice on the screen, but not enough to read it.

"Just a minute," I say, stretching the words out whilst the green light continues to mock me. I sit upright and try to clear the thought of kicking Mr Stickles to death from my mind. I hear him tut down the phone and decide to fill the silence.

"So, what can I help you with?"

"At last. Andrew, it's the quantum."

"Okay..."

The computer makes a groaning sound, like a wounded animal taking its final breath, then suddenly bursts back to life. The green light goes out and a copy of the invoice appears on the screen.

"It is not what I expected, Andrew. I'm very disappointed."

"Let's have a look then," I say.

This is all part of a game and is completely outside the remit of my work. I know it and the client knows it. These types of calls come weekly.

I scan the invoice on the screen and make positive sounds

24

like 'ah-ha' and 'right' down the phone.

"Okay," I say with finality, "I've had a look at the invoice, Mr Stickles. Is there anything in particular that causes an issue?"

The notes on the screen suggest that he has been charged exactly what he expected and exactly what he agreed to. I click and open another document. I wait for the client to sigh.

He sighs.

"It's the overall cost," he says. "I just didn't expect it to be that high."

I want to say that he knew full well what the cost would be.

I want to tell him that he is simply trying it on.

I want to tell him that I can see through his plan. That his little ruse to save money is shockingly transparent.

I want to tell him that I know the reason he is far richer than I will ever be.

I want to tell him that I hate his duplicitous nature and his trample-over-everybody-to-benefit-himself attitude.

I want to ask him how he sleeps at night.

I want to tell him that I know where he lives.

How remote it is.

I don't.

Instead, I tell him we have a document on file signed by him agreeing the overall cost. I have to remain calm, so I say, "Oh right. I think that if you look at the original advice given, you can see it states the costs."

"I'm sure it does, Andrew..."

Yes. It. Does.

25

"…but I'm still not happy."

"Right," I say, "it's just –"

"I don't really want to put in a complaint…"

He knows the exact way we work. That we have to report every single complaint to our regulatory body. That too many complaints could ultimately cause us to be closed down.

"No," I say.

He pauses for a length of time that forces me to speak again.

"What would you like me to do?"

"Well, Andrew," he begins, his schoolmaster tone now replaced by that of a sly politician soliciting a favour, "before I complain, I'd like you to let me know how much you can reduce it by."

I'm cornered. I want to scream down the telephone how unfair this is. How he should pay what he agreed. But I can't. That isn't my job. Instead, I shuffle around in my drawer and find a recent memo near the top of a pile of papers. I skim-read it and remind myself that it gives us the flexibility to reduce invoices by up to ten per cent in order to ward off complaints.

"I tell you what," I say, "why don't we discount it by, say, five per cent?"

This is my last desperate attempt to right this miscarriage of justice.

"Andrew, I have to say I find that a little derisory."

I feel like smashing my telephone handset repeatedly into the desk until the little wires and speakers are showing.

"Well, how about ten per cent, on the basis that you are such a good client." This is perhaps the most disingenuous thing I've said this year. It brings bile to my throat.

"That seems very fair, Andrew. Thank you." There is no gratitude in his voice. If anything, silent satisfaction.

"No problem," I lie.

"Perhaps you can raise a credit note?" It's not a question.

"I will. I'll get it sorted for you and send it through."

"Good," he says and the phone goes dead.

This is what I do when I'm not at home.

This is how I spend more than two hundred and forty days a year.

This is my work.

This is my life.

chapter five

I've just realised that in my eagerness to tell you my story,
I've omitted to really tell you anything about me. You will have
picked up one or two of my traits. Foibles, if you will. During our
journey you will eventually learn everything about me. That's
really the main reason that I'm writing this. I've kept this to
myself for too long. The first step to salvation, apparently, is to
admit you have a problem. I have read this online and it seems
to apply to whatever issue you may have in your life. Alcohol
or gambling or drugs or whatever. This book is my admission
that I have a problem. However, I am going one step further.
I'm laying everything bare in the hope that the following things
happen:

Somebody out there feels the same, reads this and understands
they're not alone;

By sharing this, I can offload the feelings that live inside me;

My evenings are filled by something other than endless
blackness.

To get a fuller picture, I believe it is vital for you to know a
little about my physical being. You see, people tend to make
judgements about others simply by the way they look. Take, for

example, the strong, tanned, muscular man. The alpha male. The type who wears vests whatever the weather. The one who instantly removes his top and shoves it into the front of his jeans the moment the sun creeps out from behind the clouds. I find this look hugely off-putting. Unless abroad (and usually not even there), there is something inappropriate about entering a petrol station or corner shop topless. I have queued behind these types before, and watched the perspiration in their armpit hair glisten and then drip as they reach across the counter toward the Mars bars. I have often felt moved to remark about the fact they've left their sweat on the other confectionery, but I have kept my mouth shut. Probably for fear of reprisals.

Anyway, you would expect from looking at the alpha male that he is brimming with self-confidence. His caramel-coloured skin stretches to the limit to keep his perfect muscles contained. The blue snakes of pulsating veins work without respite to provide the blood his perfect body requires. His open display of masculinity screams self-satisfaction. I have never spent any time speaking to the alpha male, but my initial reaction would be that he is the confident, self-assured type. The perfectly airbrushed female model gives the same impression from within the creased pages of every glossy female monthly. The impression of being totally at one with who she is. And we, as humans, make immediate split-second judgements of who somebody is simply by how they look. We all do it. Every single one of us.

So why am I telling you this? Well, until now you have had

no idea what I look like. And I don't feel that I am being honest with you unless I share this with you. Then, right from the get-go, you have a picture of me. You can use this as the foundation for building the picture of the whole me. Everything else I share will be unrelated to my physical appearance. The rest of me is built from emotions, thoughts and fears that my physical being simply surrounds.

It only occurred to me to share this with you because I have a very painful spot on my lip. I've come to the mirror in my bedroom to investigate it further. I have brought a shot glass full of boiling water with me. In it is a sharp needle from an unused sewing kit my mother bought for me the Christmas before last. I have a vague recollection of mentioning to her that one of my shirt buttons was loose. I opened my present, faked excitement, and she stitched it back on there and then. She then passed the kit back to me and tapped my knee twice. I think it was her way of teaching me independence. Silently saying to me, "Sewing-wise, you're on your own now." I have also brought my nail scissors and a sharp kitchen knife. I think it's called a paring knife. I have removed my t-shirt just in case any liquid is discharged from the spot.

When I was younger I suffered a great deal from ingrowing toenails. I'm not sure why, but every six months my big toenail (usually on my right foot) would work its way inside the skin and within a day the surrounding area would be a bright crimson. A day later it would be painful to touch and the day after that it would be impossible to pull on my right shoe. It all seemed to happen so quickly. My father would 'operate' at that stage. This involved a cup of boiling water, tweezers and nail scissors. The operation was a straight cut from the top of the nail about five millimetres from where the nail entered the skin. My father would then cut vertically all the way down to the cuticle.

The pain was unimaginable.

In between cuts he would dab the area with cotton wool balls soaked in boiling water. Once he had finished his incision, the infected area would in effect be fully separated from the rest of the nail. A picket line between good and bad. Using the scissors, he would then flick at the underside of the 'bad' nail to detach it from the skin behind. Once he had successfully prised it away, it flapped aimlessly, the blood rising through the skin below. He would then use the boiling water to wipe away the blood, before grabbing the protruding nail with the tweezers. At that stage my insides would tighten and I would mentally shut off.

Then, in one sweet movement, he would pull the nail, ripping it from deep within the bed of skin into which it had forced itself. I was allowed to shout out in pain, but tears were unacceptable. Thick lemon pus would escape the cavity where my nail had once been and mix in with the blood. My father would smile as he held up the piece of nail in front of my face. I would like to point out that my father took no sadistic pleasure from the whole operation. Rather, I like to think his smile was

31

of simple satisfaction. This recurring experience taught me not so much about feeling pain, but about hiding its visibility from the outside world.

On closer inspection, the spot lives right on the border, halfway on my face and halfway on my lip. It sits proudly, pulling the skin around it tightly toward its yellow summit. The skin that surrounds it is sore to touch. I move my face from side to side as I deliberate the best angle to tackle it. And it is now that I study my face for a moment. I rarely look at myself in the mirror. Sure, I neaten my hair in the mornings, but I never take more than a fleeting glance at myself. If I had to summarise my looks in one word it would be 'unremarkable'.

About a year ago, after three or four consecutive Nothing Days™ I pondered joining an online dating community. I went through the registration process but never actually finished my submission. There were various multiple-choice questions which I could answer with ease (I preferred fish to meat, music to TV and smokers to non-smokers); however, it was crucial that I included at least fifty words to describe myself. This is where I came unstuck. I didn't get past the first sentence. It was impossible to describe myself honestly without using the word 'unremarkable'. Ultimately, following five or six reminder emails from the dating agency to update my submission, my account defaulted and closed.

The reflection staring out from the wall looks empty. My eyes are so dark that it is very difficult to make out the little black full stops in the centre. I lean in closer to make sure they are still there and I can just make them out. Tiny spots in huge pools of blackish-brown. My nose runs thinly down my face. It is slightly crooked from an incident with a cricket bat when I was younger. The crookedness would not be noticeable to anyone but me. My eyebrows are equally as dark as my eyes. They begin with a thick forest of hair near my temples, which would lead you to expect that they may form one long eyebrow. Happily, this is not the case – they thin as they approach my nose, where a clearing forms.

My hair is dark and I keep it cut short and neat. I have a parting, and I brush my fringe from right to left. I've had this style since school. It's not something I've ever thought to change. I am fortunate with facial hair. It grows sporadically in little clumps. Like the work of an over-zealous gardener a few weeks after he scatters his grass seeds. Such is the nature of my facial hair, I ensure that I shave it as soon as it appears. I have nothing to tell you about my mouth. It is a mouth. I open it wide and look inside. A shock of pain emanates from the spot. I note that my face doesn't show it. The bright spotlights above me pick up my yellowed teeth. I push out my tongue. It is covered in a dense yellow film. I scratch at it with my fingernail for a second and then put my tongue away, wiping my fingernail on my pyjama bottoms.

I look down at my chest. This too is wholly unremarkable. My skin is milky and pale. Thick brown hair creates a small bird nest for each of my nipples. If I could be bothered to, I am sure I could count the minimal hairs on the rest of my chest.

My eyes scan lower. I am not fat. I am not thin. The same goes for my arms. They are not muscular and they are not weedy. I have the most common waist size. My legs, my feet, the same.

I can always get footwear at the first time of asking.

The same goes for jeans, t-shirts, trousers.

My size is always in stock.

Although I want to tell you everything, it would be superfluous to the story to describe every single part of my body. I needn't go into detail, but that too is like the rest of me. Unremarkable. Let's just leave it at that.

This is me.

I have a face that you've never seen before.

There is absolutely nothing memorable about me.

I am the person you could sit opposite on the train every single day of your life and not remember.

The one who always got picked last for football at school.

This is me.

The invisible one.

chapter six

Today is Tuesday.

Tuesday is the one day of the week that I do something. If I had a diary, it would be the only day with an entry. My diary would be six-sevenths unused. This is why I don't have one. Tuesday means a visit to my parents' house. They have given up offering me an evening meal. I suppose too many rejections have led my mother to decide it is easier simply not to make the offer any more.

On the occasion of a birthday or the anniversary of a family death, she is momentarily inspired to ask the question again. "It would be nice if we could eat together next week, you know, because..." Her voice always trails off. We both know what she is alluding to and that she has no need to finish the sentence. I know the question is coming and I've prepared in advance for it. I have a good reason why it won't be possible. The hopeful look disappears just after her sentence leaves her lips.

I pull off the motorway and stay in the left-hand lane. The traffic slows as the slip road climbs to the roundabout at the top. My heart begins to quicken, a sign that I must prepare a little list of interesting things to say. I try to focus on what I have been doing since I saw them the week before. I know they'll ask me. It reduces my anxiety levels if I feel prepared prior to spending the next hour or so with them.

I wait patiently in the queue of traffic. Smoke swirls from

the exhaust of the car in front of me and reddens in the brake lights. It then disappears into the early-evening sky.

It is necessary for me to prepare myself for my parents. My mother can tell from my jaw whether I am alright. She says that I hold my mouth in a certain way when things are not alright. She is correct. Hidden inside my cheeks, I am crushing my bottom teeth with my top. So, most Tuesdays I tend to choose music that distracts me from my own thoughts. Songs with crashing drum beats and heavy guitars. Gigantic choruses that I can sing along to. My Tuesday routine is, in the very loosest sense, akin to a boxer's prior to a fight. The boxer hears his signature tune on the way to the ring, and it helps him focus on the main event. I take myself away from my own life to put on a show for my parents. This is where the similarities between the boxer and me end.

Today has been different, however. I'm not entirely sure why. Today, I have been lost in quiet contemplation. There has been no music at all on the way home. I've allowed the radio news channel to repeat over and over. I can't remember any of the news I've heard, and begin to panic that I won't be able to remember the list I've prepared. It consists of:

Work has been busy.

I watched a good documentary about the monarchy (this will appeal to my Mum).

How tired I am.

My car needs servicing (for my Dad. He likes cars).

The traffic lurches another car length forward again and I move in tandem. I have finally made the roundabout and the traffic immediately thins out. I make my way past red-brick semi-detached houses until I reach the traffic lights. I turn left, and then sharply left again onto the road where my parents live. On the corner is a small shop that has been there my whole life. Many years ago, I used to get up before six each morning and deliver newspapers around the surrounding streets. The lights from the shop are dim, lighting the puddles a bleak cream colour. My parents have always lived in the same house. It was the house that I was born in and will be the house that they die in. The house envelops every one of their memories and I suspect the walls still whisper past secrets to my parents each day. Painting the walls doesn't hide the memories.

The house is small but perfect. If you asked a child to draw a picture of a house, they would draw the one I grew up in. I push the gate open and walk along the straight path to the front door. The garden is simple but immaculate. The lawn is cut an inch high and tonight looks like slightly damp velvet in the fading light. I notice the curtains are closed. A warm light creeps around their perimeter from the window to my right. The lounge.

I needn't knock; my parents have told me that before. I recite the list in my mind again, pull down the handle, take a deep breath and step inside. A voice comes from upstairs:

"Is that you, Andrew?"

"Yes, Mum," I reply.

I'm aware she is pretending to be busy. We always do this ritual.

"I won't be a second," she calls.

My father appears from my right. "Andrew," he says, opening his arms.

My father and I have always been close. When I reached my late teens, I seem to remember we went through a stage of shaking hands when we met. It only took a handful of life-changing events and the handshakes were scrapped and we went back to hugging. He pulls me in, the sagging skin on his cheek momentarily touching mine. His hug suggests that he is ensuring that at least physically I am still a living, surviving human being. I feel his hands move into several different places on my back. When he is satisfied that it is me, he steps back slightly and smiles.

"How are you?" he asks. He speaks softly.

"Okay, thanks, Dad," I say, returning the smile.

He nods his head slightly. "Good, good, good." His voice trails off with each word.

My father is smaller than me. He seems to shrink each time I see him. He has a happy face; the plentiful lines from his eyes and mouth are witness to this. They suggest that he has spent a good number of years laughing. I am witness to this. His hair has all but left him now, just small grey tufts around his ears remain. He wears glasses with no frames, which perch at the end of his long, thin nose. The nose he kindly passed on to me. His pale eyes shine when he smiles. The rest of the time they remain a constant matt grey colour. In company, he smiles a lot, which charges the bulb behind his eyes. Alone, I suspect the light is all but extinguished.

The stare he has fixed on me is slightly off-putting, so I put my arm around his shoulder and rotate him slightly toward the lounge. I push open the glass door.

"Let's have a sit down, Dad."

"Yes," he says, "let's."

He motions with his hand to suggest that I can have the pick of any chair in the lounge. I sit in my usual seat. My father doesn't sit; instead, he offers me a drink. He goes through all the different possibilities (coffee, hot chocolate, juice) and, as always, I settle on tea.

"One sugar?" he asks as he leaves the room for the kitchen. I know he knows the answer. He asks the question every week. I consider pointing this out but instead bite my tongue.

"Yes, please," I reply.

I am alone in the lounge. I have spent a great many hours in this room over the last forty years. Although the lounge is supposed to be a room to relax in, this one has never felt that way. Through its various stages of décor and furniture it has never seemed to achieve its purpose: a room to 'lounge' in. Presently, it is decorated in a pale green that reminds me of guacamole. The carpet is a slightly lighter shade than the walls. I am sitting in a high-backed tan leather chair. The leather looks nearly new, though the chair is around twenty years old. Testament to a room that is rarely used. The chair feels cold through my shirt. To my right is a brown three-seater sofa. My mother will sit there shortly. An identical sofa is to my left. My father will sit there. My chair is positioned at the end and soon, as usual, I will feel like I am hosting a two-contestant quiz show. Directly opposite me, at the end of a long oak coffee table, is a television that sits on top of a highly polished dark-brown cabinet. An unused DVD player and modem are visible beneath the television. Green lights blink randomly at me while I wait.

"Andrew," my mother says, entering the room.

"Hi, Mum."

She leans into the chair, putting her arms around me as best she can. I lean forward slightly to assist and put an arm around her back. My hand brushes her bra strap through her chiffon blouse and I sharply move it, catching two or three vertebrae that stick out proudly. She kisses me on the cheek and squeezes me again. She releases me and sits in her seat. Perfume hangs heavily in the air.

"How are you?" she asks.

"I'm okay, thanks, Mum. Are you?"

"I'm really well," she says.

She looks tired. It's a look she's carried for at least ten years. She has styled her hair especially for my visit, as she always does. Instantly, I feel guilty. She has a pixie-style cut, her natural grey overpowered by years of light-brown dye. The corners of her blue eyes fall downward, giving the impression of permanent sadness. Her smile gives no indication of joy. She is just about to lie.

"I'm sorry I wasn't ready when you arrived. I was dealing with some paperwork."

I see no point in pointing out her lie. It is clear she was upstairs pasting on the thick foundation which covers her face. Checking herself in the mirror before I arrived. Applying the cerise lipstick to her thin lips. And, on this occasion, to the bite of her front teeth. Emptying the perfume.

"That's okay, Mum. Don't worry."

She smiles again and leans forward to take my hand.

"So what have you been up to?" she asks. Her eyes are wide. I get the feeling she has been waiting for this moment since this moment a week before. My heart jumps and I refer mentally to the list I prepared in the car.

"Wait," instructs my father, who appears with a tray in the doorway. "I want to hear too." My heart goes again. The pressure makes me feel sick.

My father places the tray on the coffee table and squeezes himself down the length of the table toward where I am sitting. His trousers gather against the table, displaying his bottle-green socks and almost translucent shins. He sits down and begins to pour the tea.

"I was just asking Andrew what he's been up to."

"Yes, dear, I heard."

He passes me my cup and sits eagerly on the edge of the sofa. "So, what have you been up to, son?"

"Well," I say. The list. The list. "Mainly working really."

"Is it busy at work?"

"Always is, Dad."

"I expect so. Well, I suppose that's a good thing," he says.

My mother reaches forward and collects her cup from the coffee table. My father had left the spoon in for her, as usual. I watch as she stirs her coffee three times clockwise and then removes the spoon. She taps it three times on the edge of the china, making a 'chink, chink, chink' sound, before replacing it on the tray. She cradles it in her hands and looks up at me.

"So, what's been happening, Andrew?"

I really don't want to talk about work, but realise that there is little else on my list. "Oh, the usual. Lots of work on, which is good. But tiring..."

My mother nods.

Half of my list is gone. My stomach lurches. I need to divert the conversation.

"So, what have you two been up to?"

"Well, we've been really busy, haven't we, Colin?"

"Certainly have," my father responds. There's a slight pause. I think my mother expected my father to expand further.

"Tell Andrew about seeing your sister on Sunday."

"We saw your Auntie Denise on Sunday," my father says, pulling his trousers back toward his socks.

"Oh, how is she?" I ask. I don't actually care, but questions such as these reduce the pressure on me.

"She's very well –"

"No, tell Andrew about what happened at her house."

My father looks at my mother blankly.

"You know, about what happened with the water."

"The water?"

"You know, Colin, the shower." Her tone has become impatient.

He looks at her quizzically.

"The shower, Colin. The water."

There is a short pause. I'm not sure whether I should interject. Suddenly, the blank look disappears and my father bursts into life. This happens a lot these days. It is almost as if a tiny person has awoken inside his head, climbed a staircase to his brain and whispered a gentle reminder into his ear.

"Oh, yes. The water," he says.

Internally, I breathe a sigh of relief. "So what happened?" I say, feigning interest.

"Your Auntie Denise had a flood. It came through the kitchen ceiling."

"No," says my mother, dissatisfied with the truncated story, "tell it properly, Colin."

"I did," he says. "She had a flood from the shower into the kitchen." His tone has also sharpened.

"Tell him about the tiles, Colin."

"What about them?"

She nods at him, trying to project telegraphically exactly what she wants him to say. He is not receiving.

"What?" he repeats, irritation in his voice. My chest tightens.

"About how the water was escaping down the back of those

expensive tiles she'd just had fitted."

"There," says my father, turning both his hands outward.

"Really?" I say.

"Yes," says my mother. "You know she had those expensive tiles fitted? Well, they weren't fitted properly and the water went down the back of them and, well, flooded the kitchen. Didn't it, Colin?"

"Well, it made a patch on the ceiling in the kitchen," my dad says.

"Oh, that's a pain," I say.

My father pours more tea and the conversation continues in the same vein. I learn that my mother and father have been to the garden centre twice that week (they had to return an 'unsuitable' trowel) and have also been for lunch with some old friends. I am appraised of the latest situation with their friends' children, who are around my age. I am told that one of them has moved to the city for a new job. The other has her hands full with three children under six and a husband who works all hours. Every Tuesday I am given an update about the children of whichever friends they have seen that week. I am always left with a feeling that they are doing better than I am. I wonder what my parents say when their friends ask about me. I wonder whether they lie to hide the embarrassment my nothing of a life must bring. I picture my mother between mouthfuls of dessert, saying how busy I am at work.

I am fortunate that my father (and my grandfather before him) has a love of clocks. From where I am sitting I can see three. In the corner is an old grandfather clock, dating back two or three hundred years. Two further clocks hang on the wall, their internal workings on view. I watch the second hand tick by as my mother tells me about a distant friend of hers learning she has lung cancer. I am suspicious that the story is pointedly directed at me and instantly I want a cigarette. I manage to interrupt and tell my mother about the documentary. She looks pleased. My father asks about my car and I tell him that it is booked in for a service. It occurs to me that I have covered the last item on my list, but my anxiety abates when I notice the hands on the grandfather clock. They tell me that exactly an hour has passed since I arrived, and although the wall clocks disagree, I edge forward in my chair and stretch.

"Well," I say, "I'd better be getting going."

"Already?" says my mum.

Now, my dad edges forward. Their eyes drill into my cheeks from either side.

"Yeah, I think so. It's been a long day and it's an early start tomorrow."

I push myself up using the arms of the chair. Again, my father follows suit.

"Are you sure you're alright, Andrew?" my mum says. I feel my father lightly hold the inside of my elbow.

"I'm fine, Mum," I say.

"If there's anything we can do to help out, Andrew..." says my dad.

"I'm fine, honestly. Just tired," I say.

My mother is looking directly at me. She seems to see straight through my words and deep inside me. From where I'm standing I can't see my father's face, but I can feel his concerned stare. A strained, almost tortured look. A look that tells me he would step into my shoes now to make everything better. Just say the word, Andrew.

I make my way to the front door. They both follow close behind. We hug and say our goodbyes. As my mother and I part, she stares at me again.

"Seriously," I say, "I'm just really tired."

She pushes my hair to the side and rests her hand softly against my cheek. She nods. "Okay."

I can tell neither believe me.

"Take care, son," my dad calls as he closes the door behind me.

The words cripple me. I swallow hard and make my way up the path to my car. I climb into the driver's seat, pull on my seatbelt and turn the key in the ignition. The car gently creeps forward and I turn to my right. My parents stand between the lounge curtains and the window. They are lit from behind. I can't make out their faces, but I see them wave slowly. I wave back, forcing a smile, until I get out of view.

And then the tears come.

The tears for what I have done to them.

For how my actions have turned them into the people they are today.

chapter seven

Whether I actually have depression or not is debatable.

I suppose in some ways this is the reason I am telling you all of this stuff about myself. I know you didn't even suggest for a moment that I may be suffering from this illness, and maybe it's my paranoia that has forced me to bring this up. However, if you are feeling honest, you may wish to share with me that thus far on our journey together you have suspected this. Your partner may have spotted you reading my story and asked what you were reading. You may have innocently turned to them and said something like, "It's a story about this man who is two different people in his home life and work life." Then you may have innocently added as a postscript, almost in a whisper, "I think he's got depression."

I want to tell you that it's okay if you did. I really don't mind. You haven't broken any confidences. In fact, if you know without question that I do have depression then it would be helpful if you got in contact and let me know. I can then get the help I need.

I've done a lot of research on the internet about how I feel. I've been warned against this by numerous sources. There is a growing trend of self-diagnosis, and by definition it's dangerous. Giving medically untrained hypochondriacs access to that type of information can only lead to trouble. You know the type: they go online because they have a small lump on the sole of a foot and within twenty minutes have diagnosed foot cancer. Their next search after that? Flowers and coffins, guaranteed. The actual diagnosis? Hard skin.

My situation is slightly different. I acknowledge that something isn't right. I am aware that during the night hands creep from the corners of my room, dragging a translucent grey sheet over my life whilst I sleep. Acceptance is the first step to solving my problems, so I'm told. I can't decide, though, whether the fears and anxious feelings coupled with overwhelming waves of desire to be dead are just normal. Just feelings that we all have.

I mean, do you ever feel like this?

The reason I don't know whether this is 'normal' (a most-hated term of mine, used here solely for colloquialism) is that nobody shares these feelings. In general, society induces us to conceal our deepest thoughts. This is another reason I am telling you this. I want to normalise it. I want to lead a huge parade of people who are totally open about those feelings. One by one, we can all stand up and tell the world the thoughts that circle and swoop around in our confused brains. However dark those thoughts may be. The mind is so powerful – it controls us all; but we focus on the physical instead. We daren't deal with our minds. Surely now, though, we have almost conquered the physical. There aren't many illnesses that we don't know how to treat. But the mind, oh no, we don't want to talk about that. And I don't know why.

Take the following examples. The only background you need

is that in both I am telephoning the office because I won't be working that day due to an overwhelming feeling of panic. It takes all my fortitude to even pick up the phone.

"Good morning, you're through to reception, how may I help you?"

I put on my croakiest, drowsiest, most fatigued voice. "Hi, Jo. It's Andrew."

"God, you sound awful. Are you okay?"

"Not really. Is Nick there?"

"One minute."

[Hold music.]

"Hi, Andrew. It's Nick."

"Hi, Nick." I pause breathlessly for effect.

"God, you sound terrible."

"Yeah, I'm not so good."

"You not coming in today, then?"

I cough. "No."

"Okay, well, let me know how you get on."

"I will."

"Get well soon, Andrew."

"Thanks."

Or try:

"Good morning, you're through to reception, how may I help you?"

"Hi, Jo. It's Andrew."

"Oh, hi, Andrew. You okay?"

"Not really, to be honest." My voice cracks. "Woke up feeling really, really panicky today."

"Oh no. I hate it when that happens. I was the same last week."

"Were you?" (It's not really a question, more a show of solidarity.) "Nightmare, isn't it? Is Nick there?"

"Yeah, sure. It'll pass soon, Andrew. You take care."

[Hold music.]

"Hi, Andrew. It's Nick."

"Hi, Nick. Sorry, I'm not going to be in today."

"Oh, right. Everything okay?"

"I've just woken up feeling really panicky. It's taken me ages to catch my breath to call you."

"Right. I can't say I know how you feel, because I don't, but my wife and daughter suffer terribly from anxiety."

"Do they?"

"Yeah, sadly – it's a nightmare at times." He pauses as if he's thinking. "Must be awful. Listen, see how you feel tomorrow and give me ring then, will you?"

"I will. Thanks."

"Take care, Andrew."

I saw a story on the news the week before last. It was about a local girl who went missing one Friday night. She was thirteen. The day after her disappearance, the whole of the local community turned out to try to find her. Organised troops trekked miles over the countryside, searching every inch of area. Closer to her home, people searched sheds, garages and other outbuildings. Posters were prepared and put up in windows everywhere. Groups huddled in the streets, holding steaming cups of tea, taking a brief rest before resuming their search. Neighbours met neighbours they had never spoken to before. Four days after she disappeared they found her. A few miles from home. Hanged inside a disused farm building.

The next day locals interviewed on the news said how much she'd be missed. How lovely she was. Numerous friends assembled to share their grief. To share their memories of her. Once again the locals gathered, this time outside her family home, and laid flowers. The grey-looking house on some ramshackle street was suddenly lit up by colour. Bouquet after bouquet arrived. The television crew filmed some of the cards. The messages all spoke of the girl, how much she was loved, how she'd be missed. That type of thing.

I couldn't hold back my anger. I found myself standing a few feet away from the television screen screaming at the people.

"Why didn't you tell her?"

"It's too late now!"

"Why couldn't you have shown this love before?"

I couldn't understand it.

I still can't.

What are we waiting for?

Why do we live in a time where we only say what we feel

when it's too late? We have evolved. We can split atoms and cure diseases and travel to other planets. Yet we can't say how we feel. We can't tell one another who we really are and be accepted for it.

I had to turn off the television.

I was worried I might put my fist straight through it.

chapter eight

The drive home from my parents is always the same. I know what to expect. I have a lit cigarette in my right hand at all times. I drive in silence, the thoughts of my past spinning around the boundaries of my mind like the horses on a merry-go-round. I have tried so many times to break the pattern but it really is impossible. I cannot be distracted from this repeated thought process. The guilt I feel every time I see them. The guilt that drives me to want to leave even before I arrive. That makes it impossible for me to relax around them. I wonder whether any other person has to prepare a list in advance of seeing their parents. A list simply to distract them from their own guilt. I wonder now if my parents are sitting at home in silence, on opposite sofas, just staring at one another.

To try to break the cycle, once or twice I telephoned them from the car to see whether everything was alright. This just confused them further. They couldn't understand my asking this question when I had only just left them. I suppose that I was really ringing to ask them the question literally: was everything alright? Had they forgiven me for what I had done?

I am more distracted than usual and nearly miss the final turn toward home. Well, I say home. I don't think that our definitions of home will be the same. In the interests of clarity, for me home is simply a synonym for house. Or dwelling. There is nothing homely about my house. I get no feeling of joy or satisfaction when I push open my front door. There is no welcoming smell or feeling of warmth. It is simply the place where I shelter from the weather outside. It is the place where I sleep. I have no emotional connection with it. That being said, I have decorated it to my taste. I have painted most of the rooms. I have lined some of the walls with bookshelves and put up pictures that I like. I have a matching kettle and toaster set. I even bought myself slippers. So you see, I have tried. It just hasn't worked.

My house is a shell for storing my things. A larger version of the brown cardboard box that a man fills on his retirement day at work with the few personal items that have been scattered around his desk for the last thirty years. A couple of out-of-date photos of his wife and kids. Maybe a few business cards and a handful of ties.

This is my home.

I put my things in it.

I sleep in it.

I shelter in it.

I feel nothing for it.

I'm still locked in thought when I pull into the space outside my house. I'm hungry and I have a sudden urge to cook fresh vegetables with fish. The house looks miserable. Dark and sullen. The curtains hang sadly at the lounge window. I have often thought about getting some of those plugs with timers that will switch on my lamps to greet my arrival home. From the outside, it would warm up the look of the house. It may even look inviting. At least then I wouldn't have to walk directly into the darkness when I arrive. I am sure I have added them to my list of things to do at the weekend before. I make a mental note that they would be a helpful addition to the household for nights like today, when walking into warmth could be all it takes to save me. I disregard the fact, for now, that the lights cannot possibly judge my mood in advance. I remain in the car, staring at nothing. This happens to me a lot. I find that my eyes fix on something in the distance and I just stare. It is only when my eyes begin to blur and sting that I even realise I am doing it. I rub my eyes with my shirt sleeve and notice that nearly five minutes have passed. I remove the car keys and collect my cigarettes from the passenger seat.

I see movement to my right; it's Stuart, a neighbour from across the road. He's waving to me. I am unsure how long he has been standing there repeating his arm movement from left to right like a human metronome. I wave back and pretend to look for something in the pocket in the door of the car. Without looking up, I can feel him approaching. The remaining light outside somehow gets dimmer, and then I hear a tap made with the knuckle of his first finger lightly against the glass. I look up, feigning surprise. He smiles. This is all I need.

I push open the car door, edging him back as I do so. I glance down and hope he doesn't see that the side pocket is completely empty.

"Hello, Andrew. Good day?" he says. Stuart is about my age but acts as if he is in his late fifties.

"Y'know," I say, "work…"

"We all have to do it!" He chuckles, as if accepting his fate far too easily. I am not sure what he does for a living, but it seems to involve wearing a suit, driving a Mondeo and being at home during the day quite a lot. I suspect it is something to do with property. I've never been inclined to ask him. His next sentence adds to my suspicion, however.

"They're talking about building more houses on the field at the bottom."

I close the car door and walk onto the pavement. He follows me waiting for a response.

"Oh," I say. I want to add the word 'really' and a question mark, but I can't bring myself to do it. I categorically don't care, and pretending I do is not being true to myself.

"Yes," he says. He draws a dramatic deep breath before continuing. "I saw some papers." He winks and taps his nose: a code.

I edge closer to my front door. He catches my eye, and I raise my eyebrows to appease him.

"Wouldn't be so good for you and me," he continues, his finger flipping between pointing at himself and then at me. For the first time in the half-light I notice his hands are green and there are small pieces of grass caught in his hair.

I get my key into the door.

"No," I say, trying not to be rude. Butterflies lurch up inside my chest. I need to get inside now. I push the door open, hoping it indicates to Stuart that I wish to get inside. He takes a step toward me.

"You noticed number thirty-eight's got a new Saab?" he says, nodding in the direction of the house he's just mentioned.

I haven't. I shake my head. My breathing quickens.

"Yep. Silver. It's spot-on. Must have had a pay rise," he adds.

"Oh, right," I say. I wonder what else I can do to show Stuart that I need to get inside. Now.

"Yep, one-five plate. Alloys. You'll have to have a look when he gets back."

I have known Stuart for years and I have nothing against him; I just don't want to be around him. My mistake was lending him a ladder a few summers ago. Sadly, he's never forgotten my act of kindness. I have no doubt it will live in his mind for the rest of time.

"Listen, mate" – I use the second word in an attempt to soften any rudeness that may have crept into my voice – "I've got a phone call to make, so I'm gonna have to go."

"No worries, Drew," he says. I have no idea when he decided to shorten my name.

I'm half inside.

"I know what it's like, Drew, getting in from work after a long day. You just want to get comfy and –"

"See you," I say.

"You will. Keep smiling, son."

I get inside and close the door.

I held it off just long enough.

I am instantly destroyed by its power. A bowling ball

launched from the darkness at the other end of the hall going straight through my ribcage – that is the best way I can describe the feeling. A full physical pain in my chest. I am winded. After the initial impact, the ball bursts inside me, releasing a million more butterflies. I stand motionless in the hall, unable to move, resting my hand against the wall to steady myself. I am barely inside the door.

My head and chest are suddenly blazing and sweat trickles down my neck. I claw at the buttons of my shirt, desperately unfastening them one by one. I remove one arm. I pull the other inside out. It catches on my watch, and the button pops off the cuff. I throw my shirt to the floor. There is a target painted on my chest. It is black around the perimeter. Inside it is a smaller white circle. In ever-decreasing circles there is white, then blue. Red. White. Finally, in the centre, the smallest circle is yellow. This is where the butterflies gather. All fighting for position in the smallest area, which is painted directly beneath my ribs. A few flutter around the larger circles, pushed back by the others, looking for a route back to the centre. I can hear their wings flapping inside me. I cannot move. I take exaggerated deep breaths, each one designed to suck the butterflies from position. It doesn't work; today they seem far more agitated.

This is one reason that I smoke. I know the risks of smoking. I have been told them so many times before. My dentist reminds me that I am damaging my gums and that I have a heightened risk of mouth cancer. My family and friends tell me that my lifespan is being shortened. My colleagues tell me that I should think about stopping. My doctor simply shakes his head. Jesus, even posters at bus shelters depict children looking sad because, before she died, their mother smoked. The cigarettes do seem to suffocate the butterflies, though. Nobody ever reminds the world of that. For the time I am smoking, I am sucking in a poisonous gas that even the butterflies cannot withstand, and for a moment they subside. Hiding away at the edges of the target, scattered in tiny groups. And their impact lessens.

I push myself back from the wall so the weight is evenly distributed on my feet and slip off my shoes. I walk through the darkness of the hall and flick on the light switch as I pass through the lounge toward the kitchen. I cannot tell whether it is actually me who is walking or whether I am being carried along by the butterflies. In the kitchen I reach into the cupboard above the kettle and grab an already opened packet of cigarettes. I put one in my mouth and light it. I unlock and push open the door which leads into the back garden and breathe in long and deep, imagining my lungs expanding as they are flooded by thick grey mist. I hold the smoke in for as long as I can and breathe out. For that moment, the butterflies retreat. I suck in again and make a slight noise of satisfaction when I exhale.

I continue the process, lighting another cigarette from the dying heat of the first and smoke it all the way to the bottom, knowing that the period of respite is now over. I feel slightly sick. I take one last draw and flick the cigarette into the darkness of the garden. It flies in a direct line and skids along the floor, spraying little orange sparks as it makes contact with the ground. As I close the door, the butterflies gather again and then swoop toward the bull's eye. I can't control them. They are now working in tandem with my brain.

Thoughts orbit around the inside of my mind at frightening speed. Information arrives and is processed in milliseconds. Always the same: logic, rationality and sanity are sieved out; only black, corrupt thoughts are allowed in.

Who am I?

What purpose do I serve?

Would anyone really care if I wasn't here?

Why do I have these dark feelings?

Why is every day a struggle?

Why do I have to suffer?

The thoughts gather pace, a hundred plates spinning together inside my mind. The butterflies join in, telling me I don't have to suffer any more. That it's okay: they can help me feel nothing ever again. They tell me that nobody would miss me. They encourage my brain to skew my perception further. The once-logical thoughts I had have now slipped from my mind, down my throat and into my chest, to be savagely fed on by the butterflies.

I slump onto the kitchen chair. I cannot let them win. Not again. I hold my head in my hands and rock forwards and backwards, squeezing my temples with my hands. I will not let this happen.

Suddenly, I stand. I must try to get on with the evening. I move over to the fridge to get something to eat. I open the door and am momentarily blinded by the bright light. I stare inside and cannot remember why I am there. A red glint catches my eye and I reach into the fridge, concluding that if I opened the door, I must have required something. I open the can of Coke and throw a mouthful down my neck, hoping to drown the butterflies. It doesn't work. I no longer feel hungry.

I move into the lounge and switch on a lamp before sinking onto the sofa. My brain continues to whir and the intensity grows in my chest. I reach for the remote control on the carpet beside me and press the red button. I'm cold and I pull a blanket from behind the sofa. The TV comes on. I recognise the newsreader, a black man with slightly greying hair. His mouth is moving but I can't hear him. I watch in silence for about twenty minutes, unable to take in anything he is saying. I can only hear the sound inside my head. A whooshing sound, like a flock of birds rising and swooping in unison.

My thoughts are now reaching a crescendo. The masses of them that I started with have made their way down an imaginary funnel in my mind. There are fewer to deal with now. They continue to rotate, one by one disappearing as my mind rejects them.

Until there is just one.

One conclusion.

chapter nine

I breathe deeply and push the office door open.

"Morning, everybody," I sing.

I am met by a very unusual sight. The path to my desk is blocked. Elaine and Martin have dragged their chairs into the walkway and are sitting directly opposite Jess. They are deep in conversation. On the periphery, Claire and Jacob have slid their chairs in closer to Jess. I can tell she isn't enjoying the invasion of her private space. The tension on her face suggests that they shouldn't move even an inch closer.

"Am I missing something?" I ask.

"Pull up a chair," Jacob says. "Big news."

I squeeze my stomach in as far as possible and shuffle behind the chairs. I slide my chair alongside Elaine's to join the group.

"So, have I missed much?"

All heads turn in my direction. Martin answers.

"You'll have not seen your emails yet –"

"Being three minutes late," snorts Elaine, tapping her watch. I notice that the fatness of her wrist has begun to swallow her thin silver watch. I ignore her comment.

"– but, it seems Alan is on his way," Martin continues.

Alan is my boss. Next week he will have been at the company for exactly thirty years. I have no idea how he has lasted this long; it seems he has spent the majority of his time at the company rebounding from one corporate disaster to another. Most of the projects he has managed have ended in abject failure, and after being switched from position to position around the company, he finally settled as manager of my department. His levels of incompetence have reached almost mythical status in company folklore.

Alan is one of the most affable people I have ever met. He is a true gentleman, chivalrous to the point of obsession. Each week, Alan brings in his wife's offerings of homemade flapjacks and buns. He gives the impression that they were surplus from the weekend's baking, though it is quite clear that they were specially made. I have already decided that, should my employment status ever come into doubt, I will spend each evening baking. It seems that flour, eggs and icing somehow make an individual unsackable in the eyes of his superiors. Alan is the first to offer help in any situation, either at work or otherwise. It is irrelevant that his help is generally of no use. I suspect it is for these reasons that his employment was not terminated twenty-nine years and eleven months ago.

Jacob has printed a copy of the email and he passes it to me. I scan through it. The business is to hold a small drinks party the following week over lunch. The company is not in a position to recruit someone full time to replace Alan. There will be an internal appointment from the existing staff in the department.

"Interesting stuff," I say.

"I like the wording." Martin reads from the email: "'Not in a position to recruit someone.'" He chuckles. "More like, nobody knows what he does all day!"

Clare giggles and then scans the room as if checking for bugs.

"I've emailed them," Jess says. "I don't want to do it."

She pushes her chair back slightly to indicate that she wants nothing further to do with the conversation. It is an overt way of asking everybody to leave her alone. To stop invading her space. Jacob and Clare don't take the hint. Jess tuts.

Everyone else is silent. I take this to mean that everybody else is interested in the role. As we haven't seen Alan in months and are already working together as a team to do his role, I suspect everybody would like a pay rise for effectively nothing.

"I want it," says Elaine aggressively. I imagine her spotting an enormous chocolate cake through a shop window and using the exact same words in the exact same way.

The first challenger has just stepped forward.

"I reckon you'll get it too," says Clare. "You've been here the next longest."

"I doubt very much it'll come down to just that," Martin says with authority. "It can't just be decided on how long you've been here. It's whether you're the best for the role. Simple as that."

"Well, would you do it?" snaps Jess.

"Yes, I most certainly would," he replies.

Challenger number two.

I feel the mood change very slightly. Elaine repositions herself in her chair, pushing her chest out and folding her arms. Martin leans back and looks around the room.

"I used to work in a company," begins Jacob. "It was a while ago now. When was it? It was about eight, no, nine years ago. It was a chemical production company. Well, I say production. It was more testing, I suppose."

Jess stretches her arms out, her elbows indicating that it is time for her to get her space back. She starts typing. Clare slowly slides her chair back toward her own desk.

"Anyway, I used to work there with a guy called Paul. I think he'd been there about five or six years at the time. Nice bloke he was – from somewhere near Worcester, I think. His dad was actually –"

"Is there a point to this, Jacob?" Martin interrupts.

Jacob seems nonplussed. "Yeah, he was going to be promoted. He'd been there the longest. Everyone thought he'd get the job. But he didn't. Someone else did. Can't remember his name."

"Fascinating," says Jess. "Look, can you move back to your desk?"

"Uh, yeah, sorry."

"So would you do it, mate?" I ask.

Jacob considers it for a moment. "Yeah, I think I would."

"Me too," I say.

Elaine grunts.

And now there are four contestants.

"Well, better get some work done," I say, standing.

We all move behind our desks and the pathway through is clear once again. The room is silent apart from the continuous tip-tap of computer keys. Within just a few short moments the

65

relationships built over years have changed.

Out of the corner of my eye, I notice Clare pick up her phone. She runs her finger down a list attached to the wall next to her and then punches the numbers into her keypad. There is a pause.

"Hi, Janet. It's Clare from Compliance...I'm ringing about the email you sent this morning. You know, about Alan...Yes, that one. I'd just like to say I'd like to be considered for it... Thank you."

She places the telephone back down on her desk carefully. The mood in the room shifts again.

A fifth and final competitor has entered the arena.

The office has been near-silent for the entire day. An air of division hangs in the room. It is an uncomfortable feeling. Eyes seem to follow my every move. Sly glances are shared as people overhear their rivals arranging meetings on the telephone. As the day draws to an end, I decide to break the silence.

"Everyone listen," I say.

One by one they stop what they are doing and look at me suspiciously. When I have their attention I continue:

"Look, I just wanna say, this thing with Alan. I just think whoever gets it, y'know, deserves it."

Jacob smiles at me. He seems to appreciate the gesture. I get the distinct impression that any trust the others had in me has already gone. My statement is greeted warily or, in the case of Elaine, outright ignored. As if I am trying to somehow gain an advantage over them.

"Anyway..." I go on, "I'll be seeing you all on my return."

It appears that everybody has forgotten that I will be away from the office for the next few days. No-one seems to care enough to ask me where I'm going.

chapter ten

I've never explained this to anyone before, so I'm afraid you'll have to bear with me. I didn't realise until you and I sat down together how difficult all of this would be. Don't worry, I'm not about to give up, not yet. I just didn't expect that putting all my trust in you would be so complicated. I can't remember now whether I've always been like this or whether it's happened in my more recent past. In fact, I find it difficult to remember very much at all nowadays. I find this very strange. Most days I'll overhear conversations in which people recall memories from their past with great precision. Regardless of whether the event they are referring to happened twenty years ago or twenty months ago, they remember.

My mother is an absolute expert at this. And I suppose I see it as both compelling and murderously irritating. My mother can tell a story right down to what clothing I was wearing when we were abroad in Egypt thirty years ago. She can remember colours and makes of cars we've rented on holiday and when. She remembers the names of other families we met when I was six. She remembers the names of tour guides on our journeys to obscure Tunisian monasteries. If her recollections are true, this is an exceptional trait. I say if true, because I have no memory and therefore cannot validate the veracity of her statements.

My father lost interest in the vast majority of what my mother says long ago. Thus, he just nods in agreement, pretending to listen, when she retells a story. I do believe her, though. She is not the type of woman to simply make things up. That being said, hearing such superfluous minutiae of every memory soon begins to grate. I know she doesn't include such details to gloat, it's simply how she brings it back from her own memory. The small facts build the bigger story. Unfortunately, because of her delivery the impact – and indeed the point – of the bigger story is fundamentally lost. I feel my insides tighten within a few sentences. I tense up further with each unnecessary fact, until now I simply interrupt and tell her to get to the ending. She doesn't like this, but it's preferable to strangling her.

I say my mother is exceptional because of the amount of detail she retains about every aspect of her life. It seems to me that people, in general, retain memories of their past holidays, their illnesses and any significant life achievements. People spend hours reminiscing about past conquests and their life before marriage. It seems that a great deal of the populous are mourning past times, locked in how things used to be before they took the step of becoming part of a couple. If you listen out for it, you'll notice how much of a pandemic this is.

I don't do any of this. My past is a grey fuzz. I can remember some things but in no great detail, just that I was there. With who, why or how I felt are all out too.

Just, I was there.

I have to expend a huge amount of effort to get through the static and white noise to actually draw up an old memory. So, I tend not to do it.

The reason I am telling you this is that I can't remember anything at all that happened today. I don't remember being at work. I don't remember the journey home (though my previous therapist said this was normal). He said it was something to do with 'subconscious memory' and the fact that 'the brain learns habitual behaviour so we don't need to think when taking part in repetitive activity'. Or something like that.

As I pull up outside my house I already know that the evening ahead will be difficult. It always is when my thoughts are scrambled.

I check the digital clock on the dashboard. It is 17.45. That means the traffic was good; I'm home nearly half an hour earlier than usual. If you are paying attention, you'll know that today isn't Tuesday and therefore by default I am free for the evening. I leave the car, unlock the door and step into the darkness of my house. I slip off my shoes and switch on the light. Then, as is usual every night, I head immediately upstairs to get out of my suit and into my pyjamas. Just to be clear, my pyjamas are not the type my father wears. They are not a matching striped two-piece. They are not the buttons-up-the-front-of-the-top-lapels-and-collar type. I've not yet sunk that low. Instead, they are checked bottoms with a plain t-shirt to match. I saw somebody wearing them on TV who looked happy. I bought some on the off chance that the key to happiness was something as simple as pyjamas. It wasn't. Nevertheless, I like how comfortable they feel and revert directly to them (and the other three pairs

I have) when I get home. I hang my suit carefully, catching the trousers as a combination of the weight of the belt and gravity allowed them to slip momentarily from the hanger.

I go downstairs and switch on the kitchen light. The large analogue clock on the wall tells me it's now six o'clock. I switch on the radio and open the back door. I light a cigarette, pondering what to do with the evening ahead and the extra time I've managed to acquire. I click on the kettle so it can boil whilst I smoke. This ensures I don't waste any time. It's too precious.

My phone beeps. I collect it from my pocket and look at the screen. It's a text message from my friend Ian. He's asking whether I am around for a chat this evening. Ian lives abroad and always texts in advance to arrange our conversations. He has a family and children, so I never ring him, just in case it is inconvenient and he has to make excuses not to speak to me. I wouldn't want to put him this position. It's an escape route so he doesn't need to feel guilty for not taking my call. Like I would.

I expect that Ian will think I am travelling home in the car from work. He knows that I prefer to talk whilst driving. It's a good use of my time, combining the drive with communication. It means the time I have later is my own. In all honesty, I don't like talking on the telephone. Generally, I like to get to point as quickly as possible and then end the call. I don't like to talk about everyday things. I have nothing to say.

I much prefer conversations face to face; they are somehow

more honest. I feel less on edge when I can see the reaction to my words. On the telephone, there is nothing to stop a person from rolling their eyes or holding the phone away from their ear or, worse still, mouthing something unpleasant about me to someone else in their vicinity.

Nevertheless, I tell myself, to maintain friendships there has to be an element of communication. And Ian is my closest friend. Emotionally, that is, not in distance. In distance, he is without question my furthest friend. I finish my cigarette and toss it, still lit, into the garden. It lands on a damp blanket of previously smoked cigarette ends. I reread Ian's message and consider my response. I know categorically that I do not want to talk. I don't want anything to eat into my unexpected time this evening. I consider texting him to say that I am not feeling too well. But that may worry him. Maybe I should tell him that I'm out with friends, or maybe at my parents. Or perhaps still at work. Any of these will do. But none are true. I stare at my phone, suddenly frozen by my response. I begin to worry about what to do. The simple truth is: I don't want to talk. I begin a text message saying exactly this. Then I consider how Ian will feel when he receives the message. I know my message will cause him to worry about me. I don't want this. I also don't want him to think that something he has done has caused me to become suddenly taciturn. I can't decide on a response, so instead I switch off my phone and replace it in my pocket. That way if he ever asks, I can honestly tell him that I was sorry I didn't respond to his message, but my phone was switched off.

The kettle clicks, reminding me that I wanted a cup of tea. I drop two sugar cubes into a cup and pour the water carefully. I then stir the water, watching closely as the sugar cubes disappear to nothing at the bottom of the cup. Only then do I add the teabag.

I have an almost infinite mental list of potential problems that can occur and immediately ruin my day. This is probably the reason that I have no room in my mind to store memories. I constantly plan ahead so such problems don't occur. Discovering sugar cubes permanently crossed off one of the problems on my list. Until this time, I had wasted such a lot of my time spilling teaspoons of sugar over the work surface. Usually when I was distracted, or even due to something as simple as snagging my sleeve on the small chip at the edge of the work surface. I would feel an instant wave of anger, which quickly turned to tears as I wiped the grains away with the dishcloth. The time wasted clearing up the mess is time that I can never get back. Sugar cubes instantly brought salvation. One problem dispelled. No doubt to be replaced by ten more.

I like my tea strong, so I leave it to steep and light another cigarette. I check the clock again and realise that the half hour I have gained this evening has now been extended to thirty-three minutes. I smile. I think that I might watch a film tonight. That is quite a major decision for me. It takes a large commitment on my part to give up two hours of my time. I finish my cigarette and declare out loud that I will watch a film. I believe my own authoritative tone, and thoughts of doing anything else subside.

I have committed to the film. I pour milk into my tea, make my way into the lounge and lie on the sofa.

I bring up the menu on the screen and ponder what type of film to watch (usually thriller or horror). I scroll down the screen, reading the brief descriptions of each and mentally storing those that I haven't seen and look interesting. Some have the option of watching the trailer, which I do. My list of possibles reduces to zero once I've seen a two-minute snippet of each film. None appeal, so I look through other genres. Drama is next, followed by war. I absolutely refuse to watch comedy. I don't share the same sense of humour as the general population. My brain doesn't allow me to accept the ridiculous situations comedy characters find themselves in. I end up shouting things like "That wouldn't happen in real life" or "Yeah, right" at the screen. No, comedies bring out feelings of pure negativity in me. That's why I don't watch them.

I scroll the menu and watch the trailers until my list is down to four. Three are dramas. One is a war film.

I get up from the sofa and collect my laptop from the dining room. I pull up a couple of film review websites that I trust and begin to read the reviews. My first choice was unanimously criticised by the press and I immediately discount it. My second, third and fourth choices all received reasonably favourable reviews. A couple of comments in the reviews concern me slightly, so I read more. This causes me to discount another one of the films on the basis that it sounds a little too arty for me.

I am down to two.

The first, a war film. The second, a drama about the return of a child who disappeared more than twenty years previously. Both are true stories. I like true stories; they give me points of reference for my own life.

I can't decide which, so I take a sip of my tea. A few minutes pass and I realise I have been staring at a mark on the wall for a while.

"Just pick one," I say out loud.

Moments later, I am watching the war film. There is a massive explosion and the opening credits begin. The lighting in the room isn't right, though, so I pause the film and get up to correct it. The main light is off, the lamp on. That's better. I perch on the edge of the sofa and scan the room to ensure that everything is now perfect. It seems to be. I finish my tea and lie back down. I begin to watch again.

A minute passes, and I pause the film. I can't concentrate. I know the empty cup is just beneath me on the carpet. A moment passes, then I get up and take the cup into the kitchen and drop it in the sink. Back to the film. I stop as I reach the lounge door, turn and return to the sink. I wash the cup thoroughly and leave it on the rack to dry. Then I return to the lounge.

I stand in the middle of the room, a US marine staring at me, and put my fingers to my temples to concentrate. I do this sometimes to help me focus. I draw thoughts to the front of my mind, quickly checking off any possible problems that could arise to spoil my enjoyment of film.

I decide to go to the toilet and squeeze out what I can from my near-empty bladder. Such is the lack of pressure that I end up slightly wetting the leg of my pyjamas. I go upstairs and change and return to the sofa. I am now ready.

I continue to watch the film. I say 'watch', but in reality the film is just happening in front of me. I am finding it hard to follow. The soldiers all look very similar in their uniforms. They all have beards. The more blood that covers them, the more difficult they are to differentiate. The sound of mortars and constant machine-gun fire makes it difficult for me to hear what they are saying. I can't work out which one has a wife and kids at home waiting for him, and which one is the maverick that they never thought would make it through boot camp. To me they are all the same. I rewind segments over and over in an attempt to follow the story.

Half an hour has passed. My chest has tightened to the point that the muscles in my arms and legs feel taut. I have had enough and decide I am not in the mood for a war film. I stop the film in frustration and go into the kitchen. I light a cigarette and open the back door, noticing that the time is now past seven o'clock. Tiny colourful butterflies appear in my chest to laugh at the fact I have lost all the extra time I had.

I smoke quickly, realising that my evening is rapidly disappearing. I have to leave for work early the next day so must be in bed by ten at the latest. I return to the lounge and flick to the other film. I reread the synopsis. It does sound appealing.

Just then, the evening news appears in the top right-hand

corner of the screen. There is something about the news that sucks me in. The stories are always dismal accounts of tragedy and desperation somewhere on the planet. I watch and listen to an account of disease and starvation in some war-torn country in Africa. The look on the journalist's face is grim as he describes the unimaginable suffering going on in the vast camps behind him. I wonder what he will eat after his segment has been filmed. The picture changes, showing children and parents crying, holding one another. The voice over informs the world that the two adults we can see are husband and wife, and the child they hold is the only survivor from their family. Just a few days earlier the couple had five children. I watch and listen, trying to understand their suffering. I feel disconnected from it.

I once had a wife and child. Actually, this is not quite true. I once had a wife. I still have a child. I just don't know where he is.

The rest of the news passes me by, something about an election in Russia and a mining disaster. I don't remember much else. I decide to watch the film and flick the menu back on, only to realise that the film will overhang my ten o'clock cut-off by sixteen minutes. I discount the film.

I spend the next two hours scrolling up and down the seemingly endless channel listings, trying to settle on something to watch.

There is nothing. I choose a programme, watch for a few minutes and then move on to something else. I cannot find anything to watch. The butterflies are enjoying my indecision. They dance in delight as I discard each programme.

I notice that it's now fast approaching half past nine. It is too late to begin to watch anything now. I consider going up to bed to read. This might be the best option now. The butterflies are playful at the moment, but I know only too well how they can turn. They seem friendly enough, and then from nowhere their innocence will suddenly be swallowed by darkness. Giant grey shadows will be cast over them and they will disappear into the mouths of ugly, contorted beasts, their enormous bodies lined with coarse slate-coloured hair. The repeated sound of their giant flapping wings will deafen me. Their hunger to get out from within will splinter my ribs as they pound repeatedly inside my chest. My only thought is escape. Away from them permanently. I need to get to bed before they turn.

I switch off the television and smoke my final cigarette of the evening as quickly as I can.

I switch out the lights and race up the stairs.

When I reach my room, I realise that I have nearly forgotten to pack for my trip the next day. I pull down my case from the top of the wardrobe and open it. My bag of toiletries is already there from my last trip. I grab a change of clothing and my spare rucksack and place them inside. I collect my duffel coat from a hook on the back of my bedroom door, fold it into quarters and push it into the case. It zips closed easily. I take a couple of books from my bedside table and put them into the rucksack that I will use as my hand luggage. I place the rucksack on top of the case. On top of that I put my passport.

I suddenly feel very tired and decide to go straight to sleep. The sooner I am asleep, the sooner a new day begins.

I have three ways of sleeping. I always attempt them in the same order, trying each for several minutes before resorting to the next.

The first is a Superman-type pose. I lie on my side and straighten my right arm, my hand in a fist. Then I force it between my two pillows and rest on top of my arm. I think that subconsciously, just before sleep, I am trying to convince myself that I have the power of Superman. It rarely works.

Next, I simply cuddle myself. I lie on my side, my right hand on my left shoulder, my left hand on my right shoulder, my arms crossed like a corpse in a coffin. Protecting myself from the world outside. This usually works.

I take the third and final option at desperate times. Here, I lift my head about six inches above my pillows, holding it up with my neck muscles. Then, I asphyxiate myself. Seriously. I hold a pillow tightly so it covers my mouth and nose so I cannot breathe. I hold this pose for as long as I physically can. About a minute and a half. Eventually, as the dizziness overtakes me, I give up and my head falls down into the pillows below. Usually, that is enough for me to fall asleep.

As I lie under the covers, the butterflies continue their dance. Only lightly. Just enough to remind me that once again I have lost another night.

I close my eyes, push my fist through the pillows and

feel confident that, for this evening at least, I can just about overpower them.

chapter eleven

I don't take too many holidays. There is a very simple reason for this. It isn't really a holiday. I'm there.

Sadly, by definition when you book a holiday, you are required to go along. My very presence there makes it anything but a holiday. I've often thought that it would be good to book time away from yourself. To leave the real you at home, doing what you always do, and go to some faraway destination as someone else. Unfortunately, as I write this, technology has not evolved to allow this, and so I sit in the airport, staring at the brightly lit departure board with myself.

I have brought a book and my iPod for company. I find the checking in and passing through security fairly straightforward – I manage to mutter less than a handful of words throughout the whole process. I don't bleep through the machine, which speeds things up nicely. I am at the relevant gate at the moment it opens. I sit and half-read, half-listen to what is going on around me. A small child wails behind me and I hope that it is not near me on the plane. I have nothing against children; I just don't want the nearness of noise whilst trapped inside a metal cylinder for two and a bit hours.

A man and a lady, I assume is his wife, sit across from me. Our feet are nearly touching. I pull mine in under my seat. I pretend to read whilst surreptitiously scanning their faces. They are in their early fifties, and each holds a can of Stella

Artois. They are laughing. The woman pulls at the top of the man's arm tightly. He smiles at her. The man nods at me. He seems to smile at the same time, but this could be a fade-out from the laugh he has just released. I am unsure how to react, so I raise my eyebrow just slightly in acknowledgement. I quickly divert both eyes firmly back to my page. I hope that they are not near me on the flight.

I am the first on the plane. I stow my hand luggage firmly under the seat in front and clip my seat-belt. My seat is next to a window and I gaze down to the wet black tarmac below. In several places, orange light shines onto the tarmac, reminding me of pools of spilt marmalade. I have my book clutched between my knees and the seats to my right remain empty. As the plane begins to fill, one of the cabin crew announces that "today's flight is full" and requests that "people try to be seated as soon as possible". The announcement is a slight disappointment to me. I was hoping that, for no other reason than my own comfort, at least one of the two seats next to me would be vacant.

As I wait for my fellow passengers to board, I recognise slightly too loud laughter coming in my direction and spot the couple from the airport making their way down the aisle toward me. Instantly, I open my book. The man carries a leather luggage holdall clutched to his chest and accidentally barges into the back of an oversized lady who is rummaging through her handbag. In a typically British way, both parties swiftly apologise to one another and the man turns and pulls a slightly sarcastic 'oops' face to his wife. She stifles a further laugh by biting her bottom lip. I cannot see the expression on the oversized lady's face. The man clarifies the seat numbers with his wife and stows his leather bag in the overhead locker. He plonks himself down next to me.

"Alright," he says. His breath smells of alcohol.

I nod. "Hi."

We are led through the safety procedures, and half an hour later we are cruising above the clouds. My book has been my saviour so far. I fold the cover back over the spine to obscure the title. I don't want anyone around me to know what I am reading. This is not because of the subject matter (though reading about serial killers is seemingly frowned on by society. Apparently, it's not 'normal'). One of my reasons for reading in public is to send a clear message to my fellow passengers that I am busy. I am ensconced in something and do not want to be disturbed. I have been interrupted before by some nosy stranger who sees the cover and suddenly develops an interest my book. Once I was travelling, I forget where, when the person next to me had previously read what I was reading. She decided she wanted to discuss it at length. I was too polite to decline and ended up talking about the book for two hours. She even spoiled the end. I won't make that mistake again.

We are near the back of the plane and so the hostess service arrives with us almost immediately. On this particular airline, the service is called a 'bistro' service. I make a mental note to look up the definition of the word as soon as I have chance. I am convinced that the dictionary will not describe a 'bistro' as a small four-wheeled trolley rammed with chocolate, peanuts and alcohol. I order a cup of tea and a packet of shortbread. The man and his wife top up on Stella. Two small cans for him, one for her. They open them in unison and take large gulps.

The woman passes the man her can and stands. She removes the bag from the overhead locker and retrieves something. She replaces the bag and sits back down. Her husband unclips her tray from the seat in front of her and places her can down. The woman has a book. She folds it back on its spine and begins to read. I can't see the title. The man leans into her and whispers a few inaudible words. Out of the corner of my eye it is clear to me that she doesn't want to speak. He sits upright, staring straight ahead. This is not a good sign. For a few moments he picks at a sticker on the head rest in front. He isn't the first. His interest soon wanes and he turns to me.

"So, you taking a holiday?"

I pause briefly, feigning deep concentration in my novel.

"Oh, er, yeah, kind of," I say. I hope it's enough to leave the conversation there.

It isn't.

"Have you been before?" He smiles.

"Yeah, a few times."

"You must like it then." He extends his hand to me. "Sorry, I didn't catch your name?"

"John," I lie.

"I'm Paul," he says, "and this is Sharon."

I half-expected her to be called Ringo.

He nudges his wife and she looks up from her book and smiles. I smile back.

I've instantly forgotten his name.

"You must like it then, John?" he says.

"Yes, it's good. You'll enjoy it." I hope that he now has the message that my closed answers are trying to give.

"What do you recommend doing?" he says.

Jesus.

I want to say that I'm only on the trip for cigarettes. I'm not sight-seeing; I'm here to stock up on ridiculously cheap tobacco that would cost me five times as much in England. I have no interest in the city itself; I am here for a couple of nights for one simple reason. I quickly bring to mind some of the sights I am aware of in the city.

"The usual stuff really. The castle, the Charles Bridge, the old town." If I sound vague, it's because I haven't seen any of them.

"Right," he says. He turns to his wife. "John says we should go to the old town and to the..." He turns back to me. "What was that bridge called?"

"The Charles Bridge."

"The Charles Bridge," he says to his wife.

She smiles again, widening her eyes and nodding at me. She begins reading again. I follow suit, hoping he'll get the message.

"What's in the old town?" he says to me.

"Old stuff," I say without looking up.

"Oh," he says and gets up to go to the toilet.

chapter twelve

The blackbird lands on the fence.

He peers at the house for a moment or two.

Something is different. There is no activity inside.

He stares intensely at each window, one by one, looking for a flash of movement.

Nothing.

He lurches forward onto the path and then hops the last few steps down the garden. He flaps his wings enough to lift himself onto the kitchen windowsill. He springs backwards and forwards, following the edge of the window.

The house appears empty.

He opens his yellow beak and begins to screech.

chapter thirteen

I am in my hotel room. It is actually very nice. Although my trip is primarily a way of saving money on tobacco, I do like at least to stay somewhere comfortable for the thirty or so hours I am here.

The room is large and painted totally in white. It has twin beds and a large white metal desk. On the desk are square tea and coffee cups and a white kettle shaped like a pyramid. Nearby in a white wooden box, there is a scattering of tea, coffee and sugar sachets. The hinged lid has stark black lettering that simply says 'DRINK'. There is a mini-bar – well, fridge. The bathroom is nicely done in tasteful sandstone throughout, with two sinks and a large bath. I smile. I don't like taking baths, but find on these city breaks that the anticipation of having one, along with the preparation needed – bubbles, gauging temperatures, preparing a drink, ensuring a towel is nearby to dry wet hands, collecting my book, choosing my music – is a good way to pass time.

I remove the change of underwear, socks and t-shirt from my case along with my spare rucksack and put them in the cupboard. It is late, and I climb into bed, ready for my cigarette mission the next day.

I tend to take these city breaks two or three times a year, purely for the purpose of buying cigarettes. I can save around one to two thousand pounds per trip even after costing in flights, taxis and my accommodation. When I first decided to take the trips, I worked out the cheapest countries to get to, with the cheapest tobacco, and then visited for three or four nights. A different place each time. The idea was to collect the cigarettes on the first day and then take in the sights of the city. But after perhaps the third city, I realised that I was kidding myself that I was enjoying seeing all these 'must-see' places that people back home talk about so much.

I would race from place to place just so I could say to whoever asked, with some degree of honesty, that I had been there. I was in and back out of Kunsthistorisches Museum in Vienna in half an hour. I briskly moved from one picture to the next, repeating "Seen it, seen it, seen it" over and over in my head. In Poland, I did Auschwitz in just under two hours. I couldn't have done it any quicker (I didn't realise the sheer scale of the camp; the time I spent there was purely down to the distance to walk). Conversely, I did the Colosseum in Rome in just eleven minutes.

I realised that the reason for my lack of enjoyment at these historic places was twofold. The first was that I worried that the cigarettes I had purchased could be stolen from my room whilst I was out. I did consider buying them on the last day instead, but that added the extra worry that there may be a sudden shortage in whatever city I was visiting and I would return home empty handed. I quickly deduced that the real reason, though, was because I was there. I was there in the city. And it is close to impossible to enjoy anything with me around.

My parents don't approve of my cigarette missions. They don't approve of me smoking full stop. When I was younger, each year they would take me abroad and force me to visit sights I didn't want to see. Now to keep things simple, I return to Prague (and visit none of the sights) each time. I suppose it is a minor act of rebellion. Perhaps, in some way, smoking is too. I don't really think anyone understands the importance of my missions. They bring me a small modicum of happiness, a feeling of relief that I have stocked up for a good few months. A worry to strike off my to-do list. Something that I need not remember to buy from the dreaded supermarket. Buying large quantities of any commodity in advance (I do this with most non-perishable products: toiletries, tins of soup, toilet rolls, cans of fizzy drink) also allows me to avoid unnecessary human contact. If I were to visit a shop each day, that would add a further unwanted and unnecessary conversation every single day. Stockpiling allows me to avoid this.

The other, more pertinent thing that people don't understand is that the cigarette mission (and smoking generally) allows me to be a conscientious participator in my own long, slow suicide.

The next morning, I wake later than expected. It is not often that I get the amount of sleep that I desire. On mornings when I have to be up early for work, I feel like I could hibernate through the rest of the year. At weekends, sometimes I wake just an hour or two after falling asleep and remain awake for the rest of the day.

I am therefore pleased that it is now just before lunchtime. I shower and pack one rucksack into the other. The weather looks cold outside, so I add an extra jumper before pulling on my large duffel coat. I head downstairs and I am quickly out of the hotel door, before the receptionist can greet me.

An icy wind whips my face and I turn left for the short walk to the tabák. I stop briefly in an alleyway and light a cigarette before pulling on my gloves. I walk back into the wind and make my way down the road, head down. I turn left at a small stone monument and reach the street where the shop is located. From a hundred yards away I see that the gold-backed blue T on the sign is not lit. I march on, sucking in my own death. When I reach the shop, it isn't open. Permanently. I throw down my cigarette and cup my hands around my eyes so I can see through the window. The shelves remain in the centre of the store, but they are empty. Post has gathered on the inside of the door. My heart races.

I look around. People are milling up and down the street, but I don't speak their language. I suddenly feel extremely alone. Lit up in the centre of all this activity. I decide to walk on further, looking for another outlet. A few minutes later, I come across what looks like a small supermarket. Large, bold stickers in the window proclaim PIVO and ALKOHOL and from outside I can see numerous bottles lining the shelves inside. It looks a likely target. Tobacco is usually not far behind alcohol. I push open the door and a long, repetitive beep sounds.

A small, slightly balding Asian man, Chinese, perhaps Korean, appears from behind a curtain and sits at the low counter. He says a word I take to mean 'Hello' and I say "Hello" back to him. Behind him, cigarettes line the shelves. My heart rate reduces.

"Cigarettes," I say.

"Mmm, cigarety," he replies.

"Lucky Strike blues."

Without looking, he reaches awkwardly above his left shoulder and pulls my brand from the vast selection of cigarette packets behind him. I am immediately impressed. He puts the packet on the counter.

"Do you have more?"

"Ninety-one crown," he says, tapping the price on the side of the packet.

I ask the same question again, using my hands to try to communicate 'more'. I resemble a fisherman showing a gathered crowd the size of the one that got away.

The man smiles – a smile of confusion. It is his turn to repeat. "Ninety-one," he says.

"A carton? Do you have more cigarettes? A carton?"

The man's expression changes and he repeats the word 'carton' in broken English. He reaches under the counter and pulls out a carton of Lucky Strike blues from underneath. Ten packets of cigarettes in one box. He places it down. I smile. We are making progress.

"Nine hundred ten," he says.

"Do you have more cartons?"

"More?" His eyes close slightly.

"Yes, more."

From a fist, I peel out my fingers one by one, counting the number I want. I actually want sixteen in total, but obviously this is not possible to show without removing my shoes. He copies me, and looks under the counter again. Seconds later there are three cartons on the counter.

"More?" I ask.

He shakes his head. "On-lee three."

"Okay," I say, unzipping my rucksack and putting the cartons inside. I pass him my credit card to pay. He waves his hand in front of him.

"On-lee cash," he says.

"Oh," I say, patting my pockets for effect. "I don't have any cash."

Instantly, the man realises that I have the cigarettes in my rucksack and could make a break for the door without payment. It is clear this is something he has experienced before. He grips the side of my rucksack tightly and points to a bank across the road. I let him keep my rucksack and go and retrieve the cash.

His grip relaxes as he sees the notes I hold tightly in my hand. I pay him and he releases the rucksack back into my custody.

"Where else can I buy cigarettes?" I ask the man.

He shakes his head, continuing to smile. It is the same smile of bemusement. Realising that I am unlikely to get much further with this conversation, I thank the man and leave.

I head left, in the opposite direction to my hotel. The cold wind blows directly into my face. Before very long, I spot a similar shop down a side street on the opposite side of the road. The word CIGARETY is printed in red on a white sign above the door. Inside, the shop is almost identical. As is the shopkeeper, again Asian, this time with a little more hair assembled into a tuft at his crown. We have an almost identical conversation which concludes with him providing me with five cartons. I pay in cash, to avoid the awkwardness of the card conversation and to keep communication to a minimum. I safely stow the cigarettes in my rucksack and return to the cold outside. I have never noticed these little shop doors on my previous visits. They seem to be grouted in between the regular high-street chains and smaller electrical and clothing outlets. The shop doors, often without even a window for company, open up into an unexpected vastness of vices for sale. The interior belies the near-invisible exterior and each shop sells almost exclusively alcohol and tobacco. The linoleum floors are often torn and always dirty and the items on the shelves are packed far too high, ready to topple at any moment. I don't doubt that you could probably buy drugs and perhaps even introductions to women inside. I don't enquire about either.

The shops become my only goal. I no longer see the large, well-lit shop fronts; instead my eyes scan and search for the little doorways. In and out of them I go, collecting a carton or two in each. In some of the shops I am greeted by a shake of the head and an offer of two, three or maybe four single packets. This is no good. Single packets have a tendency to get crushed on their journey home. The cartons retain their sturdiness.

Further I roam.

Greeted by an Asian man.

Buying him out of Lucky Strikes.

Down a side street.

Another shop.

Another walk.

Another turn.

Another sign.

Another purchase.

This theatre continues for most of the afternoon. I stop for a quick drink from a bottle of Coke I took from the hotel minibar. I am temporarily shielded from the wind in the entrance to an underground car park. I crouch and open each rucksack. The one I have carried on my back contains nine cartons. The zip strains as I pull it closed. The rucksack I have carried in my hand contains four. Three to go. I light a cigarette and stand for a second. The rucksacks aren't heavy, but their cargo makes them cumbersome to carry. Especially two at the same time.

I suck in the smoke and poke my head into the wind. I look up and down the street. The majority of the shops seem to be situated in the direction I have walked from. I notice a sign ahead. I am convinced small text at the bottom says ALKOHOL. I have to tell you that my eyesight is excellent. It is one of the things about myself that I actually do like. I like the ability to see words in the distance before anybody else does. I feel it gives me a slight advantage. I am not sure, however, what, if any, value this has. Usually, I would be able to read the sign easily, but the light is fading now. It is the first time that I have noticed it is beginning to get dark. The sky has turned an ominous battleship-grey. I throw my cigarette to the ground and the wind blows it across the street before I can put it out with my foot. I turn in the direction of the shop and walk directly into the wind. The first flakes of snow begin to fall, wetting my cheeks and lips. My eyes begin to water.

I reach the shop in less than five minutes. As I approach I let out a little chuckle – an audible pat-on-the-back for myself – I was right about the sign. I push open the door and step inside.

There are bottles of spirits stacked tightly together on either side. I cautiously remove my rucksacks and hold one in each hand as I squeeze through toward the counter. I cannot contemplate a discussion over an accidental breakage in two different languages. We have the usual conversation, and the man happily hands over his last (and only) carton of Luckies. I pay cash and put the cigarettes into my rucksack, then thank the man as I leave. The sky has closed in, surrounding me in black. It has happened in an instant and the darkness slightly unnerves me. I hadn't planned for any of this activity today. On my previous visits to this city, the cigarette run was a formality, over and done with in less than twenty minutes. The rest of my time would usually be spent in the hotel room, half-guarding the cigarettes, listening to music, reading and, of course, bathing. I check my watch; it's after five. I realise that I have absolutely no idea where I am. The most sensible action would be to go back in the direction that I have come from. But I am two cartons short. I cannot go back without them. My heart rate begins to quicken. That would be just another abject failure. I must go on.

I look down the street. It is lined with tall stone buildings which stretch down each side. Most have black wrought-iron balconies which look down onto the street. Cars are parked tightly together on each side. Further up the street on my side, large bins have burst from an alleyway onto the pavement. One lies on its side, spilling litter across the pavement, beneath the cars and into the road. There is no way past the obstacle and I suddenly consider that it may be a trap. A place I could be ambushed. I quickly cross over and make my way up the other side. I walk into icy puffs of my own breath that hang in the air in front of me. I pass the bins unscathed.

It is getting darker, and as I walk the spaces between the lampposts grow. It is getting colder. Darker. A small black dog potters down the street past me, looking for food. It circles me, sniffing closely at my jeans. I stop, for fear of falling over it, and notice the area I am now in seems largely residential. The snow continues to fall. I decide to continue, peering up and down the streets that criss-cross the road I am walking down. The dog joins me for a short while and then leaves me for the scent at the foot of a lamppost. It is more difficult to make out signs now, and once or twice I stop and narrow my eyes to try to draw the letters on signs closer. Most of the streets do not look inviting, and small groups of teenagers have begun to gather on the stone steps leading to the entrances of various buildings, their bright jackets providing the only colour in an otherwise entirely black-and-white world. About a mile further down the road I conclude that this journey was a mistake. At the next opportunity I turn left; at the end of that street, left again.

The street I turn into is much the same as the last. Large buildings, wrought-iron balconies, dim lighting. At street level the entrances to the buildings are generally large, wide vestibules. Perhaps eight or nine steps leading through darkness to the glass entrance doors. There a keypad awaits the code to let the residents in. A hundred years earlier, these would have been entrances into magistrates' buildings or mayoral offices. Now, with the space no longer needed, it appears city planners have crammed them full of people they are not sure what to do with.

As I pass each doorway, I worry that someone may approach from the darkness. Groups of young men stand in huddles further down the street. Pockets of people unnerve me. I wonder what the living conditions are like inside to make people prefer to stand in the wind and snow outside. The next doorway I pass has the same access as the others, though the glass doors are no longer there, the glass instead replaced by thin-looking plywood. And as it happens, that is the last doorway of its type. The buildings have now changed; single doors and keypads line the way. The buildings are concrete. There are no more balconies. Graffiti adorns both the walls and the doors. I walk more quickly. I preferred the previous street. I look to my left, desperate for a left turn to take me back onto it.

I am approaching the groups of people now. The snow has begun to settle and crunches as the soles of my shoes force it into the pavement. I consider for a second that I could be robbed. My heart begins to pound. Butterflies emerge from their slumber. At least I have the cigarettes to give to them. I hold the strap of the rucksack tightly with my right hand. I pull the other rucksack to my chest and wrap my free hand around it. I lower my head and march toward them.

When I am around fifty feet away there is a left turn, which I gladly take. And then, a few feet away, the word CIGARETY, brightly lit on a sign.

I exhale my relief, push open the door and approach the counter.

"Lucky Strike blues?"

The Asian man shakes his head. "No carton."

I mishear. "Yes, a carton."

The man raises his voice. "No carton."

"Oh –"

"No, carton! I say," he shouts angrily.

I am surprised that my question has caused him to become so irritated. The man pulls down from the shelf behind him the only packets of Luckies left. There are six packets of twenty cigarettes. Four short of a carton. Fourteen short of the number I require to finish the mission. I really don't want single packets, but the walk has caused me to reconsider my action plan.

"You buy." He points at the packets. It is not a question, it is an instruction. He stacks them together in a block. A kind of mini-carton shape. He grips my wrist.

I pause for a little too long.

"You buy!" He glares at me. "I say, 'no carton, no carton, no carton' today."

I suddenly realise that we have met before. Sometime earlier in the day, it seems. I have been in so many of these shops that I haven't taken the time to register the features of each shopkeeper. This one, however, obviously recognises me. The English stranger who asked for a carton of Lucky Strike blues twice in one day.

"Yes, yes, of course," I say. The man releases his grip slightly. I reach for my wallet. "It's okay."

The man nods and rings the price into the till. I don't want to complete the mission now. I need to abort. I want the comfort of the hotel room now. In fact, I want to be back at home.

You'll find that this is a continuing theme for me. Somehow, I always want to be in a different place to where I am.

When I am at work, I want to be away from it.

When at home, I want to be anywhere but there.

When abroad, I want to be at home.

The grass isn't greener on either side, because whichever side I'm on, I am there. And that's probably what spoils it.

(I hope you realise just how honest I'm being with you.)

"A carton of Marlboro lights?" I say. I'll settle for my back-up brand to get the day over with.

The man looks at me wearily. I think he is trying to work out whether I am being sarcastic or funny or even ironic. I nod to confirm he heard me correctly. He reaches under counter.

"One? Two? Three?" His raises his short, fat fingers with each word.

"Two," I say.

I pay the man and leave the shop, back into the unusually dark evening. I realise that if I have visited that shop previously, I must be heading in the right direction to get back. Large snowflakes fall, lit beautifully by the lampposts, which are now getting closer together. I breathe a sigh of relief that's so deep I suspect it will still be hanging in the air long after I've returned to the hotel. I begin to recognise the doors of shops that I've visited. It's Hansel and Gretel-esque, the bread replaced by tobacco, leading me back home.

Within twenty minutes, I am in the warmth of my room. I dump the rucksacks on the floor and remove my coat. It's just before eight. I lie back on the bed, kicking off my shoes in the process. I stare at the ceiling, considering the afternoon and what could have happened on the rough-looking back streets of the city. I conclude that actually, in hindsight, nothing interesting did happen.

In my life, it never does.

There was no great adventure.

There never is.

There is no story to tell anyone when I get home.

And even if there was a story, if there is no one to tell, perhaps it would not even exist in the first place.

I get up from the bed and set the bath running.

chapter fourteen

A crash on the motorway means that this morning I am forty minutes late for work. It only takes me a minute or two to notice that there has been a seismic change in the office. I have been away for just a few days.

"How we all doing?" I say cheerily to the middle of the room.

Jacob is the only one who answers. "Good. You?"

"Really good, thanks. How's everyone else?"

There is no answer. I see Martin's left hand move and tightly clutch an unopened pack of Post-It notes. Jess reaches for her phone and pulls it to her ear, though she doesn't appear to dial any numbers. It is clear that something has happened in the office whilst I've been away. This seems to be a more than reasonable conclusion. I have never known the office to be this deathly quiet. Before I speak again, the thought suddenly strikes me that perhaps this isn't something work related. It is possible that something has happened outside work which has impacted on my colleagues today. The funereal atmosphere unnerves me.

I know nothing about the lives of the others, aside from what they choose to share with me. The same applies with me, of course. I would not want any of them to know anything of my private life. I am happy putting on my mask of happiness daily. I have concluded that it is by far the simplest option. Pretend for the eight or so hours I am there each day. I am sure that is what everybody else does. Then we all leave and live our real lives outside of office hours.

I remember in my previous job there was a women who was consistently spiteful with everyone she came into contact with. From time to time a colleague would take exception to this and challenge her about her attitude and general demeanour. At that point she would collapse in a flood of tears and be shepherded off to a meeting room to be consoled. Each time, those at the hierarchical summit would leap to defend her. She would frequently be sent home for the rest of the day to recover. The following day she would return to resume her hateful attitude. Nobody could understand why she was tolerated. It was only when she left the company that we discovered her husband – a headmaster – had been under investigation for numerous indecent assaults on the boys at his school. On learning this, we all kind of understood the pressure she had been under.

I realise that whatever mask you wear for work can slip should the pressure of your real life boil over. Of course, we all have a choice about who we are at work. I have no doubt that almost every single person invents another 'them' during working hours. We all lie about how our family lives are; how many glasses of wine we had the night before; how much overtime we did; how happy we are. I therefore feel qualified to say that who we are at work is not the whole story.

I never did find out what became of that woman, or her husband for that matter.

I walk over to my desk, remove my jacket and place it carefully over the back of my chair. I catch Jacob's eye. I frown, questioning the atmosphere in the office. He pulls a face that says to me 'This is how it is now'.

"Hi, Clare. You okay?"

She hides behind her monitor. Her fingers tapping on the keyboard is the only sound that comes from her direction. I log on to my computer and turn to Elaine. I speak quietly.

"Have I missed something?"

She wipes her nose on her sleeve and looks at me. Her pudgy face is scowling, her features pulled in toward her nose.

"What like?" she snaps.

"Well, it's really quiet in here," I whisper. "Y'know, like something's going on."

"Maybe we're all just really busy. Have you considered that might be the reason that it's quiet?"

She turns away. I see her hand reach into a gap in her top drawer. A moment later she pulls out a sugar-coated biscuit and takes a large bite. I turn away before she begins chewing. For a moment, I drift into the photo that sits on my desk. I feel myself smiling at the faces in the picture.

I am interrupted by Jacob coughing. I look up and see he is nodding toward his monitor. It takes me a second to realise what he means, then I reach down and click my mouse to open my emails. I read through his message with interest. It seems that the mood in the office is, after all, work-related.

The managing director of the company, Nick (I won't mention

his surname just on the off chance there is a case for libel when he reads this), has informed the staff that he has been considering the current vacancy within the department. He and his fellow board members have considered all the potential candidates to take over from Alan. They state that they feel it is imperative to have somebody in position as soon as possible. They go on to reiterate that they will be appointing somebody from the existing team. It is vital that the individual has a wealth of experience and understands the company's culture. Therefore, the candidate must have been with the company for more than five years. In considering this, Nick goes on to say, there are only two candidates that are suitable for the role at this time. I am one of them. The other, directly to my left, is now taking a large bite out of a huge bar of Dairy Milk.

I email Jacob and he tells me that due to my lateness I missed a stand-up row between Martin and Elaine. They now appear not to be talking to one another or anybody else. Apparently, a few home truths were shared, and Elaine went on to tell the department how unsuitable I would be for the role. Aside from the lack of her level of experience, she cited the fact that I was 'habitually' late and my demeanour was 'too friendly'. As she succinctly put it, I was 'simply not business orientated enough to succeed'.

I can feel the anger rising in me as I read each word. As I reach the end of the email, I see that Jacob has asked me to permanently delete the message. He is, no doubt, fearful that this information may be traced back to him. I understand his concerns and thank him for passing the information on, telling him that I won't say a word. I delete his email, and then remove the deleted email from the recycle bin.

I am furious, and this isn't helped by the constant chomping and slobbering coming from my left. I am also constrained by my promise to Jacob not to raise the issue with Elaine. Not to disclose my source.

In my anger I follow suit with the rest of my colleagues and spend the entire day in silence. Not for the first time, I find myself wanting to be somewhere different from where I am.

chapter fifteen

I've managed to make it through another day at work.

The return journey has been uneventful, but as I turn the corner toward my house I get a deep sense of foreboding. It's something the size of a fist that just magically appears immediately below my ribcage. It's not actually a fist, I am simply telling you that as a point of reference. It is a large, heavy weight hanging awkwardly inside in my chest. I call it the fist for ease. I am certain that physically it doesn't exist. If a surgeon was to open me up now, there would be nothing there. I've spent many nights poring over forums for a solution to this problem. One or two people, I electronically 'met', seemed to suffer with the same condition. We all agreed that it wasn't actually there. Tumours cannot appear and disappear like the flash of an indicator light. But before we go on, you have to try to understand that it feels like it is there. And when that feeling arrives, it forces my mind to think in ways I hadn't otherwise anticipated.

There was a time, a few years ago now, that I got sucked into the internet forum storm. If you are not familiar, bear with me while I explain. A forum is simply a group of people who 'chat' by typing messages to one another. Each member can use either their real name or a pseudonym. There are thousands of forums, each dedicated to a specific subject like football or being a mum or running or baking. I was born before the internet. It didn't exist. We all pretty much kept our feelings to ourselves. And then, in the same way that a bird decides to eject the contents of its bowels onto your car windscreen, it just appeared. The internet had arrived, and not only that, there were millions of people sharing their deep thoughts, innermost feelings and despair with strangers from God-knows-where. Don't get me wrong, I am sure an equal number of people were sharing random moments that brought delight to them (the first snowdrop of the spring; a card from a long-lost friend; an unexpected delivery of flowers), moments of happiness that their oh-so-perfect lives bring to them daily. It's just that I didn't use the search engine to find those people.

Anyway, suddenly there were people worldwide claiming to have the feelings that I thought were unique to me. The people in the DarkLife Forum. And those very same people were befriending me. Telling me that Andr3w1974 should never feel alone. They felt the same as me. I had them now. We had each other. They would listen to Andr3w1974 and understand. But, you see, here lay the fundamental problem. We were all connected because we shared the same issues, and to be frank, none of us had a bloody clue how to solve our problems. We thought we had found friends, confidantes, but instead we had just found people so fucked up that they had nothing else. We all had nothing else. We were happy to listen to each other, just so we could get our own points across. We never got to solving anything.

From time to time, some members of the forum reported

positive news to the group. As soon as they did, they were castigated with sarcastic comments along the lines of 'Well, jeez, that sure must be swell for you' or 'Glad your life is going good'. They soon disappeared (perhaps to join a 'some days are bad/some are good' group).

I also found that the friends I had made felt a competitive urge to keep up with the other purveyors of misery, with whom they hung out in the forum. On one particularly bad day, I decided that instead of being on the outskirts of the group I was going to post about my day. It was my first attempt at trying to be honest about my feelings. A precursor to this book, if you like. Before now, it was the first and only time I had ever shared anything. I typed my post and told them about the fist inside me and how it made me feel anxious and at times hopelessly desperate. I received a couple of responses along the lines of 'That's too bad' and 'Jeez, Andr3w1974, I don't know how you've coped'. And then came the initial trickle of one-upmanship, that somebody else's day had been somehow worse. If that was all I had to worry about, I shouldn't even be on the site. Those posts were in turn belittled. Somebody else had cut themselves that day with their dad's razor. That was nothing: one of them was fingering their father's gun as they typed.

I just stared at the screen.

I felt empty.

After about six months of dragging myself down further with the online company that I kept, I gave up with the whole thing. I removed myself, removed my account. Andr3w1974 ceased to exist. I really don't think anyone would have noticed.

I moved on to a different part of the internet. A place where no friends are necessary. A place where there is no participation from my side. The information is all one-way. My eyes take in line after line of evidence and statistics and data and the experiences of others. My brain processes it all at lightning speed as I tried to match myself with the data before me.

I entered the murky world of self-diagnosis. A world where I could understand what was wrong with my thoughts and feelings and fix them. Or so I thought. I'll tell you about this some other time.

I pull my car outside my house, thankful there is a space available to park in. I glance around me as I remove the keys from the ignition. There's nobody about. Quickly, I get out of the car and head to the front door. As I reach the door there is a metallic click to my left, and then a squeaking sound. I realise that Stuart has opened his gate and I fumble with my keys in the lock. A rumbling sound from the same direction suggests he's dragging his wheelie bin out a day early, as usual. I just make it into the darkness of my house before he sees me.

I spend the next half hour in the kitchen, smoking and mentally fighting the fist inside me. I don't know why it's there and my mind dips and swoops like a stunt plane, trying to find a reason for its appearance. The physical heaviness the fist brings renders me incapable of thinking of anything else except my past. I process thoughts to try to understand why, from nowhere, I suddenly feel this way. Nothing seems to fit. I tense up. Eventually, I feel like the kitchen is closing in around me and, in desperation, I move into the lounge to change the scenery.

I reach behind the sofa for my old blue blanket. I'm not sure where I acquired the blanket, but I like it. It's enormous. I lie on the sofa, aware that my suit is getting crumpled. I pull the blanket over me, covering the grey blanket which I feel permanently covers my life. I pull the edges of it under my feet and tuck the sides in. I want to be alone in my own private universe, with no air entering from the room around me. I pull the blanket over my head and breathe. My breaths are deep and I can see each pushing and then pulling the blanket. I am now entirely surrounded by the blanket, cocooned within, with just my thoughts. I have trapped the fist inside here with me, in this small, enclosed area. I am aware of the paradox. From experience, I know it wouldn't matter whether I was enclosed or not. The fist wouldn't fly free because there was open space around me. I have to rid myself of it. I close my eyes.

I'm not sure whether a minute or an hour has passed. The light outside is not noticeably different from when I arrived home. The fist is still inside me. I am on the street outside. I pull the front door closed behind me and press the button on my keys. The car winks at me, almost seductively, and invites me in. I don't need asking twice.

And then I'm in the car, and I'm driving. Some time has

passed; how much I'm not sure. I'm not checking the clock. But I do know that the bright lights of the area where I live are far behind me. Hedgerows and vast, gaping fields line both sides of the road. My car is taking the road that runs between them, making its path like the first push of a lawnmower through uncut grass. I look in the rear-view mirror, but can see nothing of where I have come from.

Time jumps forward again – it has to – as I am now many miles from home. The landscape has changed again. I am surrounded by trees, their bare branches arching over the road. Nothing in this journey is smooth. Everything blurs, and suddenly I have jumped in time and landed in another part of journey. Although I cannot feel myself driving, I know that I must be. The fist remains. Stagnant, hard, insistent. My mind has done everything it can to try to work out its existence. I have played with past memories, present thoughts. There is no reason for it to be here. Nothing happened to put the fist in my chest at this moment today. There was no trigger that made it appear the moment I got home from work.

I have exhausted all thoughts. Having eliminated every single thought that has ever entered my mind, I've concluded that there can only be one reason that the fist is here. And that, I believe, is the reason I am driving.

I jump forward in time again. It's dusk and I am nearing where I believe the fist wants me to be. I pull out from under the canopy of the trees and into open countryside. The roads are narrow here, and my headlights illuminate wooden fencing

113

a few yards to my left. A small drop from the road separates me from them. A grass verge and endless hedging follows the road to my right. And then, for the last time, I jump time again. My breathing becomes heavier and I round a corner, which takes me onto a very steep road. I stop and get out of the car.

I am in the middle of nowhere. I recognise the area. There is nothing around me but the road I am on and fields. The headlights illuminate the road as far as I can see, beyond which, the tarmac fades to an unseen, distant grey. Straggled wooden fence posts are separated by twisted barbed wire which has been pulled out of shape by many years of exposure to the elements. It is suddenly cold and I blow into my hands. I have my last cigarette. Then I take one last glance down the steep hill and get back into the car.

I take off the handbrake and begin to accelerate. I know this road so well.

A red light beeps on the dashboard in the shape of a man with a seatbelt pulled across him. I continue to accelerate. As the car moves faster, I change into third gear and increase my speed again. As I push the pedal down, the fist begins to dissipate and the hardness in my chest softens.

Into fourth gear, the needle on the dashboard is well over halfway to the full distance it can stretch.

I push down further, and the beeping and flashing quickens. I ignore it.

I am looking for a chipped wooden bench on my left.

Ah, here it is.

I press my foot to the floor and swerve to my left. The wheels hit a mound of dirt as I leave the road. It is almost perfect. The car lifts slightly and then entirely.

My back wheels catch the barbed wire of the fence below, straining two wooden posts before catapulting them into the sky after me.

The car is now turning into the open sky. I am no longer getting higher but I am getting further away from the ground. I know this because this is how I planned it. The drop after the bench is sheer. A hundred or so feet to the small stream that trickles unsuspectingly below. I push my head deep into the headrest and close my eyes.

The feeling inside me is now gone.

There is nothing there.

For a split-second I consider plugging in my seatbelt to quieten the beeping. Silence at this moment would signify total perfection. I have thought about this moment so many times, though I never imagined that I would have so much time to think, to wait. The seconds pass so slowly. Yet I feel entirely relaxed. I quickly discard the idea; the beeping will have to stay. The seatbelt could bring about an ending that cannot be considered.

The car lurches and I feel its drop increase.

I am moments away.

And then I feel the impact, jarring for the briefest of moments before I am propelled forwards. My face shatters the glass in front of me. And then, as you would expect, everything is black.

I am soaking wet. Everywhere. My trousers are saturated, stuck to my legs with what feels like tree sap. My upper body is the same. Sticky. Wet. Liquid drips from my hair down behind my ears, little drips of water forming their own deltas on my neck. It drips into my eyes. I am suddenly hot. I open my eyes and kick off the blanket, gasping for breath. I claw at my shirt, fumbling at the buttons to allow cold air to reach my skin. I pull at my tie, which seems to have tightened to the extent that it is now almost choking me. I unzip my trousers and lift myself from the sofa to allow me to pull them to my knees. The air rushes in. It feels good.

I stare at the ceiling and breathe until my intake of air is back to normal.

Before you think that I have just been dreaming: I haven't.

I wouldn't insult your intelligence with some lazy-Hollywood storytelling. It wasn't just a dream.

In my mind, it happened.

I felt it.

I was there.

And the fist is still here to remind me of that.

chapter sixteen

I want you to close your eyes and picture the scene I'm about to describe.

Imagine a small, grey, windowless room. There is one door. Nobody ever visits the room. Trapped within are six humans. I am one of them. There are two further men and three women. We have to spend eight hours a day in here.

We only communicate with one another when we absolutely have to. When somebody does speak, the answer they receive is short and discloses the absolute minimum information required. Coupled with this, the other inhabitants greet both the question and answer with grunts, sighs or tuts.

Because of this, it is now rare for any speech to take place at all during the eight hours that we are all trapped.

It feels like an experiment to reverse evolution.

Now imagine that the only sound you hear is the consistently monotonous noise of forty-eight fingers and twelve thumbs colliding with plastic keyboards or clicking the buttons on their mice. This noise beats throughout the day. It is interrupted from time to time by the telephone ringing. Whichever of the inhabitants receives the call chooses to end it immediately and leaves the room to redial in private.

Except one. Elaine. She has taken it upon herself to become leader-elect. Elaine takes great pleasure in speaking more loudly than she needs to on the telephone. If the caller is important within the company, she overuses their name so the rest of us know to whom she is speaking. She makes regular veiled, maledictory statements about everyone else in the room. She snorts and laughs at comments to which we are not privy, in a way that you would expect if she were communicating with a stand-up comedian.

The group has no leader. No direction. Four of the individuals realise that their entire future hangs on the elected leader. For this reason, they don't speak so as not to alienate their own future position. There are no sides. Everyone is together, alone.

Tap, Tap, Tap, Tap.

Ring Ring.

Tut.

Grunt.

Tap, Tap, Tap, Tap.

Tut.

Tut.

Tap, Tap, Tap, Tap.

Tap, Tap, Tap, Tap.

Ring Ring.

Tut.

Snort.

Tap, Tap, Tap, Tap.

Tap, Tap,

Tap, Tap.

Tap, Tap, Tap, Tap.

I look around the room. I feel like I am slowly losing my mind. The noises generate a constant rhythm. It is almost musical. The room is so quiet that I begin to feel I can hear what other people are typing. I have now identified that the space bar makes a different sound to the other keys. As does the shift key.

Tap, Tap, Tap. Space bar.

It is hypnotising.

Tap, Tap, Tap.

Tut.

The day drags and drags.

   Tap, Tap, Tap. Space bar.

      Tap, Tap, Tap.

         Tut.

         Snort.

            Space bar.

            Tap, Tap, Tap.

               Space bar.

               Tap. Tap.

                  Tap.

The little clock in the bottom right-hand corner of my monitor finally changes. It is five o'clock. Five chairs slide backwards. Five fingers push buttons on PCs to send them to sleep. Four inhabitants leave the room in silence. I linger.

Elaine remains and feeds a quiet tut to each of the departing.

"Well, goodnight," I say.

She looks at her watch and grunts.

I have no doubt that in five minutes she will also leave.

Five o'clock today has brought the best feeling I can remember experiencing for a long time.

chapter seventeen

I call in to the petrol station on my way home. I am slightly annoyed with myself as I have already called in to the same petrol station on the way to work. This instantly changes my mood for the worse. It is a waste of time, and you already know how precious time is to me. I curse myself for failing to remember on my earlier visit, that this morning, I used the last of the toilet roll.

I pull the car up alongside the tyre-inflating machine and get out. The petrol station has been converted into a mini-supermarket slash off-licence. The lighting in the shop is far too bright. Similar to the blinding light from an open photocopier. I make my way down the aisles, passing packets of cereal and kitchen cleaning products, to the toilet rolls. There are two rolls left. I grab them quickly, almost in expectation that someone else is rapidly approaching from behind me. I clutch them tightly to my shirt and make my way to the counter.

The girl behind the counter is frowning. She is trying to replace the till roll. She looks up. "Won't be a minute, love," she says.

Her face is a deep orange. Her brown hair is pulled up on top of her head. She wears deep-crimson lipstick. It is thick and wet looking. Her eyebrows are thick black lines. Whatever it is she uses to draw them on covers her real eyebrows and bleeds onto skin. They are perfectly rectangular. They remind me of burnt French fries, like the ones trapped in the hinge of my oven door. I watch her for a moment as her chubby fingers coax the till roll under a small rubber cylinder. The colour of her hands could not be a more different shade to her face. In fact, her hands are pink. A completely different part of the colour spectrum. I wonder if I should tell her.

I don't understand make-up at all. It is a complete lie that is so openly accepted and is a near-integral part of being female. At some stage many years ago (when, I care not) a woman began to change the parts of her face she didn't like. She began to apply all kinds of powders and bits of plants and bits of animals and strange potions to make herself look different to how she actually looked. And at that time, other people would have noticed and commented on how attractive the woman now looked. If you think about it, this is a huge insult. It is basically saying that (now she had painted over the cracks) she looked good, the inference of course being that before she looked bad.

And so, many years passed and generations of women gained some kind of security from being able to 'make up' (hence the name, I expect) their features. My lips are too thin – paint on fatter ones. My skin is coarse – plaster over it and smooth it. My face has wrinkles – fill them in. My eyes are surrounded by dark patches – lighten them. My eyelids are bland – colour them in.

It's a very clever, and universally accepted, way of changing exactly who you are. And as you know, we already hide too much of our real selves in creating characters that we want

122

the world to believe we are. The last thing we need is a world that perpetuates the acceptance of a lie about our external appearance as well.

This is why I am here.

This is why I am telling you this.

It is time for us all to tell the truth.

And it has started with me.

Because I seriously cannot take much more.

I catch my reflection in a small mirror which is angled down to the counter from the top right of the cigarette kiosk. I lift my head slightly and my hair disappears from view. I stare deeply into my eyes and for a second I'm transfixed. It is only an interruption that breaks my stare.

"Is that it, love?" says the girl.

I turn to look at her. Her face reminds me of a well-trodden autumnal path.

"Sorry?"

"Is that it?"

I panic. I feel that the purchase of just two rolls of toilet paper is not enough for her. I grab a discounted and partially dented can of Coke from the counter. "Oh, and this," I say.

She sighs. I grab another can and pass her that. I hope it will appease her.

She takes my money and gives me the change. As I carry my bag toward the door, I can still hear the heel of her hand repeatedly hitting the cover where the till roll is inserted.

I climb into the car and throw the bag over my shoulder

towards the back seat. As it leaves my hand, the bag catches my shoulder and the impact smashes the misshapen cans into my cheek. It hurts, and I curse myself out loud for not taking the simple option of opening the back door and placing the bag in the rear foot-well. I check in the mirror for bruising. At that moment, my eyes make contact with those in the reflection and I wish with all my heart that I could use make-up to change the way I feel inside.

I put the car into gear and move slowly from the petrol station forecourt to the main road. Pyramids of orange light, cast from the lampposts, illuminate the wet road below. I wait until the traffic clears and turn right toward home.

It has not been a good day at work.

It will not be a good night.

I cannot face seeing my parents tonight. I decide to text them later and lie about being held up at work. I'm sure they'll understand.

The contradiction is evident to me. I don't want any company, yet I am dreading the solitude in the darkness of the place I call home.

I travel the short distance home and turn left onto my street. I am immediately greeted by an audience of bins. They stand on the pavement facing toward the road, like a crowd at a parade. They are brown. It is the plastic and glass recycling collection tomorrow. The bins are equal distances apart, straight and neat as their owners left them. Around where I live, it is likely that by the morning several will have been kicked over by over-exuberant teenagers impressing their friends with pseudo-karate moves. I hate bin day. The routine eats enormously into the little time I have to myself. I will explain why.

My bin – well, actually bins (green, brown, blue, black) – are all situated in my back garden. On bin day, I have to enter the house from the front, remove my shoes and make my way to the kitchen at the back. Then I have to retrieve the padlock keys from the kitchen drawer, put my shoes back on and traipse out into the back garden. I have to unlock the padlock and unbolt the three bolts that keep my gate shut. I then have to drag the bin to the end of the row of terraces, along the side of the end terrace and then back up the street to leave it outside my house. My terrace is halfway up the row and thus I have to travel three sides of a rectangle. It all takes so much time. You'll appreciate that, from time to time, I have been sorely tempted to drag the bloody thing straight through the house.

I unlock the back door. The blackbird is sitting on top of my gate. As I approach the bin, he hops sideways across the top of the gate and onto the wall. I unbolt the gate and, as I open it, I look up at him. I nod. I swear he nods back.

I pull the bin into position at the front of my house. My bin has a large sticker on it that is supposed to make it look like a leafy ivy bush. My father surprised me by applying the sticker one day when I was at work. Sadly, against a red-brick background it only amplifies just how out of place the bin looks. A large foliage cuboid. Once the bin is in place, I usually go back into the house through the front and perform the shoe removing and bolting and locking ritual in reverse. Today is slightly different.

"Nice bin."

The voice comes from behind me.

I turn. About three bins away is a woman, aged around thirty. I've not seen her before. She is perfectly lit beneath the spray of light from the lamppost. The romantics amongst you may see this as a sign. An angel lit in gold. A defining moment from a cheesy film where a burst of light comes from the clouds and lights up whatever it is the film director wants you to see. I can assure you it is not.

She is short and is wearing a dark hoodie. It has a white logo that I cannot make out as the design indents between her breasts. She is smiling.

"I said, 'nice bin'," she clarifies.

This feels awkward. Her sarcasm isn't lost on me.

"Hmm," I say. I am conscious that the noise doesn't come out right at all. Her next statement confirms this.

"I'm sorry," she says. "I didn't mean to offend you."

My chest tightens. I'm immediately angry that I gave the wrong impression.

"It's okay," I try, hoping that sounds better.

She walks toward me. She is now less than a bin away. I notice that her hair is ginger. It is pulled back into a ponytail. It looks unbrushed.

"I'm Carly," she says.

"Andrew," I say, holding out my hand in the same way I would greet an important visitor to the office. She takes another step forward and reaches out her hand. I shake hands with the cuff of her hoodie. It's slightly damp. I wonder if she's been sucking on it. Like my son used to.

"We've just moved in," she says.

"Right."

"It seems alright 'round here."

I lower the corners of my mouth, raise my eyebrows and rock my head from side to side. It is supposed to give the message, 'Yeah, I suppose it's okay.'

She giggles. I wish I'd just said the words instead of trying to mime.

"What's up? Is there something I should know about living here?"

"Nah, not really," I say. I know that wherever I live, sadly I'll be there too.

She giggles again playfully. Her mouth and cheeks move up and down simultaneously. She reminds me of chipmunk. Or a red squirrel.

"Come on, Andrew. Spill the beans."

"It's nothing," I say, partially because I don't know what else to say. I think. Hard. "There are plenty of worse places."

I'm thankful she doesn't pick up on such an obvious statement. Of course there are. Her sarcasm could have ripped such idiocy to pieces.

"Yeah," she says, looking skyward for a split second. "Yeah."

She takes a step backward. I do the same. We are two bins apart.

"Well," she says, "I'd better get back inside. Can't leave my little girl for too long."

"Yeah. No problem."

"It's been good to meet you, Andrew" – she cranes her head around to see my front door – "of number forty-four."

"You too," I say.

"I'm at number fifty."

She smiles again.

I try my hardest, though I suspect rather than a smile my mouth looks more like a broken zip.

She pauses. "Well, I'll see you."

"Yeah, see you," I say.

I turn quickly and walk into my house. I shut the front door and stand behind it for a second. I control my breathing, which is initially deep and heavy. I slip off my right shoe, using the carpet for leverage. I then post my big toe into the side of my left shoe and remove it. I stand for a second or two longer, wondering whether she is doing the same in her hallway.

chapter eighteen

It was work.

Absolutely nothing happened.

Aside from the cadence of keyboards, which I firmly believe is beginning to affect my brain.

I don't see that there is any point in wasting your time trying to relate something from my day that may be interesting to you.

There was nothing.

I arrived.

I worked.

I left.

chapter nineteen

My daydream of a perfect world is ruined when a rapid blur of silver flashes across my eyes. I am instantly back in the real world. The car in front of me has swerved sharply to the right. In that split-second, I act instinctively and swing my car in the same direction. The car in front then swerves back across the lane I have just left and screeches to a halt on the hard shoulder. I copy the manoeuvre and swing back to the left, returning to my lane without crossing the continuous white line. In my rear-view mirror, I see the empty cardboard box we've both just skilfully dodged. I can also see a lady at the wheel of the silver car, aged around fifty, with her head in her hands.

Through my sunroof I see grey clouds race across the sky. I hope it won't rain. I pull off the motorway and coast down the slip road toward the roundabout that leads me home. This is my favourite part of the journey. It takes me away from the pick-up-speed-slow-to-a-crawl repetition of the motorway and through sweeping countryside. The roads are narrower and the feeling of control over the car becomes more thrilling. The motorway reminds me of a conveyor belt – the cars, boxes, all moving the same way at the same speed. The open roads on the final part of my journey twist and curl, challenging me to accelerate and brake at each turn. I come off the roundabout onto the straight stretch that begins the four miles of open countryside. To my right is a large field of cows. I study them as I go by, hoping they will solve my weather conundrum. I estimate that roughly half are lying down, which suggests rain. The other half are standing. Some help they are.

I continue up a steep hill, ignoring the sign that limits my speed to fifty. I press the buttons on my steering wheel, changing the view on the screen in front of me to a digital speedometer. It vacillates between sixty-two and sixty-seven. A few spots of rain hit the windscreen and the automatic wiper springs into life. I consider turning around to congratulate those cows that chose to lie, but decide against it. I really could do without the rain. I have promised my father that I will cut his grass for him after work tomorrow. A total washout will mean that I will have to endure his calls each day, asking when I will be over to cut it.

He used to love cutting the grass. It was one of his favourite hobbies until sciatica put an end to it. I often wonder whether he enjoyed the task so much because it was the only one that allowed him to be truly alone. The noise of the lawnmower drowns out everything, my mother included. Every other job he may attend to, whether it be car washing or weeding, she's there too. She stands a few feet behind him, either commentating on his every move or disseminating vapid information. Don't get me wrong: she doesn't criticise. She just speaks. Constantly. Like the buzz of the motorway.

He has never disclosed to me why he loved cutting the grass so much and I've never asked him. I suspect I'm right, though.

I know that he used to take at least an hour longer than I take. And this is nothing to do with age. It has always been that way. He'd prolong the experience, squeezing out every last moment of solitary pleasure. He would also cut the lawn at the first sign of growth – in the summer, sometimes every other day. And now each time I cut the grass he follows me around the garden. From the moment I pull the cord and the petrol engine bursts into life, he is there. As I push the mower up and down the garden, he walks a pace behind me. Living the experience vicariously. From time to time, I stop suddenly and he walks into my back, as if trying to hug me from behind. It makes me feel slightly uncomfortable, but I suppose I don't really mind.

The sky cracks and the raindrops instantly become bigger, bouncing up from the road in front of me. My mood begins to sink when I realise that soon the weekend will be upon me. The truth is, I take little pleasure from the weekend. Two days without the distraction of work. Two days by myself. Tiny palpitations begin in my chest and I know that as the evening goes on the feeling will only grow. I push the pedal harder to the floor.

I fumble with the stereo, scrolling through the music for something loud. Something heavy. I am half watching the road and half the list of artists on the screen to my left. There are nearly ten thousand songs on my iPhone. I scroll through the entire alphabet, unable to find anything I want to hear. I swerve to miss a small branch that has become detached from one of the many sycamore trees that cloak this stretch of the road. I twist the knob to begin scrolling back towards the top of the list. The feeling in my chest begins to increase and a hot, burning sensation rises toward my neck. I post my finger down the front of my tie and pull it loose, momentarily leaving the car to steer itself. I grab the wheel again to correct my angle away from the grass verge, and then, using my thumb and forefinger, unbutton my shirt. I still feel hot. My left hand continues to scroll and I alternate glances between the screen and the road. In this instant, I feel dangerous. A turn of the dial lands the red cursor on Nirvana, and I push the knob to select it. The music needs to be loud. I want to sing or screech or scream the words at the top of my voice. I want to shout out the feelings that are rising inside me. Spit them out of me.

There is a list of songs and I begin the scroll again, looking for my favourite, 'Territorial Pissings'. A whiny voice opens the song, sarcastically mocking The Youngbloods' classic, and I turn the volume up to three-quarters. The fuzz of guitars is quickly overpowered by frantic, urgent drumming and the car is filled with sound. It is loud, and I shout along with the singer. I feel the song. I feel the torture that the singer endures. I want to scream until my throat bleeds.

A minute into the song:

It's not working. It's wrong. It's the wrong song. This isn't what I wanted. My heart beats faster. I am getting hotter. Anger rises inside me. I turn the fan up to six, the temperature as cold as it will go. The blast of cool air causes my fringe to lift and then hover. This song won't work.

"You fucking idiot," I spit. I hate myself for choosing the wrong song.

As the car leaves the row of trees I accelerate again, knowing this is the last stretch before the beauty of the countryside is exchanged for the drab grey houses of my town. I scroll frantically for another song, up and down the names. I realise that I don't want to listen to Nirvana after all. No, I need to find something else. I prod the screen, moving back to the list of artists. I'm cold now, so I turn the dial the opposite way. Full heat. I lower the fan speed and my fringe falls. I choose Pearl Jam and begin to scroll through the songs. I settle on 'Daughter', one of my all-time favourites. The familiar guitar opens, but I'm too unsettled now and it doesn't sound right. I leave it for a moment longer and then, concluding that once again I've made the wrong choice, I slam the palm of my hand into the knob, instantly turning the stereo off.

A few minutes later I am sitting at a red light, waiting to turn onto the road that leads to my house. The car is silent. I turn off the fan and light a cigarette, my fifth or sixth of the journey. I have an indentation in the shape of a circle in the palm of my left hand. I think I can hear the sound of my heart. Outside, a man in a damp grey coat stoops down to collect what his dog has just left. He nods at me. I nod back. The traffic begins to move.

I do not want to go home.

I have no reason to.

I indicate left and turn into my road, creeping slowly toward my house. I wish my heart would follow suit and reduce its speed to match my car. As I pull in, I notice a woman on the pavement. I turn off the engine and get out of the car.

"Hi," she says, smiling.

"Hi," I reply. I notice that she is wearing a hair slide in the shape of a peace sign. It's luminous yellow. It clashes with her hair.

"Another meeting by the bins, eh?" she says, winking.

I like her.

"Yep," I say. I manage a smile back.

"You walking 'round with me then?"

"Why not?" I say.

"Get your posh bin then."

"You're just jealous," I say, grabbing the wet handles, the only part of my bin not covered in ivy.

She grabs her bin and pulls it behind her. She is wearing a Nirvana t-shirt under her brown cardigan. I like her a little bit more.

We begin our walk down the damp pavement toward the end terrace.

chapter twenty

Today is going to be a good day. I can't explain why I feel this way, I just have a feeling as I walk up the stairs to the office. I pause briefly and widen my mouth into my morning smile. I'm not sure whether the anticipation is driven by some kind of change that I feel, but it's clear from the most recent emails that Alan's replacement is going to be appointed soon, perhaps today.

I'm not actually sure whether I want to be in charge of this department. It's hardly something I dreamed about as a child. We were all footballers, train drivers or rock stars back then. I do remember a boy at school – he was called Francis – saying he wanted to work in the sewers and drains beneath the town, but he was just, well, weird. Plus, his dad did that job, so it may have had a bearing on Francis's choice of future vocation. I know that I have a poor memory, but I don't ever remember saying that I wanted to grow up to be the head of a complaints department. Nevertheless, here I am, and to be fair the recognition would be nice.

I open the door and walk into the department. It occurs to me that some of my colleagues may have seen me through the two thin panels of glass that run vertically down the side of the wooden door. If they did, if they saw my routine, then so be it. I do it every day. A long, deep breath through my nose, smile and enter.

"Morning all," I say cheerfully. I still insist on greeting the team with an almost sarcastic joyfulness.

Today, my greeting is met with more enthusiasm than in recent days. I get one or two direct responses. Even a nervous smile from Clare. There seems to be a slight shift in the atmosphere. My colleagues are more relaxed. I wonder whether a further email has been sent to all of us. Maybe today our futures will become clear.

I walk to my desk and sit down.

Elaine is grunting and sighing. I reach down under my desk to switch on my computer and twist my head so I can see what she is doing. She is repeatedly prodding the screen on her iPhone with her chubby forefinger. I close my eyes for a second and then lift my head back up. I log on to my machine. She grunts and then sighs again. I am used to this routine. The grunt is actually a question. It says, "Will you help me, Andrew?"

I really don't feel like assisting her, but something inside me tells me I should. I have ignored this routine once or twice in the past and it simply led to me becoming more irritated.

She holds her phone outstretched in her left hand and prods frantically at the screen. She grunts again. I decide to help her if for no other reason than wanting to stop her grunting. I know already that my irritation will reach its peak at the end when, after I've solved the problem for her, she announces to the room that she already knew how to fix it.

"Got a problem, Elaine?" I ask.

"It's this bloody new phone," she spits. "There's something wrong with it."

I know for a fact there isn't.

"Why? What's it doing?"

"The screen, it doesn't work properly." Her chubby face is screwed up tightly and sweat runs down her temples. She bears a passing resemblance to a pregnant sow.

"Ah, right," I say.

"It was doing it last night." She sweeps her hand forward and slams the phone down onto a pile of files that are stacked like pancakes on the corner of her desk. "Bloody useless."

I pause, considering whether I should warn her that her actions could break the phone permanently. She pulls the phone back up and gingerly turns it over. A small look of relief is visible when she sees the screen is undamaged. She snorts. It makes a change from the grunts.

"Do you want any help?" I offer.

"No, it doesn't work. Cost me seven hundred quid as well. It'll have to go back."

I slide my chair closer to her and hold out my hand.

"I had the same problem," I lie so as not to make her feel stupid. "Let's have a look. I might be able to fix it."

She turns the screen toward me, but won't release the phone. My hand remains outstretched and anyone entering the room now may believe they are interrupting me asking her to dance.

"So, what are you trying to do?"

"Get into my emails. There's an important one to my home address from Nick," she says pointedly. She prods at the icon shaped like an envelope on the screen again. Nothing happens. "You won't be able to fix it," she snaps.

I ignore her tone. I am used to it. She sounds like the most spoiled, immature child that ever lived. Crossed with a pig. I cannot describe how awful it is.

"Let's see," I say calmly. She moves the phone closer to me, her fat pink hand still gripping tightly. Each finger is half-covered with gold rings. A wave of skin laps from her hand and surrounds the rings, sucking them in. Her hands are swallowing her jewellery. There is no question that to remove the rings you would need to remove the fingers.

I lean in, catching a slight smell of body odour.

"So you're trying to get into your emails, yeah?"

"I've just said, haven't I? Bloody screen doesn't work."

She prods the screen again randomly.

"Why do you have to be so fucking rude?" a voice says from across the room.

We both turn. In unison, so does the rest of the room.

"Well?" Jess continues. "He's trying to help you and you're talking to him like shit."

Her words are precise and direct. Elaine's face flushes. Jess is staring at her; there is no expression on her face. I flash a smile at Jess. She ignores it and looks back at her monitor. The room is silent.

"Okay," I say, adjusting the screen slightly in my direction.

Elaine still won't relinquish it. I reach and press the letter icon on the screen precisely. The screen changes and her inbox appears.

"How did you do that?" she says. There is a discernible change in her tone. Slightly less aggressive.

"I just pressed the icon."

"Well, it doesn't work for me."

I want to say that it's because her fingers are too fat to make contact with a single icon alone. That when she presses the screen she hits two, sometimes four icons. That the phone is confused by the sheer size of her finger ends and doesn't know how to respond. That the anger she has stored inside her for whatever reason should not be taken out on her phone in the form of spiteful, vicious prods at the screen. I say none of this.

"Hmm. It might be because of your nails," I say diplomatically. I've noticed her ridiculously long and quite obviously fake black nails.

"What do you mean?"

"Well, the angle that you tap the icons at differs because of your nails." I tap the screen; it responds. "See? I don't have any nails so it's not a problem."

"It's a design fault then," she mutters.

"I can increase the size of the icons to make them easier to hit," I say.

"Hmph. Well, I tried that, but I suppose we can try it again."

I ignore the lie she has just told and scroll through the settings. She still grips the phone.

"There you go."

She taps the screen. It works.

"Well, it'll have to do," she says. "Like I said, I'd already tried that."

"Er, thank you, Andrew," says Jess, staring directly at Elaine. I imagine lasers powered only by hate coming from her eyes.

Elaine stares back. "Oh yes, whatever. Thanks, Andrew."

"It's fine."

"See, that didn't hurt, did it?" says Jess.

I slide back to my desk and begin to work through my emails, confused as to why Jess has suddenly become an ally.

Five hours and six Camel lights later, I get the call I was hoping for. It's Nick. He wants a meeting in fifteen minutes to talk about the replacement for Alan. Before we end the call he asks me to inform Elaine that she too will be needed. I turn to her. She is talking to Clare.

"It's a design fault," she says. "What good is a phone that women can't use because of fingernails?"

Clare nods in agreement. She looks genuinely concerned.

"It's crap. Useless waste of money,"

"So are you going to send it back?" Clare asks.

"Well, Andrew made the icons bigger and it works better now," Elaine concedes.

Clare's face brightens and she nods again.

"Of course, I knew how to do that."

I've heard enough.

"Elaine, Nick just rang. He wants to speak to us in fifteen minutes."

"Ooh, okay," she says. She picks up the phone on her desk. "Hi, Janet. Cancel all calls for me and Andrew. We have a very important meeting with Nick."

She turns to me. "I've told reception not to put through any calls."

The whole office is staring at us. You can feel the anticipation. I catch Jacob's eye. He nods and smiles. It gives me a warm feeling of confidence.

I decide to have a cigarette prior to the meeting.

Standing outside for the five minutes or less it takes to smoke a cigarette somewhat ironically saves my life on a daily basis. The pressure that builds in the office has to be defused somehow. The reward of a cigarette does this. As I've already said, I don't have a particularly stressful job. The stress comes from keeping up the charade all day. The joyous happy-to-be-alive-and-thankful-for-each-day me. I undertake a particular piece of work with two things in mind. The first is to do a good, precise and thorough job. I am being paid to do this and as such I perform every task to the best of my ability. The second is the reward of the cigarette when the task is complete.

I prefer to smoke alone, but this is not always possible. A handful of people in the whole company are still fatally addicted to this pursuit. We gather randomly at the allotted smoking area at the far end of the building, next to a large green metal dumpster. A place allocated by management for the damned. Today, happily, I am alone.

I cannot tell you just how much pleasure I get from being alone out here. I lean against the red-brick wall, the foundation of a short-lived smoking shelter which was built when the smoking ban was first introduced. It used to have a curved plastic roof to protect us from the rain, but it was destroyed by local teenagers soon after it went up. We arrived one morning to find nothing but broken shards of plastic on the floor. It's never been replaced. The red wall is all that remains.

The sun beams down on my face. I light my cigarette and breathe in the smoke. The first draw doesn't have any impact, so I pull on the cigarette again, ensuring that I can feel the smoke filling my lungs. I hold it for a while, shut my eyes and then release it. I feel free. Standing in the warmth, eyes shut, I could be anywhere. I allow myself to dream about living trouble-free somewhere in rural Iowa, surrounded by open fields. The type of place where you may not speak to anyone for a few days, maybe a week. My dream is sabotaged by the scraping of a fire door. I open my eyes. A fellow smoker has arrived. I can't remember his name. I nod at him and he returns the gesture. I take the last draw of my cigarette before dropping it to the ground. I check my watch to see whether there is time for another cigarette. There isn't: my meeting starts in six minutes.

Back at my desk, Nick has already arrived. He looks at his watch, a cowardly way to suggest that I am late. In fact, he is early, but in the interests of my job I decide not mention this.

"Been smoking, Andrew?" says Elaine, knowing full well this is the case. This is typical of her spite. I seethe inside.

"Hi, Nick," I say.

"Right, I need to talk to you both," he says, indicating that we should move into a private meeting room elsewhere in the building.

It is extremely rare for Nick to be in our department. In fact, it is extremely rare for anyone else from the company to be in our department. Nick's appearance causes the staff to behave like meerkats. Alert heads pop up from behind the monitors on each of the desks, and eyes dart between one another. It's decision time. I have no nerves whatsoever, though I'm thankful that the meeting was arranged at such short notice. We enter the meeting room and Nick closes the grey door firmly. It clicks loudly into the lock.

"Sit down, Andrew, Elaine," he says.

I breathe in.

It's time.

Around an hour later, I am back at my desk. My new boss is addressing the department for the first time. We all look on. I am half-listening. It may just be me, but the expressions of each of my colleagues seem to replicate my feelings. We are all utterly astounded.

"So," Elaine continues from behind her desk, "I will be making a few changes, but you'll hear about those later."

This is because she has no idea what they may be.

"And," she continues, "I just want to say that all your jobs are safe."

I am aware that her role does not extend to hiring and firing staff. She takes a huge bite of a sugared chocolate doughnut that was lying on a white paper bag on her desk. We all watch as she chews, making a clack-clack sound.

"For now, though, it'll be B-A-U."

"Sorry, what?" says Clare.

"Business as usual." I watch a small piece of chocolate leave Elaine's mouth and stick to her monitor.

We all turn back to our screens. It seems the speech is over. It was hardly Martin Luther King. It's time for a cigarette. I stand.

"One final thing," she says. I am standing a few feet away from her. From this angle I can see a dozen or so granules of sugar caught in the coarse black hairs that protrude from her chin. "There will be no smoking during work hours." She turns to me and smiles. "Except at lunchtime."

I look blankly at her.

"What?" I say.

"No smoking during office hours, Andrew. It's unproductive."

The audience of meerkats has reappeared.

"I'm not sure you can do that, Elaine," I say calmly.

"I just did, Andrew." She draws out my name for extra effect.

I remain silent and continue my stare. I hope that the expression on my face says: 'What the fuck are you doing?'

"Do you want to call Nick and ask him?"

"No," I say, "I don't."

I sit back down. A barely audible hush is released into the room. I decide for now that this is not a battle I want to take on. It's just past four o'clock and I can wait until I leave for the day to smoke. I begin amending a report.

Elaine resettles her huge frame in her chair and spends the next twenty minutes on the phone telling people within the company of her promotion. Simultaneously, she releases pungent odours which remind me of dough and sprouts. I continue to make corrections to my report, ignoring the enemy assault on my senses.

She finally puts down her phone and links together her fingers, before inverting her arms and stretching them out in front of her. She lets out a loud, satisfied sigh across the room. Then she stands and makes her way across the room to a small partitioned area where the photocopier is. The photocopier – or multi-functional device, as we are now supposed to call it – takes up most of the area. It is a huge machine that all the computers in the office print to. We can also fax, scan, photocopy, you name it. It has five trays filled with various sizes and colours of paper. Alongside the partitions are various boxes full of reams of paper. There is a small desk. On top of it sits a franking machine. The partitions were installed six months ago when Clare anonymously complained that she couldn't concentrate due to the noise. Her complaint described how close she sat to the photocopier, which made the anonymity of her complaint wholly pointless.

Across the room I see Jacob shaking his head. We look at one another, incredulous. I can't help but smile. I turn back to my screen and scan my report. It won't be finished today. My eyes are sore from staring at the screen and I can feel my concentration waning. I decide to spend the remainder of the afternoon checking it by hand, and hit print.

I rest my hands on the edge of my desk and just sit for a moment.

My eyes are closed.

I wonder what the future now holds.

We'll see.

After a few moments, I push against the desk and my chair slides back, the wheels squeaking slightly as it moves. I stand and make my way around the corner to the photocopier. When I arrive, I am greeted by the sight of Elaine lying on the floor. She resembles a huge clothed slug. Her face is red and sweat has wet her hair across her forehead. She looks up at me.

"Is it jammed?" I say.

"What does it look like?" she grunts. The bottom tray is pulled out and she has her arm pushed deep inside it, clawing at the inside of the machine. She pulls out a small section of A4 paper which the machine has half-eaten. I can hear her breathing short, fast bursts through her nose. I imagine her heart is pumping for all it's worth. She changes position,

147

struggling onto her side to get a better angle on the paper. The machine bursts into life. I am fortunate to be printing from the top tray.

"You should be doing this," she says. From above, I can see straight down her nose.

"I'm happy to help out," I reply.

"I'm fine," she snorts. "I might be the boss, but I don't mind getting my hands dirty." She continues to fumble around inside the machine, trying to remove the paper that remains.

"Okay," I say. I reach over her to retrieve my report and turn away.

"Ah, got it!" she shouts out happily.

As I move away from the photocopier I swing my leg forward then use the back of my heel to shut the open photocopier drawer. I connect with some power. It is my attempt to help – to save Elaine from having to close it. I fully expect to hear the click as it slides back into place. Instead, I hear a scream.

I immediately turn to discover her face has reddened even further. She is breathing very heavily. My eyes follow her head to her shoulders to the top of her arm. I realise – to my horror – that this is as much as I can see. I cannot see the lower part of her arm, it is caught somewhere inside the drawer and the belly of the photocopier.

"Oh my God!" says Clare, who has approached after hearing the scream.

I reach down to pull open the drawer and release her arm. As I do Elaine screams again, this time louder than the initial cry.

"Don't you dare touch it!" she bellows.

"Oh my God," repeats Clare. She begins to cry.

I turn to Clare. Behind her the rest of the department are peering silently around the corner.

"Just get him away from me," shrieks Elaine.

chapter twenty-one

Not for the first time recently, I cannot wait to leave work.

I am away from my desk and into my car like my shoes are on fire. I slam the gear stick into first and hit the accelerator. I am ashamed to say that my tyres screech as I pull out of the car park. I didn't actually mean that to happen, it was a misjudgement, but for a moment I was the same as the youths that fly around my local town centre in twenty-year-old cars with body kits. I feel a sudden sense of relief when I can no longer see my office in my rear-view mirror, and I slow down. By the time I have reached the junction onto the main road, I am calm again. The traffic lights are on red as I approach them and I stop behind a white van that is advertising gardening services. I am second in the queue. My trousers have bunched up uncomfortably around my groin, so I lift myself slightly out of the seat and remove my hands from the steering wheel. I tug at the creases on the thighs of my trousers to loosen them. I relax back into my seat. It hasn't worked: I am still uncomfortable. I lift myself once again and feed my hand down the front of my trousers, inside my boxer shorts. I adjust myself and lower my boxer shorts so they are no longer tight around my groin. I hear the sound of a car horn. I look up. The white van has disappeared. The lights have turned to green. I quickly shuffle back into position, put my car into gear and lurch the car forward. As I cross the opposite carriageway, I change into the wrong gear and the car jumps and then stops. I've stalled it.

The horn sounds again. Long. Aggressive.

I look up and see the angriest face I have ever seen. It belongs to a man in the car behind me. In my mirror, the face is only inches away from me. It is already crimson and the man's mouth is shouting silent swear words. I push the gearstick back into first, raise the clutch and drive away, concentrating as hard as when I took my driving test. I check the mirror again. The angry face is still there. The man seems intent on remaining as close to me as possible. His car cannot be more than a few inches from mine. As I change up through the gears, the face reduces in size, and then enlarges. I wouldn't be surprised if the man hit the back of my car very soon. He is gesturing and pointing with his right hand, beckoning me to pull over to the side of the road. I expect he wants to tell me face to face what he thinks of me. Worse still, he may wish to take his anger out on my person. The rage which envelops him frightens me. I cannot imagine feeling the way he does about something as simple as being held up in traffic for no more than thirty seconds. As I watch him in the mirror, glaring at me and spitting out swear words, I begin to wonder what his life is like. He is wearing a shirt and tie, and his car is close enough for me to make out that the shirt is pale blue with white cuffs and his tie is maroon. He has neat brown hair and is wearing glasses. He looks my age. I expect that he must be some kind of salesman. He's driving a mid-range executive car, the type

151

that is economical on fuel for hour after hour after hour of daily driving. I imagine that he spends the vast majority of his day driving from business to business, trying to sell whatever it is his employer manufactures.

My mind begins to wander. Each day he leaves his home, climbs into his car and sets off to wherever his diary instructs him to go. His boss phones first thing, either to congratulate him on the daily sales report he submitted the night before, or to chastise him for not hitting the previous day's target. Whatever the previous day's results, the call ends with the salesman being told in no uncertain terms that he is expected to hit target every day. The salesman then arrives at each of his appointments and, in simplified terms, begs his customers to buy something from him. Each and every day, he drives his silver Ford Mondeo into another car park in another town. He straightens his tie, sprays breath freshener into his mouth, affixes a smile and then enters his customer's premises.

His ego will never let him accept it, but he is of no real importance. Let's be honest, if the customer is desperate for more product, they will simply ring his employer. So he sits and he waits, busying himself on his tablet with one eye on the clock on the reception wall. Perhaps twenty minutes after his appointment time, a weary-looking buyer – or, more likely, office manager – greets the salesman and beckons him into a meeting room. There is no apology for keeping him waiting. The salesman then goes into his charm offensive, describing the company's products as if he lives and breathes them.

As if the world simply can't do without them.

As if he's selling earth's final supplies of oxygen and water.

Then, after showing his customer various aesthetically pleasing charts and diagrams, he may or may not secure a commitment to buy. If he does, his mood will improve in synchronicity with the sale. If he sells nothing, he slumps. His sales graph directly echoes his emotional state. When he leaves each customer, he is already late for his next meeting. He spends the next hour in the car, accelerating to make up time and telephoning apologetically to rearrange his appointments for the reminder of the day. I glance in my mirror. He is still shouting. And pointing. My lack of response seems to be adding further fuel to the fire that is raging inside him. The sweat that drips from his temples suggests it's getting quite hot in there. His forehead is wet and shiny. He continually removes his glasses, wipes his eyes and then replaces them. I get to thinking about what his home life is like.

I imagine that he has a wife and perhaps three kids, all younger than eight. I glance in the mirror to see whether I can spot a gold band on the finger next to the middle finger he is currently holding up. This isn't a sensible move; I get the impression he thinks I am trying to provoke him further by staring, so I look toward the road again. Each evening, he pulls his car onto his gravel drive and parks in front of his mock Tudor house. His family are inside, waiting for the dull thud as he slams his car door. From the moment they hear the car, their moods are also synchronised with his sales graph. His wife waits nervously, hoping that the sales have been good that day. His older children look forward to his arrival to share with him reports of their day at school. As soon as the front door shuts, his wife instantly knows whether to shepherd the children into a different room. She justifies this using statements like "Daddy's had a busy day at work" and "Let your daddy get through the door".

On a good day, he appears at home with flowers, wearing a broad smile as he enters the expansive modern kitchen – the kitchen that his wife accepted in return for his long hours and mood swings. He feels safe in the knowledge that he can afford the mortgage repayments for at least another few months. The man swerves his car as if to overtake me, and then quickly drops back as a blue Land Rover comes from the opposite direction. The man beeps his horn frantically, blaming me for the appearance of the other car. He is furious. I look at him long and hard and wonder what can possibly drive people into such rage. What lives inside them that makes them behave this way? His anger has become contagious and his actions over the last ten minutes have begun to affect me. He is overstepping the mark. He is completely unhinged, a danger to himself and others. I continue to stare at him. Again, he points to the side of the road.

I have had enough. He knows nothing of the struggles of my life. If slowing him down for a matter of thirty seconds is enough to send him into a rage where he wants to physically hurt me, then let's have it over with.

I have never been in a fight.

I do not know what I am capable of.

The salesman makes me want to find out. I have always thought that if the time ever came for me to fight, I would win. Not because I am the strongest or best equipped, but because I have so much tension and pressure inside me that once released would swamp me. I would not know when to stop. I would literally have to be dragged off the person I was fighting. I would be covered in their blood. On my fists, my shoes, my clothes. I would still be stamping on my opponent's pulped head long after they had lost consciousness. It would take five or six people to pull me away.

I make a 'wanker' sign in the mirror and turn in my seat to look at the salesman. There is a microscopic change in his expression. I turn back to the road, and then turn again and point at him, and then to the side of the road. I want him to stop. I want to scream into his face. Tell him how his actions have made me feel. He reminds me of the bullies at school. His mouth is now closed. He grips his steering wheel with both hands. He is looking away. I can almost see his resolve crumbling.

I slam on my brakes and swerve my car half onto the pavement.

I have lost control.

I throw my door open and leap from the car into the middle of the road. The man swerves around me, resisting my invitation to discuss his actions. He doesn't look at me as he passes. I watch as his car disappears over a mini roundabout and down a hill and out of sight. I am left standing in the road with my arms aloft. Cars creep past me slowly, their drivers eyeing me cautiously.

I tuck in my shirt, adjust my boxer shorts around my groin and climb back into my car.

I feel good.

chapter twenty-two

I fix my smile and walk into the office. Something is going on. As I enter the room, my colleagues are huddled together around Elaine's desk. As they notice my presence, they begin to slowly slide their chairs back using their feet to propel them. They remind me of synchronised swimmers returning to the edge of the pool after meeting for a group routine. I have a feeling that they believe I cannot see what they are doing. As I approach, Jess and Martin give up on the charade and wheel their empty chairs back behind their desks. I wait until everybody is at their own desk before greeting them.

"Good morning, everyone!" I say, smiling slightly more widely than usual. I hope that they can see the element of sarcasm in my smile.

I receive one or two responses from the usual sources. Jess glares at me. It appears her allegiance to me is already over.

"So, what were we all talking about?" I say to no-one in particular.

Elaine answers.

"Alan said to ring him as soon as you get in," she says.

I look over at her. She is sitting taller than usual. I suspect she has used the lever under her chair to literally elevate herself to match her new status. She looks like a fat lifeguard.

"Right," I say.

I remove my suit jacket and place it over the back of my

157

chair. Various items of post have been deposited on my desk since the previous day. I shuffle through them while I wait for my computer to boot up. The department is silent.

"Er, Andrew…" Elaine says, trailing my name annoyingly.

I turn toward her, and notice that her enormous thighs are wedged between her chair and the underside of the table. It looks painful but she obviously feels it is worth it. She smiles at me, a sour smile, like she is holding a quarter of a lemon between her teeth. She doesn't show her teeth.

"Yep?"

"Alan said as soon as you arrived."

"Well, he won't know I'm here yet, will he?"

She turns to her screen and immediately begins typing. A few seconds later she clicks the mouse, releases a satisfied sigh and leans back in her chair. I suspect she has just emailed Alan.

At that moment, my phone rings. I glance at its digital screen. It's Alan. My paranoia may just be spot on this time.

"Andrew," he says, "are you free? It's important."

This is not really a question. It's just phrased that way. I don't believe I have any choice.

"Yeah, sure," I say.

"Good," he says. "We'll meet immediately in the small boardroom."

"No problem. Do I need bring anything?"

"No, I don't think so."

I replace the phone.

"Alan?" says Elaine.

"Yeah. How did you know?"

She ignores my question.

I stand and put my jacket on. I collect a pad of paper and a pen from my desk and walk the length of the office.

"I've got a meeting with Alan. I don't know how long I'll be," I say as I reach the door at a volume that everyone can hear. No-one responds.

I open the door.

"Andrew?" Elaine has chosen the moment that I'm furthest from her to ask her final question. "Can you ask Janet to call me once you've done?"

"Er, yeah, sure," I say.

I haven't realised the implication.

The journey to the small boardroom is through a rabbit warren of thin corridors lined with doors. All the walls are painted light grey. The doors are dark grey. The carpets match. This part of the building has recently been refurbished and the skirting boards and architraves gleam in a resplendent white. There is no natural light, and I could be forgiven for thinking I've walked into a world with no colour, a 1950s' film where the entire world is monochrome.

I have no idea whether natural light is available behind the thick grey doors that I pass. Equally, I have no idea what is behind them. Each has two small rectangles of glass, one above the handle, the other below. Blinds on these small windows conceal whatever activity is taking place inside. The only difference between each door is a small white plastic plaque with black lettering, which is the code for the room. I pass BC1, BC3 and BC5. There are no doors on the other side of the corridor and I wonder who within the company has an aversion to even numbers. I run my finger along the wall as I walk, following the door frames. I round a corner, and pass CC1 and CC3 on my left. Directly ahead of me is the small boardroom (a.k.a. DC1).

The blind covering the glass is open. I knock and wait. I notice that three people are inside. Janet opens the door and holds it for me. She smiles. I smile back.

"Come on in, Andrew," she says.

I enter the room. A chair has already been pulled out from under the table. I assume it is mine. Janet stretches out her arm in the direction of the chair to confirm my assumption. She then closes the door carefully and twists a silver knob that closes the blind. Janet is tall and slim. I think she is around fifty; it's difficult to tell with amount of foundation she has applied. Her features are thin, though this could be an illusion created by her make-up. She has kind brown eyes. I suspect that she was extremely attractive thirty years ago. Her overuse of foundation is a desperate attempt to remind herself and others of that fact. To some extent, it works. She smooths the fabric of her skirt around her bottom and sits down opposite me.

"Sit down, Andrew," Alan says. His brow is slightly furrowed.

I sit.

The table is large and rectangular. It comfortably seats twenty people. The walls continue the unimaginative grey theme. The air conditioning hums behind me. Alan, Janet and the unnamed other sit opposite me. Behind them is a large glass window which looks over the small car park reserved for senior management. Every car is silver.

"Thanks," I say. I shuffle slightly from side to side and rest my hand on the table casually. That doesn't feel right, so I remove it. Instead, I take my pen and rest the nib on my pad. I'm poised, ready to write as soon as they speak.

"You've met my assistant, Mark, haven't you?"

Mark nods grimly. He is almost entirely ginger. His hair. His eyebrows. His eyelashes. Freckles dominate his face; small constituencies of actual skin-coloured skin are visible in rare sporadic patches. He too is holding a pen.

I instantly write 'Mark' on the top line of my pad. I'm not sure why. It is possibly a subconscious reaction to the fact I am holding a pen.

"Yes, I think so." I don't think we have actually met before, but I remember his face from the previous year's Christmas party.

"Do you want to start, Alan?" Janet asks.

"Yes. Sure," says Alan. He sounds anything but.

"Actually, before you do," interrupts Janet, "I'd better just say that this isn't formally a disciplinary hearing. Rather, on behalf of the company and as representatives of Human

161

Resources, we're here to collect information."

Mark scribbles frantically. I am suddenly alert.

"Sorry?"

Janet repeats the sentence.

"It's about yesterday," Alan adds.

"Yesterday?" I say. In my mind, fingers are flicking rapidly through index cards. I am trying to remember whatever it is that happened the day before. I recall every single customer file I worked on. I cannot think of anything else.

"The incident with Elaine, Andrew," Janet says. "We've received a formal complaint."

"What?" I say. I am genuinely puzzled.

"The assault –" Alan says.

"Alleged assault," corrects Janet.

"Alleged assault," repeats Alan under his breath. He sounds like a scolded child.

I sit upright and drop my pen. I look at Janet. "You are joking, aren't you?"

"I'm afraid not, Andrew. This is extremely serious."

Mark scribbles.

"Is this seriously about the photocopier?"

"Multi-functional device," Mark mutters. I ignore him.

"Yes, Andrew. So that we can complete a full investigation, we need to get your side of the story."

I fold my arms. I can't believe we are having this conversation. I try to remain calm.

"My side of the story?"

"Yes, please."

I breathe out a laugh and a sigh, and raise my eyebrows. I shake my head and smile. I decide it's better, for now at least, to play along.

"Well, okay. I was working, following my meeting with Nick about Alan's replacement..."

I nod toward Alan. He nods in agreement.

"I was finalising a report, and I sent it to print so I could read through it."

Mark eyes me suspiciously. His hand continues to move across the page.

"When I got to the photocopier, Elaine was on the floor. I think she was trying to clear a jam."

Alan smiles encouragingly. I realise that, as my direct manager, he has to be at the meeting, but it all seems a little pointless due to his imminent departure. He looks very uncomfortable. He scratches at a cotton wool tuft of his hair just above his ear. Something white drops from his hair and lands on the table. He leans forward, covering it with his folded arms.

"In fact, I know she was trying to clear a jam. Anyway, my report began printing from a different tray and I collected it from the copier. As I turned away I kicked the drawer shut."

"You kicked the drawer shut?" Alan asks.

"Yeah, I thought she'd cleared the jam, so I was helping her."

"By kicking company property?" asks Mark.

"I was just closing it."

"Is it usual for you to kick company property?" asks Janet.

I feel the atmosphere in the room change.

"I wasn't kicking company property, as such," I say. "I was just trying to help Elaine by closing the drawer."

"And where was Elaine at the time?" she continues.

"Behind me, on the floor."

"Okay...and then what happened?"

"What do you mean?"

"What happened then, Andrew?"

"Well..." I choose my words carefully. "When I pushed shut the drawer, Elaine's arm must have still been inside."

"It was inside," confirms Mark.

"Yeah, I think I trapped it accidentally."

Alan nods and slides back into his chair. He glances at the table. The white thing has gone. He smiles and looks back up at me. "So, let's summarise, Andrew. Elaine had her arm in the photocopier drawer and you closed it and trapped her?" His tone suggests that he has concluded the investigation and there is nothing further to say.

"Accidentally."

"Sorry, accidentally," he says.

"That's right."

An hour, maybe longer passes. During this time, Alan has checked his watch three times. Each time he has tried to do it surreptitiously by casually sliding his cuff up against his knee and glancing at his wrist. Each time I've spotted him. Janet has maintained an almost fixed look of understanding. I suspect that she practices the look in the mirror at home. She reminds me of a politician nodding in agreement before putting across the opposite view. Cursed with insincerity. Mark has now completed eleven A4 sides of notes. I have repeated my version of events at least three times.

At the end of the meeting, Mark shuffles his papers together and places them in a neat pile in front of him on the boardroom table. He puts down his pen perfectly parallel with the top edge of the paper. For the first time, I noticed that his hands and fingers are a similar rust colour to the rest of him. Janet closes the meeting.

"Well, thank you for your time today, Andrew."

"No problem," I say. I think I am in a state of shock. I cannot believe the time we have just wasted. "What happens next?"

Alan rubs his eyes.

"Due to seriousness of the allegations we have to investigate further, I'm afraid."

If – at that exact moment – you had walked into the room, you could be forgiven for thinking that I had just been accused of a string of rapes.

"Right. What does that mean?"

"Well," says Janet, "we'll have to interview the other staff members that were present at the time. And then we'll make our decision."

"Decision?"

"Yes. Whether the matter will be escalated."

"Escalated?" I curse myself for continually repeating the last word of Janet's sentences.

"Yes. Elaine's allegations are very serious."

"Okay. Can I just make it clear again that it was an accident."

Alan nods. Mark doesn't bother to note this.

"Are we done then?" I say.

"For now," says Mark, almost certainly overstepping his authority. Janet shoots him a glance and he lowers his head.

"Right, well, er, thanks." I stand and collect my pad from the table. The word 'Mark' looks lost on the otherwise blank page.

I leave the room and head back to my office.

I push open the door and the chatter of the department is instantly muted. It is like being temporarily deafened. Elaine immediately picks up her phone and punches at the keys. I walk through the department slowly. By the time I reach my desk, she has immersed herself in a meaningless conversation with a person unknown.

I look directly at her as I walk past.

She doesn't look back.

chapter twenty-three

It's Sunday. I couldn't tell you what happened to the last few days. I keep losing them recently. I honestly don't know why.

I wake and instantly recognise this is a Nothing Day™. I rub my eyes and look around my room, as if taking it in for the first time. It is warm beneath my red-and-cream-checked duvet and I do not feel like moving. I am sorry: I realise that I have omitted to tell you anything about my bedroom. I suppose that is because in many ways it is irrelevant. However, I do spend a vast amount of my time in here so I'd better at least tell you a bit about it. I would like to make it clear that I won't go into any detail about 'things' that have happened in here. You know, sexual things. That whole area of topic embarrasses me.

I would just like to add that I am not breaking my promise to reveal everything to you. As far as sex goes, I simply don't feel comfortable telling you about it. I have nothing to hide. I am extremely normal in this area. If you'll forgive my shyness, I'll tell you that nothing of a sexual nature has happened in this room for four or five years. Even if you pressed me to tell you more, I don't think I'd be able to remember. Except that it was normal sex, went on for a normal length of time and I felt normal when it finished.

There.

Back to my bedroom.

The last woman I brought back here described it as a student's bedroom. It hasn't changed much since. As I scan the walls I can in some ways accept her description. Directly ahead of me, at the end of the bed, is a chest of drawers. On top of it sit my television and three cans of deodorant. My aftershave stands alongside them; Hugo by Hugo Boss. The bottle reminds me of a hand grenade. That's why I bought it. Above my television are four shelves that run the length of the wall. They are filled with books. I generally read novels, or true crime. It is not often that I finish a novel. I tend to lose interest toward the end. It's different with true crime books; I always finish these.

I don't read them for the grisly details of heinous crimes; in fact, I usually skip the graphic descriptions. No, I am most interested in why the criminal acts the way they do. What drives a person to commit a crime? Why does somebody one day decide that they're going to leave their house and injure or, worse still, take the life of a total stranger? It fascinates me. I often think I may have been better suited to a career in psychology. It's too late for me to change direction now, though.

I am also interested in the chase. You know, how the criminal gets their comeuppance. This is less satisfying for me as the books are all written from the side of the investigators. We never get to hear about how the criminal felt as the net tightened. Could they sleep? Could they feel the world closing in? As their time ran out, did they consider just one more kill before being caught? Here the books fall short. I always close them at the end with a slight feeling of emptiness. A 'To Be

Continued' that never will.

Opposite my books is a feature wall. I only have one because I saw some home decor TV programme that mentioned them. Until then, I never knew they even existed. Anyway, one weekend soon after I brought the last woman here, I decided I would decorate my room (it was probably something to do with her comment). I went out and bought a few tins of paint and the necessary rollers and brushes. I finished the feature wall in a deep chestnut colour. I bought a clay colour for the other walls. Those tins remain at the back of the cupboard under my stairs. I never did paint those walls; they remain the same pale blue they were when I moved in. I lost interest after the feature wall.

To my left is my wardrobe. On the wall adjacent to it are my pictures. There are only two. They mean everything to me. The first has a thin pine frame within which are tiny indications of the things I've done. A bus ticket from Rome, a ribbon from some rock festival years before, cinema stubs. The rest is filled with gig tickets, from the days when I used to go and see live music. A lot of the tickets have begun to fade, the sunlight sweeping over them and turning black ink a light maroon. Soon the names will be gone forever and I will be the only man in England who has a frame full of white rectangles of paper.

The second frame is similar to the first, except in this one I display my photographs. I remember the night I put it together. I sat on the floor in the lounge and removed the board at the back. I collected all my photographs and put them in a pile in front of me. I swept through them randomly, like stirring a huge pot with my hand. I picked each one up and stared at it, trying to remember the event it depicted. This proved hard. As I went through them, I chose a couple from holidays abroad with my friends. They were the usual group shots, at a festival around the tent or in a bar somewhere on the slopes. We all held bottles of beer. In each, the same friend leapt centre of the shot, a wild 'we have to look like we are having the best time ever to make everyone who didn't come jealous' look on his face. The rest of the group crowded in around him, arms around one another. And then there was me, trying my best. In some shots, I pulled a wild, wide smile or was captured mid-shout – but I just didn't look right. Unnatural. I was always slightly out of the shot. Subtly disconnected from the group.

You probably wouldn't even notice unless I pointed it out.

But I noticed. To me it was obvious.

I used Blu-Tack to attach the photos to the board and looked through for others. My idea was to create a montage of the people in my life that, to the very best of my emotional ability, I loved. I found a picture of my parents. They looked smart. Dad in a cream suit, Mum in a blue flowered dress. They were on the deck of a cruise ship somewhere. Their faces shone like polished mahogany. The sea was lit by the moon behind them. I stuck that on. And then, after delving to the bottom of the pictures, I found one of me holding hands with a small child. He was no more than two years old, his face hidden by long blondish-brown hair. He wore a blue parka, blue jeans and red wellies. He was looking at me. I was smiling at him. I stuck in onto the board.

For the next hour, I looked through the remainder of the photographs. There were no more that meant anything to me.

And so, the large framed picture still hangs on the wall today. Four photographs fill its top left-hand corner. They partially cover the large picture of a man, woman and child that was in the frame when I bought it. Their teeth are perfect. They look happy, in an airbrushed kind of way. The rest of the picture is incomplete. I suppose that says it all.

I'm in the kitchen. Regrettably I have had to leave the warmth of my bed to smoke. Associated habits ('Wake up. Smoke. Finish a meal. Smoke. Before the film starts. Smoke. Last one before bed. Smoke.') are one of the main downsides of smoking. The brain is a very clever thing. It stores the routine, everyday things that we do so we can instantaneously access knowledge. Take, for example, driving a car. Once we've learned, we don't even think about what we are doing. We simply get into the car, our brains take over and we drive. That's why we can sometimes finish our daily commute to work and have no memory of even making the journey. That's why we can swim a year after previously doing it, or ride a bike twenty years later. I suppose this instinct kicks in after we take our first breath. And sadly, this instinctual storing of habitual behaviour forced me to leave the warmth of my bed and go downstairs.

It is drizzly outside. The mud that I call my garden shines.

It is wet, having soaked up the continuous overnight downpour. I draw smoke into my lungs and stare at the sky. It's blanketed in a grubby blue colour. I wonder whether something far more exciting is happening on the other side of the blue. Somewhere far away in space.

The blackbird lands on top of the wall. As usual. He hops from one foot to the other, and then lowers his body to the wall. He is facing away from me, staring down the rows of fences that separate the back gardens of my neighbours. I stare at the side of his head. If he were human, I would definitely get the feeling that I had in some way upset him. He seems to be purposefully ignoring me.

I nip the end of my cigarette and throw it onto the mud. The blackbird turns his head slowly and, with his blind eye, stares directly at me. The eye reminds me of an oil spill. I raise my eyebrows, coaxing him to make his point. I am half-expecting him to speak. And then he does. He opens his yellow beak and makes three long cawing sounds somewhere between a scream and a command. He lifts himself up onto his legs and turns to me fully. I shuffle backwards, preparing myself for attack.

I grip the edge of the door, ready to close it should the blackbird take flight. He sits back down and looks at me quizzically.

"What?" I say out loud.

The blackbird rises swiftly and disappears over the wall into the alleyway behind. A moment later he reappears, gracefully rising into the air above me. His wings are stretched out wide and he flaps them to gain more height. Perhaps he is going to investigate whether something exciting lives high above the clouds.

I watch as he disappears from view. He doesn't look back.

The weather has again denied me the chance to cut my parents' lawn and I am now at a loose end. I considered visiting my parents to say hello, but put this idea on hold for now. Instead, I tidy the house and do the usual Sunday chores of hoovering and dusting and cleaning the bathroom and kitchen. I am very neat as a rule and so, much to my disappointment, this only takes an hour.

I flick through various television programmes (none of which I can concentrate on) and pick up two different books, a novel and a true crime book (neither of which can hold my attention).

It is now one o'clock.

Bedtime seems a lifetime away.

I walk from room to room, muttering under my breath about nothing in particular. I am a bored child sitting at a window in the summer holidays whilst the rain pours down outside. I am listless. I cannot think of anything to do. My mind turns to work. Strangely, I am looking forward to it.

I straighten my shoes in the hall.

Then something hits me. This happens to me quite regularly. A feeling inside my chest like a blow from a child's fist. When I am unable to make a decision, like now, I feel that the skin inside my stomach is stretching wider and wider. Getting tauter. Then there is a small popping sound and it is my body's way of saying, "Get on with something. Now. You have no choice. If you don't, your day will collapse. You will sink to depths from which you may not recover."

I have learnt from experience that I have to listen to my body when this happens. I am afraid of going to that dark place. The place that the other me inhabits. I must react quickly, so I grab my car keys from the side, pull on my shoes and slam the door behind me.

chapter twenty-four

I have absolutely no idea where I am driving to.

I wish that the above statement were true, but I suspect you know enough about me now to realise that it is not true. After all, maverick actions like driving to nowhere are not in my nature. No, I will come clean with you. I do know where I am going. My drives always start the same way. Pick an album (today it's Augustines) and turn up the volume loud. The idea is that the noise attacks my senses and thus interrupts unhelpful thought patterns. Then I drive out of the town that I live in, onto the open road.

I have a genuine fear of being too far away from home. This is because I am not always in control of my brain. I worry that I may be miles from home when my brain chooses to remind me that I may have left the oven on at home. Or maybe I didn't lock the front door. Either of these (or similar) events would throw me into a state of panic. The last thing I need is distance being added to the equation. That is the reason I do not drive far. My brain makes choices for me. Choices I cannot control. My mind has driven me to do many things in my past. Things that I am not quite yet ready to tell you about. But I will.

I tend to drive within a twenty-mile radius of my home. I rarely take the same route, but I end up using the same roads, albeit in different orders. I can't always remember which road leads where, but ultimately they all intertwine; small veins crossing and connecting to the main artery. The wide, winding country roads all look quite similar.

As I drive, the rain begins and my wipers come on. After two staccato drags across the window, part of the right wiper detaches itself and hangs limply down from its fitting. It looks like a liquorice stick. I am immediately anxious, realising that I will need to buy a replacement. Another job on my to-do list.

Butterflies sweep up inside me and instantly overwhelm me. They quickly fill my chest. They are telling me that I must remove the job from my list. They won't let me settle until I have done it. I drive on and stop in a small hamlet of no more than thirty houses. I switch off the engine and turn the music down to help me concentrate. I take out my phone. I will order a new set online to be delivered in the next day or so. I click on the Amazon app and search for wiper blades. The screen pauses for a moment and then is filled with pictures of black rubber. I scroll through, looking for the right set. I find it and tap it. The screen freezes. Impatiently, I tap again. No response. I close the app and reopen it. This time I don't get as far. The app refuses to open. I notice that my signal has disappeared. I will never understand this. I mean, the signal was there a moment ago and I haven't moved anywhere.

I try again and then give in. Instead, I grab a pen from the glove compartment and write 'wiper blades' on my cigarette packet. My writing is untidy and I worry that I won't be able to read the note when I get home. I rewrite it more clearly in block capitals, this time on the back of the packet, and place the cigarettes on the passenger seat. As I do, a sprinkling of dry tobacco escapes from the upturned packet. I sigh and brush it into the footwell.

You may find my behaviour a little extreme. In some ways, I do too. But this is normal to me. I may not like it, but it's all I know. I don't trust my own ability to remember even the smallest of tasks, and I live in constant fear that forgetting an unexpired job will eat into the time that I have to live my life. It is an entirely irrelevant addendum, of course, that I am an obsessive collector of free time, yet once I have it, I've no idea how to fill it.

That is not the point.

The point is, that when the moment comes where I feel truly inspired to do something – when the meteor hits me and I suddenly realise why I'm here and what my purpose is – I don't want having to shop for fucking wiper blades to get in the way. I see a couple coming toward me. They are some way in the distance, and through the half-clean windscreen it is hard to make them out. I adjust myself in my seat, so I can see above the arc of greyish-brown dirt that the faulty wiper has left. The man is taller than the woman. He has short brown hair and is wearing a black puffer jacket (The North Face, if my eyesight serves me.) His thick black arm disappears behind the woman's shoulder and reappears with a red glove resting on her waist. She is wearing a yellow and cream jacket and wearing a cream hat. Her dark hair appears from the sides. I like that. The woman is pushing a pushchair. I cannot make out its occupant but would wager that it's a boy. A crumpled plastic hood obscures visibility, but the camouflage wellingtons that poke from underneath give me a clue. The woman stops and leans over to look into the pushchair. She lifts the plastic at the side and says something to the boy. The man watches, smiling. As the woman stands, the man takes her in his arms and squeezes her tightly. She responds by holding him closely, her face pushed into his shoulder.

They part and the man holds her face in both hands. She stands on tiptoes and kisses him. Her hat slips slightly, and he pulls it back into position. They are then locked in a kiss which seems to go on forever, but in reality lasts only a few moments. They part, and the woman kisses the man again, this time on his cheek. He says something and they both laugh. The woman checks her watch, and her hands return the pushchair.

The scene is perfection and I don't mind admitting that for a moment I'm jealous. I allow myself to remember being in that same scene. Once, I was the man in that scene. My wife, the woman. The boy, my boy. None of it was true, though. Just as for the couple outside, it may not be true. I push any thoughts of jealousy to one side and recollect the lie.

The couple cross the road and walk past my car. The man's glove is now in the back pocket of the woman's jeans. She pushes the pram up the kerb. They are smiling as they disappear out of view. At that moment, to even the most cynical of humans, the couple looked the happiest on the planet. But, I remind myself, it was only a moment. What I have just witnessed was merely a snapshot in time. A picture taken that was representative of an nth of their lives. Where n is a number not quantifiable until they take their last breaths. Yes, they did look happy, but so did I. Once.

I can't say that they were simply enjoying one happy moment in a lifetime filled generally with misery. I don't know whether the man works long hours, which drives the woman to empty evenings with an empty wine bottle. Or, the man controls the woman and she lives in fear of violence if the house isn't clean the way he likes it and the child's toys tidied away out of view. I don't know whether the woman is keeping a secret from the man. The woman may enjoy the lifestyle the man's income provides, but feel a need for something more, a need that perhaps she fulfils elsewhere when the man is away on business.

I could bore you all evening with possible scenarios. God knows how many long nights I've spent mulling these over. Giving myself reasons why the couples I see aren't really happy. I don't know whether, as soon as the couple walked out of my sight, the man said something that the woman disapproved of. The woman was upset and the man told her she was being stupid. I don't know whether she screamed that he never understands her. They could now be walking home in silence, desperate to get home and out of one another's company.

What I do know is that my situation mirrored what I've just viewed. A stranger travelling in a car who passed my little

179

family may have concluded he had seen the happiest couple alive. And maybe, for that split-second, he had.

What I do know now from experience is that these passing moments are not reflective of reality. Reality is far more desperate.

I turn the key to start the car, and turn the music back up loud. I am no longer jealous of the couple. None of it was real.

I turn the car around and head in the direction of the couple. Moments later, I pass them. As I look in my side mirror, I see they are still smiling.

It's three fourteen p.m.

There are at least another five hours before the moon replaces the sun. I look up at the clouds. The rain has ceased now. I decide to head for home; I'm bored with the outside world for today. My music is abruptly interrupted by my telephone ringing. The screen in front of me indicates that my father is calling. I take a deep breath and press the button on the steering wheel.

"Hi, Dad." I try to sound chirpy.

"Hello, Andrew," he says.

I hear the same words echoed by a higher pitched voice in the background. He is in his car and my mother is in the passenger seat. I am on loudspeaker.

"How are you?"

"I'm very well, thanks, Dad. Hi, Mum," I add.

There are a few moments of confusion, where we interrupt one another and nobody is clear whose turn it is to speak. I'm instantly irritated and end the game. "Sorry. Go on, Dad."

"Your mother and I were just wondering how you were?"

"Especially as we didn't see you on Tuesday," my mother chips in.

"Oh, I'm good, thanks. Are you?"

"Yes, we're very well," continues my mother. Her voice is barely audible and for some reason I find myself squinting my eyes in an attempt to hear better.

"Rubbish weather, eh? Not a day to do the lawn," my dad says, chuckling.

"I know."

"Where are you? Are you in the car?"

"I am, yes."

I don't want to tell them that I've just gone for a drive. They wouldn't understand. To them a drive needs a purpose. Something at the end of it. A garden centre or a cup of tea. They don't just drive to kill time. It would be too hard to try to explain to them why I do it.

My mother jumps in again. "Listen, Andrew, we're only about twenty minutes from your house and thought we might pop in for a coffee."

"If you're in..." my father adds.

"Of course he's not in," my mother snaps. "He's just said he's out and about."

"Well, he might be home soon, dear."

"Well, he might not."

"That depends where he is."

"Well, why don't we ask him?" she says.

"Andrew, your mother and I were wondering if you're far from home?" says my father, apparently oblivious to the fact that I've just heard their disagreement.

"Yeah, sorry, Dad, I am." I hate myself for this answer. I could be home in less than ten minutes. The eavesdropped conversation was enough to put me off.

"Oh, that's a shame," my dad says. There is obvious disappointment in his voice. I feel terrible and momentarily reconsider my answer.

"Well, how far away are you?" asks my mum. "We could always wait outside your house for you."

"About an hour or so," I lie.

They break into another conversation about their movements for the remainder of the day and whether they could somehow juggle them to cater for me. My father ends their conversation with a summary of what I've just heard in totality.

"Right. We may be able to pop over a little later."

"Okay," I say, adding the chirpiness back into my tone.

"We'll head past on the off chance you're there. If we do, though, it'll be before six as we're out for dinner this evening."

I know this.

"No problem. Hopefully, I'll see you later on. If not, I'll see you on Tuesday." I would have thought it was obvious from this statement that I've already decided it'll be Tuesday.

"Great, well, see you soon, Andrew."

"Yeah, see you soon, Dad. Mum. Byeee."

I press the button to hang up during my final word. Heavy guitars divert me from a few seconds of contemplative silence. I take my next right and turn the car away from home.

I drive for five or six miles, singing at the top of my voice. The sun has begun to prise open the clouds and a burst hits the car, warming my face. I light a cigarette and open the window. I allow myself to imagine that I am driving on an open road somewhere in America. Across the desert to Death Valley or through the splendid isolation of the rolling grasslands of Nebraska. I don't mind telling you that sometimes I pretend I am in a music video. I spend so much of my time in the car that I allow myself to drift into a little world of my own creation. I pretend that I am the lead singer of the band. I'm being recorded by cameras at the front and side. I sing the lyrics. I smoke casually. I pull expressions of pain or anger or joy or whatever the song dictates. I tap in time with drum beats on the steering wheel. I imagine that I look cool. It feels good.

I flick the cigarette out of the window and pull into a lay-by that I have used many times before. It is far along a thin and rarely used road. The lay-by is long and wide, shaded by a group of one-hundred-year-old trees. There is a small fence that separates the fields from the lay-by. A stile leads into a wooded area behind the closest trees. The car rises and falls in the deep, muddy holes and I allow my head to flop from side to side with the uneven surface. I position the car as close to the fence as the low-rising weeds allow. My wing mirror is less than six inches from the fence. At this stage, an unanticipated quick escape from the car would not be possible. My car is entirely in the shade, hidden from cars passing from the opposite direction.

I light another cigarette and then wind my seat back a little. I see a black car in my wing mirror and as it passes I wonder whether its occupants are curious as to why I am here. Sitting alone in the countryside. Hidden. Isolated. I wonder whether I look desperate. I see the brake lights of the car light up in the distance as it disappears behind hedgerows lining the road. I flick ash out of the window and light another cigarette.

I turn off the music and enjoy the silence. For once, my mind feels empty. Resting. I close my eyes.

I hear a car approaching and open my eyes. There is nothing behind and I realise that the sound is coming from in front of me. Strangely, the noise subsides as the car gets closer. It is obviously slowing. Shortly after, it pulls into the lay-by alongside me. There are two people in the car. They are in their sixties. I sit up straight and look across the passenger seat toward them. The man stares back. The women cranes her head around the man to take a look.

For a few moments we all stare. Then the black car indicates and gently creeps forward. The man continues to look at me until his car reaches the edge of the lay-by. Then he indicates and sweeps a wide semi-circle across the road to continue on his original course.

This is not the first time this has happened. The very first time I was confused by the sudden interest. It took me a couple of days to work it out.

This place is desolation itself. It is private, quiet, secluded. It is bleak. This is a place for people who do not want to be found. This is a place for undisturbed decisions. The couple in the black car will have seen my car and interrupted their journey to turn around to see whether I was alright. They would have approached with some trepidation, expecting to find a car interior sprayed by red stains from wrists that had been cut. Or a car window open enough to fit the width of a hosepipe, the interior of the car filled with a noxious fog.

I lie back in the seat again. I feel calm. Before I close my eyes, I set the alarm on my phone for six thirty.

Sadly, I won't get home in time for my parents' visit.

chapter twenty-five

It's just before seven o'clock. As I approach my house, I flash my lights to allow a small blue car to pull out. I reverse into my parking spot, pick up my cigarettes and leave the car. Then I notice Carly standing at her front door. She is staring at the blue car as it moves to the far end of the street.

"Y'alright?" I call to her whilst putting the key in my lock.

She wipes her eyes and walks toward me. "Yeah, I'm okay, thanks."

I turn the key. Almost in.

"Aside from that." She nods at the blue car.

I know what she is referring to, but turn and follow her stare anyway. "Hmm," I say, not really knowing what response she is expecting. I push my door handle down.

"I would have thought I'd be used to it by now," she says quietly.

I let go of the door handle. "What's up?"

"Oh, I don't know," she says. "Just can't get used to Abby going overnight."

She begins crying. It is the type of crying where the whole upper half of the body shakes. I feel peculiar standing watching as she cries in front of me, so I put my hand on her shoulder in an attempt to comfort her.

"It's okay," I say, unsure whether it is.

She moves closer to me and I let her cry against my chest.

We are not hugging. She has her hands in front of her chest, like a squirrel holding a nut tightly. My arms are hanging at my sides. I feel awkward. I put my arms around her, if for no other reason than to try to stop her upper body shaking. I feel her tears through my shirt, wetting my skin beneath the cream cotton.

We stand in the street for several minutes. She begins to settle and moves backwards slightly. "I'm sorry," she says, using the heels of her hands to rub her eyes.

"It's fine," I say. Her make-up is smeared. It looks like she had put some effort into making herself look nice. Black tracks and smudges are gathered around her eyes. There are small streams of watermarking on her cheeks and chin. I notice I'm holding one of her hands.

"I bet I look a right bloody mess," she says, managing a laugh through the tears. I look at her again. She doesn't; she is naturally pretty. I want to tell her that make-up is unnecessary. She has a good base canvas to work with.

"Well –"

"Oi! Only I'm allowed to say that." She smiles.

My eyes follow from my elbow down to where our hands meet, and then back up her arm to her shoulder, to her neck and mouth. I smile back. I'm not sure who let go of whose hand, but we've parted.

"Fancy a coffee? Or a glass of wine?" she says.

"Yeah, a coffee sounds good," I say. It was a sentence I didn't expect to come out.

"Great," she says. "Give me ten minutes and then give me a knock."

"Will do," I say.

I push open the front door and head upstairs. In my bedroom, I stare into the mirror. There is a large black stain on my shirt. It looks like I have been shot by a gun firing dead spiders. I remove my shirt and ball it up, before tossing it in the already overflowing laundry basket. I reach into my bedside drawer and remove a pen and a small square of paper. I write (1) buy wiper blades (2) cut lawn (3) do laundry, on the paper and put it on the side. I go into the bathroom and wash my face and hands. I can smell tobacco on my fingers, so I scrub at them with handwash. I dry my face and look through my wardrobe for something to wear. I flick through my t-shirts and settle on a Wilco tour t-shirt. It's brown with an orange wheel on the front. As I yank it from the wardrobe, the displacement of air causes the note I've left to lift and spin slightly. I'm suddenly panicked that the note could have been lost forever behind the drawers. My heart begins to pound. I take the note and consider putting it in my wallet, but realise that I would need to write a further note to remind me to look in my wallet. In the end, I settle for placing it inside one of my work shoes. I'm sure to see that in the morning.

I take a second look in the mirror and go downstairs.

"Come in," says Carly, smiling. I notice she has painted on a new face. It looks much happier than the one I left a short while

188

ago.

"Thanks," I say.

"Sit down." She points to an armchair by the window, next to the radiator. The chair is high backed and made up of numerous small pieces of fabric stitched together patchwork-style. I like it.

"Right, Coffee? Wine? Beer?"

She doesn't wait to listen to my answer and goes through the doorway that leads directly into the kitchen (I know this because my house has the same layout). I notice there is no door on the hinges. I'm still considering her offer when she pops her head around the door frame. "Andrew?"

"Er, I'll have a coffee, please."

"Black? White? Sugar?"

I suddenly feel under pressure. "Er, white, no sugar. Thanks."

"Okay!" She smiles and disappears again.

I feel a buzzing in my pocket and take out my phone. It's Ian again. I've lost count of the number of times he's telephoned me this week. I press the red button to end the buzzing and put the phone back into my pocket.

Carly's lounge is much nicer than mine. The walls are a light green, covered with numerous pictures all in differing frames. The pictures are either old fifties' and sixties' film posters or music posters. I notice that there are quite a few Hitchcock posters and I store this information just in case the conversation drops. I consider setting a reminder on my phone so I don't forget, but decide that there are enough reminders around me to allow myself to rely on memory for once.

Carly also has a feature wall. Hers is to my right and is wallpapered in a green-and-cream tessellated design. It looks very retro. It is the type of wallpaper that I wouldn't dream of buying. The type I would consider for a second in the shop and then (not being able to picture how it would look on my wall) quickly discount. It looks great on Carly's wall. The feature wall also has a mock open fire with a small wooden mantelpiece. On top of it are candles of differing sizes and shapes, along with a picture of a small child. The room is small and cosy. Carly comes in with a glass and bottle of wine. She sits on a brown three-seat sofa opposite me. We are separated by a low wooden coffee table. A copy of Mojo and the Next catalogue sit on it.

She pours herself a glass of white wine and curls her legs up onto the sofa. She has forgotten to bring my coffee through. I get an instant hit of butterflies. I am not sure how I am going to broach this.

"So, what have you been up to today?" she says.

"Been out and about. In the car, mainly."

"Go anywhere nice?" She sips her wine and then notices my lack of drink. "Oh God. Sorry, Andrew, I've left it through…"

She is already on her feet and returns a moment later with my drink. She passes it to me and sits back down in the same position. I take a sip and she must notice me hovering with the mug, as she slides Mojo across the table toward me.

"Put it on there," she says. "Now, where were we?"

I am hopeless at listening. And I mean hopeless. As words leave people's mouths I find myself mentally drifting. I really have to focus on each word they say or I fall behind in the conversation very quickly. Then I have to add in bits that I've not heard, guessing the missing words. That works most of the time. Don't think that I am rude or disinterested. The truth is that my brain works very, very quickly. This is both a curse and a gift. When I hear a reference to some place or something I recognise, my brain races off to find a reference to it from my own experiences. Despite my speed of thought, I'm usually two or three words behind the present conversation by the time my brain connects the reference. Therefore, I am extremely happy right now to be able to answer:

"We were talking about where I had been today."

"Ah, yeah. So?"

"Just into the country. Driving. Listening to music."

"Cool. I love doing that."

I want to ask her how her day has been, but I know from the state of her make-up earlier that this may be awkward, so I decide not to.

"Love the pictures."

"Thanks. You like Hitchcock?"

"I'm not sure really. Not sure I've seen many of his films."

"What?" she says with mock incredulity. "Where have you been?"

I smile. My pocket buzzes again. "Sorry," I say and take out my phone. It's Ian again. I stare at the phone for a little too long.

"Take it if you want," she says.

"It's okay." I swipe my finger across the screen and cancel the call. I swipe again and turn off all alerts.

The next hour passes really quickly. We talk about lots of things. I say 'things' because I can't fully recall everything we talk about. We spend a short while discussing the hassle of dragging the bins around three sides of a rectangle to get them outside our properties. She agrees with me. She calls my bin 'glamourous' and laughs. I notice that when she smiles, it's almost as if two little spotlights have been switched on behind her eyes, such is the way they shine. We talk a little about films, and a lot about music. It seems we share some crossover bands, though she's never heard of Wilco so I am able to use her 'Where have you been?' line back on her. Her eyes shine after this comment too. I manage to keep up with most of the conversation, which pleases me. There are, of course, bits I missed, but nothing that matters too much, I think.

She finishes her first glass of wine and began to pour another. She stops halfway and looks at me. "Are you sure you don't want any?"

My mouth is dry from the coffee. "Er..."

She picks up on my hesitancy. "Go on. I'll get you a glass."

She springs up from the sofa and leaves for the kitchen. It amuses me how people like to drink alcohol, but generally not alone. I don't really understand why people feel better if there is someone to drink with. It must be part of the fabric of humanity: we know that drinking is fundamentally not a good thing and we feel better if someone other than us is participating because that somehow justifies our action. I have been in many situations where my peer group have pressured me into having just one more pint or to take some shots. I have never been in a situation where my mother has stood over me saying, "God, Andrew, you're so boring. Have another cuppa." Neither have I met a friend for lunch who said, "Have another lemonade, Andrew. I'm having one. Come on, get into the spirit of things. Let your hair down for once."

Carly returns and pours the rest of the bottle into two glasses. She passes the glass that is slightly fuller across the table to me.

She takes a deep breath. "So," she says, "I'm really sorry about before."

I take a sip of wine. A little voice inside my head shouts at me to focus. I realise that her statement signifies a change of conversation from trivia and I know that I must listen so I don't miss anything. Hearing and understanding every word could be vital. Either to me or Carly.

She begins to tell me her story.

It's probably a good idea if I give Carly her own chapter.

chapter twenty-six

Carly begins to tell me about her life. She takes regular sips of wine whilst she does.

Carly is thirty-four years old. She has recently moved into my street (she has been here for just over six weeks) though she did originally grow up in the area. She skips over her early life (I don't think either of us think it necessary that she tells me how many GCSEs she got or who her favourite teacher was.) Like a CV, some of the earlier achievements become less relevant, trumped by new experiences. She has an excellent relationship with both her mum and dad (though they separated when she was in her early teens). She has an older sister, Sara, whom she used to be close to but isn't so much now. Sara has been in London for the last fifteen years. As Carly put it, she is "somewhere in the capital pursuing a life of ear piercings and lesbianism". I wasn't sure whether I should laugh at this point, but the light glowed in Carly's eyes and I knew it was okay.

In twenty-five minutes, I've had a whistle stop tour through her life. I am pleased to say that I have stayed focused throughout. I drifted for a very short time, which led to Carly giggling about something I hadn't heard, so I missed my cue. It was awkward for a short moment, but she continued talking, and as far as I'm concerned the moment was soon forgotten. Carly wasn't entirely sure whether she wanted to move into my street. This statement brings us almost to the present day.

Carly has finished her wine and stands. "That was lovely," she says. "Fancy another bottle, Andrew?" Her words are ever so slightly slurred. I worry that this could slightly impede my listening skills as the evening progresses.

"Yeah, why not?" I say. My words suggest to me that I am having a nice time. Then my brain kicks into gear and tells me that I need a cigarette. Like now. I stand.

"You okay?"

"Yep, just need a cigarette." I don't like how the words sound. In my own company the justification for smoking – my fantasy rock 'n' roll rebellion lifestyle – sounds good. For some reason, I am slightly embarrassed telling Carly that I am hopelessly addicted to cigarettes.

"Yeah, sure," she says casually. "Use the back door."

I follow her through into the kitchen and she unlocks the door for me. I step out into the back garden and I am instantly hit by a bright flash of light. I stumble slightly backwards, catching my foot on the doormat. If I believed in God, I would expect his loud, deep voice to speak to me at this very moment. The whole kitchen is illuminated.

Carly giggles. "That's my dad. He insisted. For my safety."

My eyes refocus. I can now make out the black rectangular box on the wall whose light is shining directly into my eyes.

"Why did he put it there?" I ask, staring at the wall at the end of the garden.

"He insisted it shine on the door, just in case anyone tried to break in."

I think of my blackbird.

"Doesn't it come on randomly when something passes it?"

"Yeah. All the time."

We are back in the lounge, and I have a feeling that Carly is leading up to the main focus of her conversation. I suspect this because she begins at the exact point we ended.

"Like I was saying, I wasn't really sure whether I wanted to move here."

I centre all my concentration on her words and mentally promise to listen like I never have before. Carly has a boyfriend – sorry, fiancé. His name is James. They have been together for more than ten years, since university. The first moment they met, they didn't get on particularly well, but over time their relationship developed. After graduating, they both stayed in the university town and got jobs in the locality. They continued living there, along with a group of friends who did the same. They weren't ready to let university days go, so they tried for a couple of years to work but 'stay students' at the same time. It was a plan doomed to fail and they left as their friends began to move away.

They then moved in with James' parents who live about fifty miles from here. Carly tells me that she likes James' parents, they have always been very kind to her. Two years later, they had enough money to buy their own property. They moved into a 'shit tip' (not my words) and spent the next three years working and doing it up. Everything they did was focused on getting their house how they wanted it. Carly's dad spent many weekends with them, plastering and helping them paint and decorate.

They both worked during the day. Carly was a teaching assistant at the local university. James did something in an office (I didn't stop listening at this stage, I was still fully focused; I just didn't understand what his job was). Almost as soon as the house was complete, their relationship began to go downhill.

Carly isn't sure what happened. She ponders whether once she and James had nothing to occupy their time, they were hit by the stark reality of how their life together was going to be. I nod; I think I can relate to this.

Carly pours another glass of wine and leans down to her left. She scrolls through her iPod and places it into her speaker dock. I recognise Conor Oberst. I have this album. It's a good choice.

"Sorry, I'm talking too much, aren't I?"

"No, it's fine," I say, and it is.

Carly and James began to argue. Just over little things – cupboard doors not being closed (James), towels not being hung up (Carly), washing not being hung properly on the radiators (James). The list went on. They began to realise that each had numerous idiosyncrasies that irritated the other. They persisted. A few more years passed. And then, from nowhere, a night drinking bourbon and listening to old records together led to what was to become Abby.

The year leading up to Abby's birth was significantly better. The minor irritations were pushed to the back of the queue. Suddenly, there were things to do. There were plans to make. There was a focus. The study became a nursery. Carly gave up work; it didn't matter. James had done well. His salary would cover everything. Excitement filled the air.

I feel we are heading toward the crescendo of the conversation. The sky is dark outside and Carly asks me to pull the blinds down. She doesn't like it when people can see in.

For the first year after Abby was born, the good times continued. James changed his working hours so they could take turns looking after their new baby. So he could give Carly a rest. Each day, something new happened. A smile. A gurgle.

And then history began to repeat. Abby started to sleep through the night. James and Carly had their evenings together again. The novelty was beginning to wear off. Somewhere around that time, they were hit by a new reality. This was the life they had chosen together. And neither seemed satisfied with their choice. They lasted another year or so after that. The towels and cupboard doors became irritants again. Along with plenty of new ones.

Carly has now told me everything up to six months from the present day. I am extremely pleased with myself. I have retained everything so far (aside from James' job), and the way Carly talks has mostly stopped my mind from drifting. The way that her mouth forms words is captivating. They come from the back of her mouth, and her soft voice blows them out like bubbles. The words float across the room and burst next to my ears. I can almost see the words travel.

And then the arguments became more intense. She is keen to tell me that nothing physical ever happened. No, it was all verbal. And very personal. The thoughts and feelings that have been left unsaid for many years were suddenly screamed at one another on a regular basis. Vitriol that has stagnated like dark pond water somewhere deep inside raced to the surface. Carly muses that had their issues with one another been dealt with at the time they arose, they may have been less relevant in time. But they weren't. Instead, they were left to eat away at the relationship like a cancer. And of course, once the words were spoken they can't be retracted. Carly thinks that perhaps now it's too late to save the relationship. Carly shared some of content of the arguments with me, but I don't think it's appropriate to pass them on to you. They aren't really fundamental to my story, and I think she'd be disappointed if she knew that I told such personal information to you. I hope you can understand.

Needless to say, the arguments got to such a level that both James and Carly agreed it was in the best interests of Abby that they part. For now. And that is why last month Carly appeared three doors down from me.

I'm not sure where I was when Carly moved in that weekend. She informs me that her father, James' father and James himself all helped with the move. They spent three full days decorating the house and building new IKEA furniture. James wanted to make sure that Abby's room was perfect for her, to ease the transition. My mind drifts as I try to recall how I missed the move. It was only five weekends before and I have no idea where I was. I realise I am missing some of Carly's words, and to settle my mind I conclude that I was probably watching films. I am happy with this conclusion for now, but make a mental note to try to confirm this with some certainty later.

The music ends. Carly asks whether I want to choose something. I pull my phone from my pocket and press the button. The screen illuminates. I have three more missed calls. And a voicemail. They are all from Ian. This is unusual. I scroll through the music on my phone, stopping from time to time as I look for something appropriate. I can't decide. There is too much pressure. Music can alter an entire mood and I still feel that Carly has more to tell me.

"You choose," I say, taking the easy way out.

She does the same, and reaches down to restart the album that has just finished.

Although I don't really know her, I can tell that she is sad now. Her eyes have long since lost their shine. I wonder whether the consumption of more than a bottle of wine has helped. Her words now fall quietly into her lap.

"And so I'm here now," she says.

"That's shit," I say.

"I know." She runs her finger around the rim of her glass. "I suppose it's for the best, though."

"Hmm." I don't know whether it's for the best.

"I just can't do the, y'know, picking up of Abby stuff."

She begins to cry.

"It must be hard," I say.

"Yeah, it is. Really hard. You can't really get it unless you have kids of your own."

I swallow.

She tells me about Abby and how they spend their time together. She explains the little things Abby does that she recollects and scribbles in her journal each evening. She is going to present the journal to Abby when she is eighteen. Although they may seem like the smallest of things, the way Carly speaks gives them colossal importance. It is obvious that the love she feels for her daughter is unsurpassable. Abby is a vital organ to her. Carly can't function correctly when separated from her.

"It's seeing her face in the back of the car. She just looks so small. And confused."

I let her continue. She composes herself.

"I just hope that this isn't forever."

"What do you mean?"

"Well, I suppose, I hope that James and I can sort stuff out, y'know. I think I still love him."

I feel like somebody inside me has just thrown a small pebble at my heart. I am not sure what the feeling was, but it was tangible. I definitely felt it and it hurt just a little.

"You okay?"

She wipes away the tears with the cuff of her hoodie. Her face looks similar to how it was when we met in the street earlier. "Yeah. I will be," she says, smiling. "I'm just being stupid. Blame the wine."

"Yeah." The time feels right, so I say, "Listen, it's getting late. I've got work tomorrow –"

"Yeah," she says, agreeing a little too quickly.

At the front door, she hugs me and thanks me for listening. It is perhaps the first time that I don't feel a fraud. I have been listening. The whole time.

I hug her back and smell her hair. Lemon.

"Take care," she says as she closes the door.

"You too," I say.

chapter twenty-seven

Another Monday morning.

I have to share with you that I was slightly apprehensive of coming in to work today. This is unlike me. Work is usually a safe haven. I leave the car and blame my quickened heart rate on the events of the previous week. It is going to be a little more difficult than usual to make sure the mask doesn't slip today.

I don't make it through the door into my office this morning. Instead, as I make my way to the top of the stairs, I notice that Mark is waiting for me. His hair and face shine like a warning beacon. When I am five steps from the top he sticks out his index finger, points it to the floor and starts rotating it. Like he is using his finger to stir an invisible cup of tea. I stop.

"Back downstairs, Andrew."

"Why, what's up?"

He smiles. "You can't go in there today."

"What?" I say.

"Janet says, er...Janet and I have decided it's a no-go area for you today."

I screw up my face. "Why?"

"I think you know, Andrew," he sneers.

I am uncomfortable that this conversation is taking place on the stairs right outside my office. It doesn't help that where he is standing is three or four feet higher than me. The look on his face suggests that he is enjoying the elevation in his authority. I edge up one step. He notices and holds his stirring finger upwards.

"Er...stop right there," he says.

"Well, where do I work, then?"

"Downstairs, room BC3 for today."

I get one foot onto the next step. "I'll need to get my file to work on."

"Elaine has already put your files in the room for you. Turn around, Andrew."

Mark follows me carefully back down the stairs and along the corridors to BC3. He walks a few paces behind me, watching me closely. He wouldn't want his prisoner to make a run for it or, worse still, attack another innocent staff member. We reach the room, and I enter and sit down. Mark follows behind and stands over me. I lean back in my chair and look up at him, cursing the fact that he still has the height advantage.

I point to the only other chair in the room and say, "Mark, level with me, is all this really necessary?"

Mark declines the opportunity to sit. "It's company procedure, Andrew. Whilst we're still in this phase."

"Phase?"

"The investigation phase. Company procedure says that you can't work with the witnesses."

"Why?"

"Well, they all have to be interviewed –"

"And you don't want me speaking to them because…?"

"Because the procedure says that."

"Because I might in some way influence what they say?"

He looks uncomfortable. "Well, it's not –"

"It is, Mark. You think I might get them to say something different, yeah?"

"It's not me who thinks that, Andrew. It's the procedure."

I sigh loudly. Partially for effect. "Okay, Mark. The procedure says that whilst in the investigation phase I may, er, tamper with the witnesses, and so you need to keep me apart from them?"

"Yes."

"And God forbid, if they don't say what I want them to then I might torture them in the photocopier as well, yeah?" I smile.

"It's not a laughing matter, Andrew. This could lead to dismissal."

My smile disappears. "What?"

"The incident could lead to your employment being terminated."

"You are kidding, aren't you?"

"No. I'm not."

"So, what happens now?"

"We're doing all the interviews today, and then we'll schedule a meeting with you."

"When?"

"It's up to Janet," he stutters slightly, "and me, of course.

Maybe tomorrow or the next day."

"And until then, I have to work in here?"

"Yes."

I spread my arms across the empty pine-veneered desk. "And where's my computer – what do I work on?"

"Elaine's put a pen and pad in the box."

He nods at a cardboard box on the floor, which is full of grey files.

"So, I've no computer or phone?"

"Not for now." He checks his watch. "Sorry, I'm gonna have to go. We have the first interview in a few minutes."

"No computer or phone so I can't communicate with the team?" My words follow him out of the room and down the corridor.

"Yes. It's procedure," he calls back, his words barely audible by the time they've travelled back into the room where I sit.

I sigh again, close the door and begin emptying the box.

chapter twenty-eight

I climb into my car. I can't say that I have enjoyed work today. I've been pretty much alone with my own thoughts. As you'll know by now, this is not usually wise.

As I turn the key, I notice the handwritten post-it note obscuring my speedometer. I attached the note during my lunch break. Just in case I forgot. On it is one word: 'Supermarket'.

It was unlikely that I would forget: every other Monday is supermarket day. My heart rate begins to quicken and I feel nauseous at the thought of my destination. The traffic is quite heavy and I listen to some politician justifying his party's stance on immigration. As always, the interviewer stops just short of openly insulting his guest.

As always, the politician stops short of answering any of the questions posed to him. I light a cigarette and wonder why modern society has developed so-called leaders who are allowed to dodge questions which affect each and every one of us. Their inability to answer questions seems to be universally accepted. They may as well just lie. For a moment, I ponder whether I should stand in the next local election to give the electorate another choice.

I would be honest and open.

I would tell it as it is.

I see the green-and-blue supermarket sign lit up ahead of me and my heart beats ever faster. Rapid kicks from the centre of my heart. An overwhelming feeling of fear takes over me. I am not sweating, but can imagine droplets of sweat trickling down the back of my shirt collar. I toss my cigarette butt from the car and close the window. I can keep my feelings inside the car at least. I turn left, and pull off the main road. There is a sharp right turn and then I am above the roof of building, overlooking the car park. I scan the spaces; there are quite a few. The traffic is slow and I begin to queue down the slope toward the store. My breathing quickens. Ahead of me, people push trolleys to their cars. I envy them. For them, the pain is over. For me, it is just beginning. I don't mind admitting that on occasion I have got this far and then turned around and gone home. I have sat in the queue physically sobbing, such is the rapidity of my heartbeat, my mouth dry, my brain a blank. I felt that I could die, and would have taken that option if it had been offered at that moment.

The queue moves quickly and I am soon in a space.

Generally, I hate shopping. Smaller shops are usually okay – petrol station forecourts, that kind of thing. You would never get me in a retail park or shopping centre. I do almost all of my shopping online. Presently, the supermarket is a necessary evil. It's the sheer number of people around me that's the problem.

My mother says that as a child I hated the supermarket. It is one of her party stories that she likes to roll out when inadvertently embarrassing me. Apparently, I used to cry the whole way around, pointing at the ceiling and shouting that I hated the 'big sky'. Right up until I was eleven, I would eye the ceiling warily throughout the shop. I think it was around this time that the feelings began, and I learned that it wasn't the ceiling at all, it was the people around me that filled me with overwhelming dread.

I unbuckle my seatbelt and allow it to reel itself in. I like the metal on metal sound just after it passes my shoulder. I collect my mobile phone, and stretch out my legs and arms in front of me. I attempt to push my butterflies through all my nerves to the end of my fingers and toes, in the hope that they will leave my body through my extremities. I do this until my arms and legs begin to shake. I then take one large breath and hold in the air as I leave the car.

I exhale as I post the one-pound coin into the trolley and unshackle it from its family. There is a bottleneck at the narrow entrance and we shuffle through herd-like, empty metal baskets taking up the space in front of us. Once inside, the store opens up and we all separate, eager to fill our trollies. My heart is thumping in time with each step I take. The noise coming from my chest is regular. I hear the sound of steam being released as the blood rushes into my heart. When the blood arrives, my heart contracts and then expands, sounding a huge thud, like a Victorian rug being beaten over a washing line. It is the sound of a production line, an industrial factory sound, regular, almost melodic.

As I push my trolley through the welcoming rainbow of fresh fruit and vegetables, I get the feeling that people are watching me. They can hear the sound my heart is making. The wheel of my trolley begins to squeak in time with my heart.

Whoosh.

Thump.

Squeak.

Whoosh.

Thump.

Squeak.

The fruit and vegetable area is packed with people. They pause, reverse and turn to let others through. I feel penned in, caged by empty trolleys. I have to get out into the open. I begin to grab various vegetables and put them into my trolley. Broccoli. Cauliflower. Pre-chopped carrots. A stir-fry mix. I see an opening and push my way through. Steering with my right hand, I collect fruit with my left.

I am through. I realise that my heart is increasing its beat instead of slowing. It is no longer beating with my footsteps; instead it is signalling that I must move more quickly. I make my way through the chill of the cold meats, collecting steaks, sausages and bacon. At the end of the aisle are fresh pizzas and I throw three into the trolley. These are perhaps the only items I have so far collected that will actually get eaten. My mind is racing, picturing and considering possible meals as I grab tins and jars and dried pasta in the next aisle.

As I round the next corner, my very worst fear is realised. Coming in the opposite direction is a boy I went to school with. Obviously no longer a boy. I recognise Gareth instantly, even though I haven't seen him for at least twenty-five years. It's funny how nobody really changes. Gareth is around six feet tall, and he's wearing a white vest to show off his heavily tattooed arms. He's pushing a trolley directly towards me and scowling at a blond girl sitting in the trolley with her back to me. I imagine her face is covered in chocolate. Or snot. Riding on the side of the trolley is a boy. His head is shaven. He looks about six.

I manage to reverse back into the aisle I have just left. I hope Gareth hasn't seen me. Seeing somebody who expects me to speak with them is probably my worst supermarket fear. I never know what to say. I never have any questions to ask. I feel that they can smell my fear, hear my heart. Why am I so different to everybody else? On any given aisle, I see old friends, neighbours and acquaintances stopping to chat. They appear happy to see one another, happy to spend their time catching up. I always try to get away as soon as possible. Even better, avoid them in the first place. If they don't see me, they can't judge me. They can't see my weakness.

If I am unfortunate enough to get embroiled in a chance meeting, I then spend the remainder of my visit panicking about bumping into that person again on some later aisle. I worry about what to say the next time. I worry they will judge what I am buying (hence selecting fresh fruit and veg that rarely gets eaten). I worry that they will see me for exactly what I've become. A failure. I am almost on my knees, holding a tin of rice pudding and pretending to be in deep concentration as I read the ingredients. I am partially hidden by my trolley. I keep my head down and re-read the label until I believe Gareth has passed. I can distinctly hear butterflies down here. And not just their wings; I hear their hushed voices. I cannot make out their words, but I am sure they are plotting. Just as I begin to stand, I see Gareth's youngest daughter glide past. She has a chocolate beard. Gareth passes a moment later. Fortunately, he doesn't see me. I can't imagine what I would feel if he spotted me on the floor whilst he reached over me for tinned peaches.

I stand and push my trolley in the opposite direction. I pass the bakery section, grabbing a loaf and some bagels. I swallow. I begin to feel sick. Sweat forms on my forehead and starts to run down my temples. I swear the noise from my chest is getting louder. My veins suck and gush like a piston, ever quicker. The noise from my heart booms out. I am sure that other shoppers can hear me. I move faster, collecting more and more items. I can't think what I need, I just collect things. I look up at the ceiling. The bright lights seem to blur and dull. Then they brighten again, forcing me to turn away. As I walk down the dairy aisle, the product names on the yoghurts and cheese begin to blur, then brighten and then sharpen in clarity. I am suddenly surrounded by images. Product names and logos have lifted themselves from the packaging and formed a swarm around my head. I must be hallucinating. I rub my eyes. They are still there. I can hear a buzzing sound, which gets louder as the logos get closer. At the moment I feel they are going to crash into my face, they pop like bubbles and disappear. I cover my face for a moment and peek through my fingers.

They have stopped. For now. I need to get out.

The aisles begin to move. Little by little they come together to meet.

When I was younger, there was a special shoe shop in my town. It was special because it had a machine with a rectangle that you inserted your foot into. When in position, the sides of the hole moved in to measure the width of your feet. When that finished, the ends did the same to measure the length. My dad used to joke that there was a direct link between the stock room and the machine. If they didn't have your size, the machine would keep squeezing until they did. The thought of rectangular-shaped feet with matching shoes kept me awake on several nights.

The aisles are closing in ever faster and there is only enough width for two trolleys now. I decide to skip the freezer aisle and head straight for the checkout. Words begin to lift from the product lines again, buzzing around my head like persistent wasps. As I push forward, I am blocked by two ladies who have paused to chat in the middle of the aisle. They look round at me. No doubt they can hear my heart. Worse still, they seem to be blissfully unaware of the impending threat of the buzzing words and narrowing space. I cannot get past. I need to get out. I'm instantly angered that they have slowed my exit from the store. I cannot understand why they are standing and talking in the supermarket. They have come here to shop. We all have. If they want to talk, they can go to the café.

"Excuse me," I gasp, "please move. Please." The end of my

trolley makes contact with theirs.

The women glare at me, but part their trolleys all the same to let me through. I can hear the air-conditioning fan in the ceiling getting louder and louder. I look up at it. It seems the cage it is housed in is beginning to shake. I grab my trolley tightly and push forwards toward the checkout. Sweat drips from me. My heart booms and whooshes, booms and whooshes. The air conditioning sounds like helicopter blades spinning above me and I think I hear the cage rattle. I daren't look up. I expect a bolt to fall from the ceiling imminently.

I reach the line of checkouts and I am thankful to see that a number of them are empty. A woman wearing a green t-shirt stands with a giant finger on a stick, pointing out to customers which checkout to go to. The finger turns and points at me. I feel heads turn. Everyone can hear my heart. Everyone is staring at me. I keep my head down and begin unpacking my items onto the conveyor belt. The woman behind the till asks whether I need any help. I say yes and purposefully empty my trolley at a rate that forces her to pack most of the bags.

Today is not untypical of my supermarket visits.

They are not always this bad.

Sometimes they are worse.

It feels like the whole store is getting smaller. Noise seems to come from everywhere. I wipe the sweat from my forehead. My trolley is now empty and I pass the woman at the till. She smiles at me. I think it's a smile of pity. It seems to say, "Nearly there. Well done for getting this far." I smile back, but suspect

214

I look like I am about cry. I move the filled bags into my trolley and help the woman pack the last few items.

I pay with my card and make my way to the exit.

I have no idea what I have bought.

The booming rhythm again imitates my footsteps as I stride across the car park to my car. I'm outside, but can still hear the air conditioning. I open the boot and place the bags in one by one. I have no doubt that when I get home I will find bread crushed to a third of its original size and pulverised bananas, but I don't care.

I have to leave.

I have to get out.

I leave the trolley in an empty space behind my car. Somebody else can have the pound coin. I would pay any amount to be home, to be safe right now.

As I drive from the car park I notice a sign that states in late summer the supermarket will expand into online shopping and home delivery.

I sigh and light a cigarette.

Three more months to go.

Life will be better then.

chapter twenty-nine

Do you know what? I've just been thinking about how I gave Carly a chapter to herself. That's pretty generous of me. After all, we've only just met.

Carly and I, that is.

Not you and I.

I assume you are still there?

Anyway, I think it's my turn.

Here's my chapter.

chapter thirty

I'm unloading the bags of shopping from my car when I hear footsteps behind me. Due to my overwhelming desire to save time, I always collect far too many bags from the car in one go. This is exactly the position I find myself in as I turn to see Carly.

She is standing on the pavement behind me, dressed in a System of a Down hoodie and blue jeans. Salmon-coloured Converse pumps poke out from underneath her jeans. She smiles.

I am carrying five, possibly six bags in each hand and the plastic is already beginning to make grooved indents in my palms. She offers to take a bag or two, but I decline and step from the road onto the pavement. I follow this routine each week, so sensibly I already have my house keys in my right hand. I make the short journey to the front door and struggle with the weight as I raise my right hand to get the key in the lock. One of the bags slips down onto my wrist, catching on my watch.

Carly giggles. "Come here. I'll help."

"I'm fine," I insist. Finally, the key is in the lock and, as the bags cut into my flesh, I turn it and kick open the door.

I am now questioning my own routine. I suppose it's habitual. I used to believe that this was a way to save time. One or two journeys from the car laden with bags seemed far more time-effective than six or seven journeys comfortably carrying one or two bags. But I struggle to even fit through the door and have to enter the house sideways to get the bags through.

I reach the kitchen and, with a final burst of energy, I lift my arms crucifix style and deposit the bags on the side. I rest against the work surface to catch my breath. Both my hands are striped in red and white and have the texture of crinkle-cut crisps. They hurt. I rub them together to remove the corrugation and notice Carly is standing in the doorway. She is smiling and has a bag in each hand. I quickly put my hands behind my back and surreptitiously continue to knead each one in turn.

"That looked easy. I might try it," she says.

At that moment the precarious bag arrangement collapses and tins begin to fall to the floor. I use my stomach to stop a bag opening entirely and secure the contents. Holding a tin of sweetcorn, I turn to Carly and smile back.

Carly informs me that she has closed my boot and 'beeped' the car using the keys I left in the door.

"How come you've bought so much stuff?" she asks. She begins to empty the two bags she was holding onto the kitchen table.

"What do you mean?" I say.

"All this. It's a lot for just one." I sense an inflection in her voice that makes her last statement a question. I sense she is prying for information and ignore her last comment.

"I hate the supermarket. I just get in there and buy what I need."

218

"You need all this!?"

"Yeah, I think so."

The room goes silent and I suddenly feel uncomfortable. I flick on the radio next to the microwave. XFM music news sounds.

"Listen," she says. It's funny how people use the word listen to shift a conversation from one place to another. It is almost like a chapter break in speech. I make a mental note to use the word more. And then I listen.

"I wanted to say sorry about last night." She pauses, expecting me to answer. I don't.

"I was just feeling a bit down, y'know, but I shouldn't have unloaded all that onto you."

"It's okay," I say and I think it is.

Carly puts on the kettle while I unpack the bags. A snapshot in time. That's all we are. Anyone looking through the kitchen window from the outside would see a regular couple in a regular town on a regular evening unpacking their shopping. The truth couldn't be more different. I place the washing-up liquid on the kitchen windowsill and peer outside. The sky looks bright. There is no sign of the blackbird.

Carly passes me my coffee and I invite her to sit down at the little circular table near the back door. She sits and begins to scan the spines of the books on the shelves just above her. She prises out a couple of books and studies the blurbs. I continue to unpack my bags, noticing time and again that I have bought

219

items that are already available in my cupboards. I now have a national monopoly on Heinz tomato soup. I am keen that Carly doesn't notice this duplication and begin to open the cupboards only slightly to restrict her view.

"You like your serial killers, don't you?"

Now, I don't know if you've ever been asked this question – especially by an attractive woman that you barely know – but it's not an easy one to answer. The sensible answer, of course, is, "No." But that begs the question, "Well then, why have you got so many books about them?" I have to think quickly.

"I wouldn't say I like them..." My eyes scan the shelves. At least sixty per cent of my books have spines which are combinations of black, white and red. For those of you who don't know, this is a sure-fire sign of true crime content. And usually, true crime means murder (I've not seen many true crime books about serial shoplifters or trespassers).

She sips from her drink, her lips curving into a smile as they leave the cup. "It's okay, I've been asked that question loads of times."

I frown.

"You won't have seen my books. They're in my bedroom, still in boxes. Almost all true crime."

Ah. I still feel the need to defend my position. "Still, I wouldn't say I like serial killers. I'm more interested in the human condition."

"Go on," she says.

"You know, what it is that actually drives people to do these things? That's the bit I don't understand. The bit I'm interested in."

"Me too. How can somebody do a normal job and to everyone they know be, well, normal, but then kill people in their spare time?"

"Exactly. I don't really even read the graphic bits about the crime itself. I want to know why they do it, and then how they're stopped."

"Same as me," she says excitedly. "Totally agree, Andrew."

I empty the last bag, hoping that Carly didn't notice I have accidentally bought four punnets of strawberries. I push them into the fridge, knowing they will leap out to greet me the next time I open it. We chat over another two coffees about serial killers. It's an unusual subject because it's a difficult one to bring up in general conversation. You have to get the right intonation or you can end up sounding supportive of the murderer. Believe me, you get strange looks for appearing too enthusiastic about a recent slaying.

I explain in more detail my interest in what makes these types of people tick. It's beyond my comprehension that people can lead two separate lives, so disparate to one another, in this way. I cannot imagine the levels of anxiety they must suffer. Carly corrects me by telling me that these people don't have the same feelings that most people do. They literally do not care. For a second, I am jealous of this. Life would be so much easier without regularly being swallowed by anxiety. I stop short of telling Carly this. We discuss the differences between psychopaths and sociopaths. We discuss the existence and impact of personality disorders. We talk about harming animals in early childhood and starting indiscriminate fires and bed-wetting. She is clearly impressed by my knowledge and listens with interest, nodding and asking questions as I speak. For once I speak without diffidence.

"What's your job?" she interrupts.

I tell her.

"Do you like it?"

"Are you kidding? I hate it."

"Well, why don't you change it then? Do psychology or criminology or something like that."

"It's bit late to change direction now –"

"Why?" she asks. Her question is genuine.

"I've done this job for, like, more than a decade..."

"So it's time for a change, yeah?"

"Well –"

"You love this subject," she says, holding up Ann Rule's The Stranger Beside Me. "Do it for a living. I want to work for the police one day. You've got to have dreams. Life's too short."

I find myself agreeing. This is in stark contrast to my usual 'Life's too long' mantra. Her phone rings. She apologises just before picking it up. Her answers are one word. Affirmative. Affirmative. Negative. She gets up from her chair and begins to pull on her coat with one arm. It's a struggle and I help her free arm into it.

"Just one second, sweetheart."

She covers the phone with her hand and whispers to me, "It's Abby. I'll have to go. Thanks for the coffee."

She pulls me into a brief half-hug and walks through the lounge.

"Hello, gorgeous girl. How are you?" her voice sings.

I hear the front door close behind her. I realise that I've not had a cigarette for the whole two hours that Carly has been here, and so I smoke two in quick succession at the back door. I can't believe I've been able to talk so openly. For once, I felt well, normal. I didn't feel that I was being judged or classified as a potential serial killer just because of my interest in the subject. I have seen too many crime shows in which the police used a collection of books or papers or internet searches about serial killers as an indication of intent. In fact, I've often lain in bed at night worrying about whether I should give my books to charity to avoid being framed for some crime. After all, I am a loner and that's a phrase the police love. But tonight, Carly made me feel like it was okay to be interested in true crime. I smile and toss the cigarette ends onto the ground, then close the door behind me.

My mouth is dry and I head to fridge for one of the cans of Coke I put in there earlier. As I open the door I am showered by an avalanche of strawberries. The plastic packaging breaks as each punnet hits the floor and dozens of strawberries roll around my feet. I grab the Coke and laugh, breaking the silence.

I swig back a mouthful and wipe my mouth on the back of my hand.

And then.

I realise.

I am alone.

And today I don't want to be.

And it grips me.

Instantly.

A tiny feeling of fear.

(I realise now, in hindsight, that that I got completely side-tracked with what I was about to tell you. This was supposed to be 'my chapter'. It was certainly not a chapter for the Ted Bundys and Boston Stranglers of this world. Blame Carly. I'll have to tell you about me some other time.)

chapter thirty-one

Before I even open my eyes I know that today is a Panic Day™.
A thousand tiny fists are banging on the inside of my chest,
wanting to get out. I feel sick inside. My heart pumps loudly. I
begin to wonder why I feel this way. What could I have done?
What could have happened while I slept? Who have I upset?
My thoughts are interrupted by the sound of the alarm on my
phone. The additional noise is too much and my initial reaction
is to hit it. I don't mean a concerted prod to silence the alarm.
I mean slam the phone against the wall. And when it lands,
smash it over and over and over again. Stamp on it. Splinter
and cripple its casing, destroy its glass. Today is not going to
be a good day.

I resist the urge to destroy the phone and switch off the
alarm peacefully. I dreamed a lot through the night. The theme
was ominous. There were loud mechanical sounds repeatedly
interrupted by screams. The setting was harsh and desolate.
I don't mean in a dystopian way. I was certainly in the
present day, standing at my lounge window looking outside. A
procession of people walked by. Their shoulders were hunched.
They looked toward the ground. Every person stopped and
stared. Some put their hands up against the glass. All the faces
I saw were faces of despair. Each one mournful.

And that is all I know.

The sheet and duvet feel like they have been glued to

me during the night. I have to peel them away from me as I leave the bed. Panic grips my entire body. I cannot think this morning. I feel as if my head has shrunk and is now cocooned inside a larger version of the same head. Like a set of Russian dolls. The outer shell bears a resemblance to me. But inside, any words that I speak get lost on their journey from my real mouth to the larger one. The space between the two heads is padded with coarse wool, so that any noise I make is muted. I am insulated from any sounds that may be coming from the outside. Inside this shell, I am powerless. All my senses have been removed. I cannot think. I cannot think.

My subconscious helps me manage to shower and dress.

I make my way downstairs and put on my shoes. I collect my car keys and make the short walk to my car. It is still fairly dark outside. The world is yet to wake up. I press the button on the key and dimly recognise the lights flashing. They are hazy. So distant from my real eyes. I do not hear any noise.

I climb into the car and start the engine. It seems foggy in here too. I rub my eyes in an attempt to remove the film that covers them. My heart continues its rhythmic boom. I make the short journey through the twisting streets toward the motorway. I don't want today to be the way that it is. But I am powerless to change it. Music begins playing through the stereo. I can barely hear it. It sounds like it is playing through water or from inside a sleeping bag. My senses have been taken away from me. I need to get out of this shell. I feel a rage inside me and shout out loud. I don't remember what it is I shout. It's a sharp semi-moan, semi-scream. I can barely hear it. So I do it again. This time louder. The same happens. I can feel the vibration but only vaguely hear the sound.

As I reach the top of the slip road I light a cigarette.

A vain attempt to suffocate the butterflies. It is difficult to make out the shapes of the other cars passing to my right. I accelerate quickly, my mood overpowering my subconscious, and I realise I am driving too fast. I am suddenly allowed to think again. But there are conditions. Like a parent telling a child they can play out as long as they don't go past the end of the road. My mind controls the person I am now. I can think, as long as I don't try to change my path. It is time for the end. I begin to close my eyes. I tell myself that I am tired. It's dark. It's early. The dreams interrupted my sleep. I just need to sleep. I allow my eyes to reduce to slits as I join the motorway. I manage to get into the traffic. The motorway is not busy, but everything around me seems to be moving fast. All the cars in front are black. I check my mirror, the same. Continuous blurred metal passes me on my right, frightening me, almost as much as the speed of my heart. The car's tail-lights trail like sparks as it disappears into a black square somewhere in the distance. I accelerate again and move into the outside lane.

My thoughts are racing now. A twister made up of ink-black words swirling around in my head. They say nothing good to me. But I am convinced they're telling me the truth. They are raw sentences of my guilt. For the person I am. For the person I'll never be. For the person people see me as. The words spring into my consciousness and my mind forces to me to agree with them.

I am nothing.

I have nothing.

I offer nothing.

Nobody will miss me.

My foot presses the pedal toward the floor. Suddenly, the black squares in front of me begin to get bigger. Through the haze I can make out the shape of a yellow number plate, lit by a small light from above. I cannot see the lettering, it's too blurred. The vehicle moves to the left and I continue on.

There is no point.

I cannot suffer being trapped in this shell any more.

It's too hard.

It's just too hard.

I am right behind the next square; I can almost touch it. I see the blurred pinkness of the driver's hands make some gesture before he moves to the left. I do not know what he did but I know that it wouldn't have been friendly. A sentence swirls in my mind. It tells me that even people I don't know – people I haven't met – see no value in me. What is the point?

I speed up. I'm ready now. The impact will smash the shell once and for all. My decision is made. These are my last moments, and my mind graciously allows me to think of the world outside my head before the collision. My last supper, my final meal so to speak. I'm careful now. I don't want to injure anybody else. Collateral damage. It is nobody's fault but my own. Nobody else should have to pay for me being me. I think of my parents. I don't want them to have to attend inquests and listen to witnesses tell the coroner about how I sped manically down the motorway. If I can ensure that it is only me who comes out of this dead then they won't have to endure that. I slow slightly.

I think about my son. I expect he won't think of me. He can't. He'll have no memory of me. He may one day ask the question: "What happened to my real dad?" But I expect that he already believes that he is living with his real dad. He was too young to remember me.

I don't exist.

A screwed-up piece of paper tossed away years before.

Waste paper.

I accelerate again.

chapter thirty-two

I don't remember the journey into work this morning. My first memory is parking my car. I am thankful for the power of my subconscious.

As I enter the office, I am immediately startled by Jacob, who appears from stationery cupboard on my left. I have no idea how long he has been hiding in there and I don't ask. He seems quite fraught and speaks in a whisper. It reminds me of an old spy movie. He could do with a long beige mac and a newspaper under his arm.

"Andrew. A quick word."

His eyes dart up and down the corridor and he motions to a room. He enters first and hides behind the door, holding it open for me. I enter and stand right next to him.

"Are you in?" he says.

I ignore the stupidity of his question. "Yes," I say.

He closes the door carefully, ensuring there is no click as the door closes. He closes the blind. It is dark and I move toward the light switch.

"Don't," he says in a hushed voice. He looks nervous.

There are two windows opposite the door. On the other side of the window is a small alleyway which separates my office block from the next. There is little light. We are standing in a room that I expect used to be an office. Since I have worked here it has always been used to store things that have no place anywhere else. Currently, there is a mountain bike in the room, which I assume has been stowed safely here by a colleague too nervous to chain it to the railings on the main road outside. There are numerous unmarked boxes of files stacked on top of one another. A long cupboard with huge sliding doors fills the wall behind where Jacob stands. It's full of cans of air freshener, bleach, dishcloths and other cleaning products. Hundreds of toilet rolls balance precariously on top.

"What's this about?" I say.

"Did anyone see you enter the room?"

"What?"

"Did anyone see you come in, with me?"

"Er, I don't...No. No. No, they didn't." I shake my head.

Relief crosses his face. He pushes his glasses up his nose.

"Are you okay then, Andrew?" It is a question that suggests Jacob is confirming that I am okay now, because after whatever he is about to say I won't be.

"Not really, no," I say frankly.

"Didn't think so. I could tell by your face."

"Why d'you say that?"

"Well, you don't look your usual cheerful self. Has anything happened?"

I get the distinct impression that Jacob is testing me to see whether I already know the news he has to impart. I expect he'd feel more comfortable if he hadn't got it on his conscience that he's about to tip me off about something.

"No. Not really."

He screws his left eye up. His expression says, 'Go on...'

"Apart from this shit at work. It'll all blow over, though."

He suddenly looks concerned.

"They haven't told you then?"

"What?"

"Listen, don't say I told you, but I think they're trying to get rid of you."

"You're joking?"

He's not.

Jacob goes on to tell me that in his opinion the staff interviews seemed to have an agenda. He got the impression that the questions he was asked were leaning more to building a case to get rid of me rather than to get the facts. Aside from Elaine, he's spoken to all the other staff who generally had the same impression. Apparently, Clare refused to join in the conversation and left the room in tears. All the questions Jacob was asked were leading – leading to the point of proving my guilt.

"But, you were there..." I say.

"I was." He pauses. "But I didn't actually see anything. Nobody did."

"Yeah, true. But I wouldn't intentionally do that –"

"That's what I'm saying. They didn't ask us questions that allowed us to defend you. They took our first answer and moved on. That was it."

"I don't get it."

"Well, they'd say, 'Did you hear Elaine scream?' and I'd say, 'Yes.' That was taken as my answer."

"Right."

"So now they can say, 'Every staff member heard Elaine scream.'"

I feel my temper rising. "Jesus."

"They're trying to get rid of you, Andrew. Well, Elaine is."

"Fuck. I can't believe it. It's just my word against hers now."

"She's always had it in for you. You're too much of a threat, mate."

"Yeah. As if I wasn't in a bad enough mood already today."

"Sorry," he says. "Listen, I'm gonna have to go."

"Yeah. Listen, thanks."

He reaches for the handle and pulls it down precisely. "Can you wait for a few minutes after I've gone?" he says. We are back in a black-and-white Cold War drama. It's ridiculous.

"Sure," I say. I'm grateful that he's taken the time to speak to me.

He pokes his head out of the door and looks up and down the corridor. Then he's gone. I sit on a box for a few moments and consider my next move.

Ten minutes later I am outside in the smoking area. On my third cigarette. I figure that I am left with two choices. I can accept accidental responsibility, apologise forever and minimise the situation. Or I can rebel and stick two fingers up at the company. An open show of resistance to stupidity in allowing a miscarriage of justice to take place right under their noses.

Then, move on.

Find a new job.

A new path maybe.

The fact that I am smoking outside prior to even making it to my desk suggests, subconsciously at least, that I have chosen the latter option.

My train of thought is broken as a fire door at the side opens. The metal bar that holds it shut drags along the ground. It makes an awful scraping noise as it carves a path into concrete beneath it.

I think the man who appears is called Derek. I know him only as a fellow smoker. His enormous round belly pulls his shirt at an unusual angle from his ill-fitting trousers, giving the impression that he has buttoned the shirt up incorrectly. I can see his flesh pushing through above his belt. He is about sixty, his grey hair unkempt. It hasn't seen a brush for some time. He nods at me and lights his cigarette. He takes a long draw and makes an audible 'aah' sound as he exhales. I hate how he holds his cigarette. It sits between his thumb and forefinger, inside his palm, his four fat fingers canopied above it. Protecting it. Like his cigarette is the most precious thing on earth and nothing should damage it. The only other people I've seen who hold cigarettes in this way are the homeless. I can understand it with the homeless. To them, a smoke is probably one of the day's only pleasures, and all their joy would be extinguished in an instant by a unexpected raindrop.

"Heard about you," Derek says. I notice that fat has gathered in rolls beneath his cheekbones. It reminds me of wax falling over the edge of a candle.

"Oh yeah?"

"Yeah. Kicking your boss, wasn't it?" he snorts, his red face lighting up. He is the epitome of a slob. I have trouble looking at him.

"Well, I didn't exactly –"

"Heard they're gonna get rid of you."

I take one last draw of my cigarette and pass Derek to post it in the chrome cigarette box on the wall.

"Dunno. We'll see, I suppose."

I walk away. It seems that Jacob's rumour is actually common knowledge. This does not bode well. If a secret is known by everyone, it's likely that there is an element of truth in it. I have to decide whether I'll crumble and do everything I can to stay, or accept my fate.

I'm not sure that I want to leave the comfort of this job.

But then again, I don't want to be Derek.

I'm haven't even reached my desk when Elaine informs me that I'm late. I am well aware of this fact, but given that I'm considering my options, I apologise. I make up some excuse that I was checking with Janet whether I was allowed to work in the open office today. Elaine grunts. It's an excuse that I could easily be caught out on, but it buys me time. I need a little time to think. I switch on my computer and look around

235

the office whilst I wait for the desktop to load up. Everyone has their head down.

Nobody is speaking. The deathly silence is broken only by the photocopier bursting into life from time to time.

I spend all morning responding to emails and ensuring my inbox is empty. There are two emails from Janet, which I click first, but neither relate specifically to me. I have three from Elaine, which again do not relate to the photocopier incident. I am slightly perplexed. I decide to open Elaine's calendar and notice that she has a meeting with Janet at one p.m. It is marked with a threatening-looking red exclamation mark. I glance at the clock. In fifteen minutes it looks like they will take the next step up the stairs leading to my fate.

I waste time clicking through my diary. As usual, it is largely empty. I notice that the National Compliance and Complaints Conference is coming up the following week. I remember resisting being the representative for PaigeAlex for the two-day trip. I've been nominated for the last two years. The subject matter is relevant to my work and extremely dry. Put simply, it's not something I enjoy. A night away from home, surrounded by people who present themselves as actually interested in the subject. I always sit somewhere near the back and wonder whether the speakers are really enjoying the content they are forcing us to endure. I find myself doodling a great deal of the time.

There is a large sigh to my left, which causes the yellow post-it notes stuck to Elaine's monitor to flutter. She pushes

236

herself up out of her chair.

"Right," she says to the middle of the room. It is obvious she is after a reaction. Clare looks up and smiles at her.

"Here we go again." She sounds annoyed; her voice suggests 'I've got better things to do'.

I ignore her. I want her out of the way. She collects a notepad and shuffles across the office. As she reaches the door, she informs us that she'll be back 'around three'. The door closes behind her.

I spin my chair around and face the department. I ask them to spare me a few minutes. My colleagues look up blankly. As if they've heard a voice but cannot work out where it is coming from. Only Jacob smiles.

"Listen, everyone, I just want to know what happened yesterday. You know, with the interviews."

Clare and Jess look at one another and then back at me. Martin pushes himself back from his desk, distancing himself from the conversation by a few feet. He is cradling a hole-punch in his lap. Jacob rests his chin on his hand. The room is quiet.

"Come on," I coax. "We've worked together for ages."

Nothing.

"Seriously? I only want an idea of what's going on."

Finally, the iron curtain is lifted.

"We can't say," Jacob says. This seems a contradiction.

"We've been told not to talk to you," Jess adds, "about it."

"Sorree!" Clare says. She pulls her shoulders up toward her

face and attempts an expression of cute innocence. She looks like she is about to cry.

Martin appears to be staring at the ceiling tile in the far corner of the room.

I look around the room, pausing momentarily as my eyes reach each face. Clare looks down.

"You've all said that it was an accident, though, haven't you?"

Silence.

"That I didn't mean to trap the –" I refrain from using an insult, "– Elaine's arm in the photocopier. Surely."

Jess begins to type with one hand, an attempt to begin work again. Martin reaches across his desk and posts a mint into his mouth. Jacob shrugs.

It is then that I realise that I have absolutely no support. You may know the famous story about an emperor and his new clothes? If you don't, I'll tell you; it's fairly simple. There is a vain emperor who rules all the land. I can't remember where. Anyway, all he cares about is looking good to others. He hires a couple of weavers (who turn out to be swindlers) to make him the finest suit known to man. They tell him they have made the best suit in all the land, but if you can't see it, you are either stupid or unfit to hold your position. The emperor pays them handsomely and they 'dress' him in nothing. He has no clothes on. The emperor, along with his ministers and all the townsfolk, daren't speak for fear of being deemed stupid. The emperor parades through the town and the townsfolk line the streets and applaud him. A small child too young to understand pretence and self-preservation and hypocrisy sees him and shouts out that the emperor is not wearing anything. The emperor continues his procession and the crowd ignore the child's cry.

And now I am cast in the story. Elaine has become the emperor. I've become the boy who, figuratively speaking, has pointed out that Elaine is naked. The rest of the team, the townsfolk, will not speak up on my behalf. They have retreated to save themselves. Their consciences are clear. They don't know whether I did it on purpose, which is convenient as most of them have families and debts and mortgages to pay. They need their jobs. The last thing they need is to be caught up in my perfect storm. Don't speak out, don't become involved. And they won't speak out, because from the moment we take our first breath, we are preconditioned to survive. To protect number one. And because of this predisposition, I am given the role of martyr. I am about to be made into an example of how disposable humans are.

"Okay, I understand," I say.

And I do.

It's not their fault.

They were born that way.

We all are.

chapter thirty-three

A trip to see my parents is the last thing I need after the day I've had. My mind jumps from lying to them (to the extent that I ring their number twice and hang up after one ring) to just going and getting it over with. I still haven't made my mind up as I leave the motorway. My car does, however, seem to be travelling toward them.

Lying to them will just provide me with more problems. I've lied to them too many times before. If I tell them I'm not coming because I'm poorly, they'll worry about me. Then I'll be bombarded by phone calls in which they kindly offer to drop off pharmaceuticals or meals that evening. If I tell them about my day at work, they'll panic about whether I'm mentally capable of overcoming the stress. Ultimately, it will lead to them calling me at least twice daily to check that I'm okay.

My procrastination is rewarded with a beaming smile from my father as I pull up outside the house. He is clipping a small shrub with a pair of kitchen scissors. He slowly gets to his feet as I close the car door.

"Andrew!" he says. His welcome is infectious. Genuine warmth. I feel it and I smile.

"Hi, Dad."

We hug. Over his shoulder I notice that the grass of the lawn is short. I ask him about it.

"Oh, it only took me half an hour. It's not a problem."

I chastise him.

"Don't be silly." He smiles. "Come on, your mother is inside. She'll be pleased to see you."

We walk into the house, my arm around his shoulder, his around my waist.

There is no answer from my mother when we enter the house, despite us calling her. My father shuffles around the house, calling up the stairs and through into the kitchen.

"That's funny," he says.

He shepherds me into the lounge and I take my usual seat. My father is just about to sit when we hear a noise from upstairs. He looks at me quizzically. He goes back to the bottom of the stairs and then re-enters the room and sits to my left. My mother follows close behind.

"What was it you said, dear?" my father asks.

"I said, I'm on my way down."

"We were calling you."

"I know. I heard."

"Why didn't you answer?"

"I did."

"We shouted three or four times."

"I know, like I said, I heard –"

"Mum! How are you?" I say, rising to my feet. Without my interruption their conversation could quite realistically have lasted all evening.

She hugs me tightly. "Hello," she says, her words slightly

distorted by the strength of my hug. "I'm sorry, I was just dealing with some paperwork."

She smells like she's showered under a waterfall of perfume. I have to release her as I feel an immediate headache come on. I sit back down.

"Haven't you got a drink?" she asks. The empty coffee table answers her question. She turns to my father. "Why hasn't he got a drink, Colin?"

"I was just going," he says.

My father is on my left, my mother on my right. She stares at me intently. Finally, she says:

"You look well, Andrew."

"Thank you."

She looks puzzled. "I'm not quite sure what it is. But you look really well."

"Thank you," I repeat. I'm not sure what else to say.

"Is it work?"

"Is what work?"

"Is that why you look well?"

"I don't think so."

"Do you think he looks well, Colin?"

"Well –"

"He does, doesn't he?"

My father is staring at me now. I think he is trying to look for whatever it is my mother has noticed. I don't think he'll see it, though. It's a maternal thing. He nods in agreement. I suspect, like the people in that old fairy tale, he doesn't want to be the one who speaks up. I reach down for my cup and take a drink.

"Can you both please stop staring at me," I say.

"I'm just trying to work out what's different, Andrew," my mother says. She stirs three times clockwise. I wait for the 'chink, chink, chink' sound before I speak.

"Nothing's different."

"There is, you know. You look brighter."

"Brighter?"

"You know. Your face looks like it has more colour. You look more relaxed. You have a shine."

I raise my eyebrows at my father. He is still staring. I turn back to my mother.

"Anyway," I say.

My mother spends the best part of the next hour updating me with stories of interest. I listen where possible. I drift off continuously, but hear just enough to keep up with the stories. I now know that the brother of a girl I went to school with has recently divorced. I also know that the granddaughter of our old next-door neighbour has just been selected to join a national choir. Somewhere in the middle of the update my father gives up in his search for the different-thing-about-my-face and slips into a short, open-mouthed nap.

"He's always tired recently," my mother informs me.

"Well, he is getting older."

"He spent most of Sunday in bed."

"That's not like him."

"No…" she says, her thoughts drifting.

"Is he okay?"

"I'm sure he will be," she says. She taps my hand gently and then squeezes it. It's her signal that the conversation is over. It's time to leave.

I make my excuses and stand. My mother stands and walks around the coffee table. She nudges my father, and he pushes out a solitary snore and opens his eyes.

"Andrew's going, Colin."

"Oh, right. Already?" he says.

I wave to them both from the car, and as soon as I am out of sight I pull over to the kerb and take a long look at myself in the rear-view mirror. I am curious to see what my mother saw. I move my head, studying one side of my face and then the other. I don't notice any discernible shine.

As I drive the short distance home, I am intrigued by what my mother saw. I wonder whether maternal perception is something every mother possesses. And then I realise that cannot be the case. It is not something innate. It comes from pure, unconditional love. It comes from the fact that she has spent years studying me. Watching me. For more than forty years my mother been with me when I have expressed every kind of emotion possible. She has been there, watching me, through the darkest of days. She has trained her eye so that she knows how I am feeling just by the way I look. Even when I am expressionless. I suddenly find myself overwhelmed by the person my mother is. I feel a tear escape from my eye and flow quickly down my cheek. I wipe it away with my hand.

```
       T                          A
        h                          n
         e                          d,
          n,
                                     a
         a                          n
          n                          o
           o                          t
          t                          h
            h                          e
              e                        r.
                r.
```

I let them race down my cheeks and allow my eyes to fill heavily until my view is obscured. Then I wipe them away. I am not crying. There are no sounds. I am not gasping for air or trying to compose myself. There is no extra saliva in my mouth. The tears are simply flowing. It feels good.

I realise that there is something I need to do now, in order to go forwards.

But first we need to go backwards.

And we will.

Come on, keep up.

chapter thirty-four

This week seems to have passed more quickly than usual. My days at work have been uneventful. Extremely quiet; so far without any incident to tell you about.

Three nights ago there was a programme on television in which a bunch of kids ran riot in their parents' homes. I think there were four families on the programme, all of them in the US. Anyway, these kids were badly behaved. They destroyed things, wrote on walls, swore, spat – you name it. They were, frankly, horrible children. So, this doctor came and talked to the parents and decided that all the kids had some attention disorder or something. I don't remember its exact name. The doctor decided to give the children drugs to calm them down. A couple of pills a day.

The programme jumped forward in time by a month and we were treated to seeing how the kids had reacted. They had stopped their wanton destruction. They no longer swore or spat. In fact, they didn't do anything. They just sat in front of the TV. Staring. Vacant. Hollow. The parents loved it. The doctors celebrated.

And there I was at home, shouting at the television: "Don't give them pills; give them attention! That's what you've concluded they're deficient in. So give them some attention! Don't drug them so they don't require attention any more." I couldn't understand it. And then, suddenly, I stopped shouting.

I made it into the kitchen just as I was physically sick. I realised that I was a hypocrite. The way that I have acted prohibited me from holding any kind of opinion on the subject.

Since that programme, I haven't switched on the television once. My evenings have been filled instead with rediscovering some old bands, played loudly in the kitchen. Accompanied by coffee and cigarettes, of course. I am ashamed to say that I have ignored two more calls from Ian. I also haven't yet listened to any of his voicemails, which now total three. Just so he didn't worry about me, I did send him a text, though. I said I was busy and I would be in touch soon. I don't seem to be able to find the time right now.

My kitchen table is awash with papers. Mostly, they contain my scribblings. I have mapped out complex-looking flowcharts with crooked arrows that point horizontally and vertically across the page. I have scribbled page after page, summarising the decisions I have made. Writing my life down. I have made list after list. I have performed calculations. I have written letters. Most of the writing is only for my eyes. Now I see these things set out on paper, I feel worried about showing them to you. But we have come quite a long way together and I don't think it would be fair for me to suddenly renege on my promise. I've woken in the night worrying about telling you. I've been tempted just to pull the plug on the whole thing and stop right here.

I have, however, decided that I am prepared to continue.

I think it's in both of our interests.

I promised you a chapter about me before.

You are already in it.

The back door is wide open and as I smoke the sun shines directly into my eyes. I stand with my palm out in front of me, blocking the rays. I look like I am permanently hailing a taxi. My music plays loudly and I tap my foot against the door frame. It is the type of weather that attracts people to beer gardens up and down the country. Twice on my way home I considered telephoning my one friend who still lives in the area. Twice I bottled it. It's some time since I dealt with a hangover and my friend is the type that would ensure this happened.

I finish my cigarette and flick it away. 'The Girl Who Wanted to Be God' by the Manic Street Preachers blasts through the speaker and I know that I made the right choice to stay in alone. I position a chair in the kitchen facing through the door directly into the sunshine, and then walk into the lounge in search of my sunglasses. I am scrabbling around in drawers when there is a knock at the door.

"Two minutes," I shout and continue my search. There are all sorts of random things in the drawers. Underneath an old bank statement I spot my black leather sunglasses' pouch and grab it.

I open the door. It's Carly. She smiles.

"Fancy a visitor?" she says. She holds up two six-packs of Coors as a bribe.

"Come in," I say.

"Manics," she says. "Good choice, Andrew!"

Her hair is tied up in a ponytail and dark sunglasses cover her eyes. I'm disappointed that I can't see them. She wears a white vest and for the first time I see a small tattoo on the top of her arm. It's a picture of a small wooden house. A love heart, positioned above it where the sun would be, shines red beams onto the house. She wears light green shorts and flip-flops. She looks lovely and I feel like telling her. I don't.

"Come through. I'll stick those in the fridge."

"Are you sure I'm not disturbing you?"

"Nah, it's fine."

I turn the music down slightly and offer her a can. She takes it from me and we both open our cans simultaneously. I notice that her hands are tiny. We clunk the beers together and take a large gulp. Foam bubbles and pops on her top lip. She giggles and wipes it away. I put the rest of the cans in the fridge. She is over by the door.

"Jesus, Andrew."

She is staring at the back garden.

"What?"

She points and makes an 'is it not obvious?' face.

I go over and stand next to her. My naked arm is touching hers. I feel the hairs on my arm begin to rise. She doesn't move away and neither do I.

"The cigarette ends. That is ab-so-lutely disgusting."

I look down at the floor. The sun has baked the mud into

a hard, almost grey surface. Long cracks have opened up in the mud. There are hundreds upon hundreds of cigarette ends. Some have fallen down the cracks. It looks like an aerial view of a massacre. A huge battlefield, each soldier represented by a dirty orange cylinder.

"Is that why your chair is inside and not out in the sun?" she asks.

I haven't considered this before. The massacre has never bothered me. In fact, it's been there for so long that I no longer notice it.

"Come on, let's clean it up."

"No chance." I laugh. "I'm not cleaning it up."

"Well, I'm not sitting out here surrounded by these," she says.

"Well, sit inside then," I say.

I am already beginning to feel a little bit tipsy. We have been sitting outside in the sun for the last half an hour on the only two chairs I have, wooden kitchen chairs. Beneath us is a tartan picnic blanket that my parents bought me last summer. It has never been used, and now covers the battlefield. Carly says you can still smell those lost in action. I can't.

Carly has apologised at least five times since she arrived. She is sorry she left so abruptly earlier in the week. She is sorry she's not been in contact. She is sorry for turning up uninvited this evening. She seems sorry for most things. She has explained that she has been busy with Abby since Tuesday night. She has also explained that James has collected Abby this evening. She also wanted to make it clear that she didn't want me to think she was just using me when Abby wasn't there. In fact, she likes me. To be honest, I drifted off a little bit while she was explaining all of this. As soon as she said sorry, I couldn't think of anything at all she needed to apologise for, so I didn't concentrate. Now that she has mentioned using me for company she has given me something to think about. I am slightly concerned by this. It would have probably been better if she hadn't tried to apologise for something I hadn't even thought about. I wonder why humans feel the need to double-guess what their counterparts are thinking. Most of the time we have no idea what we are thinking, never mind trying to telepathically unravel somebody else's brain.

"Are you listening?"

"Yeah, 'course I am."

"What did I say then?"

"You asked if I wanted another drink."

I rattle my can from side to side. A small amount of warm liquid sloshes around in the bottom.

She laughs and gets to her feet.

"Go on then. I'll get them."

We spend the next three hours talking and laughing. It doesn't matter what we speak about; it makes me feel good. Alive. As the sun settles somewhere behind my wall, the blackbird flies high above me, its darkness silhouetted against a spectacular

251

pink sky, and the clouds ploughed into great long plumes above us.

Carly asks for a hoodie; she's a little cold. I go upstairs and open my wardrobe. I leaf through my clothes, examining each suitable top. I imagine her wearing them. I settle on a forest-green etnies top and lift it from its hanger. I sniff it to make sure it's clean. It is. I spend a moment looking down at Carly sitting in my garden. I've never seen her from this angle. From here, I can just see the upper outline of her breasts before her bra barricades my view. I move away from the window, suddenly feeling awkward about what I've just seen. I screw the hoodie into a ball and race down the stairs. I misjudge my own inebriation and almost fall down the last three steps. I want to get back to her as fast as possible. I want to see her in my hoodie.

"I think I'm a bit pissed," I say to her honestly.

Carly turns to me. She has lifted her sunglasses onto her forehead and I can see her eyes now. "Same here." She giggles, passing me a can. "Last one?"

"Yeah," I say, exchanging the can for the hoodie.

She puts it on and zips it right to the top. Her figure is lost in its capaciousness. She still looks perfect. She rubs her upper arms with both hands. "That's better," she says.

What I am about to tell you is exactly what happened next. I promised from the beginning that I would be totally honest with you. I have been and I will continue to be. I know that I have asked you this before, but I am going to ask you again. It is that important to me. I ask that you specifically try to resist another complicated part of the human condition. I ask that you try not to judge me. You have to understand that until Carly I haven't told this to anyone before. I ask that you hear what I have to say without being tempted to judge me as a person. This is how it happened.

We have just opened our final can of beer. We are listening to the Mountain Goats. Carly has never heard of them and she is giggling about how excited I was about playing them. Each time she tries to speak, I hold up my finger to silence her. I want her to hear every single lyric, every guitar strum, every drum beat.

The more I lift my finger, the more she giggles. Usually, this would irritate me. When I play music to people, they have to be silent, they have to respect what they are hearing. Strangely, Carly's giggling is not irritating me.

I hold up my finger.

She giggles.

Finger.

Giggle.

Finger.

Giggle.

She leans in to me and momentarily rests her head on my chest. Her left hand grips my hip. This is unexpected and I freeze, unsure whether I should be hugging her back. Almost as soon as she started she has moved away again, laughing.

"You're so funny," she says.

"I know," I say, the alcohol giving me a rare moment of false bravado.

"No, you really are," she says. "How come you're still single?"

I hope she didn't see the flash of pure fear cross my face.

"I'm just too funny."

"No, seriously. How come you are? And why haven't you got kids? You'd make a great dad."

I smirk, trying to deflect her questions. It doesn't work. She smiles back and raises her eyebrows in expectation of an answer.

And for the first time, I want to tell somebody. I want to tell Carly. At that moment it begins. I tell her. And I feel no fear.

Many years ago, when I was in my twenties and before that, I had a number of girlfriends. I was with the very first serious one for about two years. One day, she decided that I was surplus to requirements. I have no recollection of why. Not that it matters; we have already established that people in general don't tell the truth. In the break-up of a relationship this is especially true. We get the usual "It's not you, it's me", or "I think we both need some space". At this exact moment all the rejected really wants is some honesty. How could I improve without knowing the areas that didn't fit? At least give me a chance not to fail again.

Like I said, in this case I don't remember why; all I know

254

is that, like a used disposable barbecue, I was tossed away. I have to be honest: I didn't see it coming. I think that was the reason that it hurt so much. It was painful to be rejected, but the fact that I had absolutely no idea it was going to happen probably affected me more. After a few months of grieving, I dusted myself down and made a conscious decision that I would never fall into that trap again. I left the country for six months to travel the world. I would come back better. More interesting.

I don't remember which girlfriend came next, or in what order. I stumbled through my twenties in relationships for six months and single for a couple of years. No relationship lasted. The women never stood a chance. I was so wary that all of a sudden I might be tricked, that I had already discounted any future. I lived through each relationship guarding myself against the possibility of suddenly finding out that I wasn't wanted. Simply, I partitioned my mind. Of course I said "I love you" (girls like it when you say it back), but it didn't really count. It would have been fairer and more honest to caveat those three words with "but I don't care if we break up". I had mentally conditioned myself for it. The three or four relationships I am telling you (and Carly) about ended probably fifty:fifty between who broke up with whom. I don't remember and I don't care. What I do know is that none of the break-ups hurt. You see, I had already written then off as doomed to fail. I was prepared.

Carly stares at me intently. I am slightly worried that she doesn't believe me.

"What?" I ask.

I light another cigarette. The third since I began my story.

"Nothing," she says. She smiles sympathetically. "I'm listening, Andrew. Go on."

And so I do.

As I reached the end of my twenties, I realised that whilst I was standing still, the people around me were not. For work or love, friends began to move away from the area. The weekends that were once packed with offers of company began to empty. Friends were busy. Friends only visited one weekend in four. The group of a dozen had reduced to three or four. The rest had boldly stepped onto the conveyor belt of life. They had moved to the next stage. They were married. Their next step was children. Perhaps because of my choice to guard myself, my conveyor belt had jammed.

Weekends were instead spent in small groups with partners in tow, listening to music that reminded us that we used to be young. The impetus had gone. I became tired of being the only single one in a group of couples. The pressure began to increase. I began to feel that I was the only one who wasn't normal. I was the orphan boy outside in the icy cold with his hands cupped against the window, watching the joy and happiness shared by a family in the orange warmth inside. I don't remember making a conscious decision to change this, but I must have done. Within six months, I was one of them. To an extent I had cut away the safety net, to pursue what they all had.

We bought a house. We lived in it. We worked. We saved money. The group of friends increased, half of them people I had known most of my life, the other half the ones they had chosen to spend the rest of their lives with. We tried to replicate the lives we'd once had, but the introduction of spouses to the group changed everything. When I think about it now, it's obvious why it didn't work. Back then it was an impossible puzzle. People began to drift apart; spouses didn't like one another. We all act differently in different company. Reminiscing with friends was not particularly interesting to our spouses. Secrets were disclosed that the spouses had never heard about the ones they loved before. The nights out became fractious. The group was an intricate cat's cradle, like wool linking each finger. The wool linked the relationship between each individual in the group, but over the course of time, it frayed until it snapped. And we were left, just me and my wife. Two members of an exclusive group.

I want to make it clear that I didn't fall out with my friends; they just became more difficult to see. To replicate our past lives we had to meet without our spouses. As you may expect, this was not easy. We were limited to birthdays and stag dos. Intermittent meets somewhere in England. Of course, our relationships were no longer the same either. Most of us had changed, moved on and made new friends. The same pattern repeated and the new members of the group were summarily discarded or written off by the founding members. Friendships drifted to text messages. A few friends still lived in the area. I saw them sporadically.

By my early thirties, I began to wonder whether the orange glow actually brought any joy or happiness to anyone. It was visible through the curtains from outside, but I couldn't feel it when I was in my home. I began to spend money in a desperate attempt to find something to light up life. I'm sure that my wife felt the same; we never talked about it and I never thought to ask. We decorated the home and bought expensive pictures and light fittings. We filled it with high end electrical equipment and kitchen appliances that we never used.

Nothing worked. However many new pieces of furniture we bought, we couldn't replicate what everybody else had. I say we couldn't replicate. I can't be entirely sure of my wife's opinion here; I never asked. However, I do know that I couldn't bring the glow home. And judging by what happened next, it seems neither could she.

"God," says Carly.

Her comment makes me feel uneasy. There are so many ways I could take it. I decide to ask.

"What do you mean by that?"

"I don't know. Sounds like you've thought about this stuff quite a lot."

"Ha," I say ironically, "just a bit."

We both smile. She touches the back of my hand.

"So, where is she now?"

My can is empty. I crush it and the opening bows forward

toward Carly. "Mine too," she says, passing me her can.

Carly has been to the toilet. I have been in the small cupboard under the stairs looking for alcohol. I was sure that there were some cans of lager in there somewhere but I can't seem to find them. I crawl backwards out of the cupboard with two bottles of some oddly named stout in my hand. I remember they were a secret Santa gift at an office Christmas party. It's all I have.

I open the bottles and switch off the kitchen light. Carly shouts for me to leave it on, so I press the switch again. I go outside with my arms outstretched and pull an apologetic face for what I have brought.

"What is it?" Carly asks, taking a bottle from me.

"Dunno." I turn the label toward me. "Stout and About."

She takes a sip and informs me it tastes "a bit like Guinness". She seems okay with it. I light another cigarette and take a sip.

"So, what happened next?"

Light from the kitchen window illuminates the area all around us. I am conscious she can now see my features more easily than before. I feel self-conscious that my face may contradict my matter-of-fact delivery of the words.

I swallow.

I want to continue.

It feels good to hear myself say this.

Over the course of the next year, I saw my friends a lot more than I had previously. We were all brought together in suits

259

and ties to meet on sporadic Sundays throughout that year. They had added to their family units, little packages of joy which appeared to intensify the joyous glow coming from their windows. We had stilted conversations about jobs and cars and houses and life. We all joined in. I often wonder whether they were putting in the same amount of effort as I was to paint a picture of contentment. After each occasion, as we parted, we vowed to keep in touch. We made promises to get together again soon. Promises vacant of any truth. We went home and sent text messages now and again.

Somewhere around this time, my wife came to the conclusion that we were getting behind. It seemed that once again the conveyor belt needed oiling. For some time our evenings had been spent drinking wine and watching whatever the television spewed into our lounge. I think we both agreed that it was time to kick-start the machine again. I spent a month or two persuading myself that her suggestion of adding to the family would be the thing to finally light up our house. The pressure grew and grew, and I knew that at some stage I would have to relent. One day, she announced to her friends that we were 'trying for a baby'. It created a short-term buzz, in a similar way to purchasing a new phone or tablet. I had yet to be fully convinced, and although we were 'trying' I have to admit to you that I purposefully wasn't. Throughout that period, whilst actually in the throes of trying to create a life, I would repeat a mantra in my mind. It was simple: 'I'm not trying, I'm not trying.'

Despite my hope of controlling my own power of procreation through thought processes alone, I have to tell you I was unsuccessful. Strangely, over the nine-month period that followed my home life improved. Looking back, I think I convinced myself that a child was indeed the key. Benjamin Scott Walker was born, without complication, on the exact date the doctors had predicted. It was an easy labour. Just over two hours. Mother and son were home the next day. Easy-peasy.

I expected the orange glow to intensify significantly.

I need to ask you to concentrate especially hard for a moment now. I want you to imagine a graph. Okay, do you have it? You can see the axis, yes? The axis up the side (the y axis for you mathematicians out there) is happiness. At the top is very happy. The further down you go, the less happy you get. The axis across the bottom is time or years. The graph begins at my eighteen birthday (anything before that I cannot remember and is, frankly, irrelevant) and finishes today. If this isn't clear, reread the last few sentences or you won't follow the rest. Seriously, it's important.

The graph begins halfway up the left-hand side (generally happy) and takes a steady climb toward my mid-twenties. Yes, there are a few minor setbacks here and there. But in general it climbs nicely. And then – as life moves on and my friends go in search of the orange glow – it begins to fall. A gradual fall for a year or two, and then more steeply. By the time I go in search of the same thing, its decline is rapid. It's a triple black run, unskiable on most days. The trend continues, and by the time we try for a baby it has passed well beyond the x axis. It's unstoppable. It's avalanche territory.

For the nine months before and after Ben was born it begins to creep up again. Only slightly, but there is an improvement. A year after that, its fall is devastating.

It looks a bit like this:

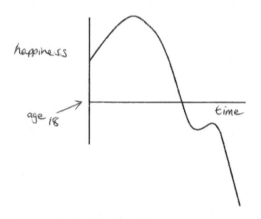

Carly reaches across and grabs my hand, squeezing it tightly.

"What's up?" I say.

"I don't know."

She sniffs.

"Just seems weird that you can talk like this."

"Weird?" I say. It's not a word I particularly want to hear.

"I'm not saying you're weird. I've just never met any..." She pauses. "Well, any man who speaks like this."

"Like what?"

"Just so...open."

She has no idea that this is the first time I've ever spoken like this to anyone. I may never do it again. She has no idea what is coming next. I wonder whether I should leave the conversation where it is. Wrap up the night. Continue (or not) some other time. But I'm incapable. The words I'm about to say have been queuing patiently in well-formed sentences in my mind for years. It's too late: I have opened the city gates. The barriers are down. The words are no longer trapped. And they don't wait: they tumble quickly from my mouth. Like sheep from a truck.

Ben was two years one month and three days old when I arrived home that day. From the exterior, nothing appeared unusual. I noticed that the hanging basket which hung outside the front door needed watering. It swung like a pendulum in the light evening wind. I opened the front door and walked into the house. It was silent.

As usual, I went straight upstairs to get changed.

I walked across the landing, looking for life. I knew not to shout out my arrival, as it may wake Ben, should he be sleeping. There was nobody upstairs. As I crossed the top of the stairs, she was waiting at the bottom. I asked her where Ben was. She told me that he was at her mother's house. She asked me to come downstairs so she could speak to me. There was an indescribable atmosphere in the house. The rooms seemed narrower, the ceilings lower. The mood was dark;

like there had been a catastrophic fire and all the smoke had risen and gathered at the ceilings, so much so that as I walked back downstairs I felt the need to duck down underneath the imagined smoke.

She was in the kitchen, sitting at the black glass table, when I walked in. I went over to the fridge to get a drink, but her face told me not to. Something was happening. She told me to sit down. And I did.

She explained to me that she and Ben were going to leave. I had little chance to speak. She seemed well prepared. They were moving away, three hundred miles away. They had a house to go to. Ben had a new dad waiting for him. She was going to collect Ben from her parents to take him there that night. She had already collected the things she wanted to take. She would come to an agreement with me about the other things. The house would be sold. There was someone else too. A lawyer. He had already prepared some documents that she passed to me in a white envelope. I took them from her. Before I could open the envelope she told me what the contents were. She informed me that our relationship was over and that I couldn't change this now. Ben's new dad had provided her with a new mobile phone; she had cancelled her old one. I could see Ben, she said, in a few weeks' time. She would be in touch.

Throughout her oratory, she would pause and look at me inquisitively. I think she expected me to say something. I just stared blankly throughout. I did listen, though. I heard every word.

When she finished, she asked me whether I had anything to say.

"No," was my only word. I couldn't think of anything else to say. When I heard the front door close, I lit a cigarette. In the kitchen. Not outside. I smoked it quickly, gathering smoke into my lungs and blowing it out. The room quickly reverted back to its normal size. The smoke that had covered the ceilings minutes before had instantly lifted. I flicked the ash onto the cream kitchen tiles. When I had finished, I dropped the cigarette on the floor and crushed it beneath my foot. I lit another.

I repeated this until there was a small pile of filters on the floor.

I felt nothing.

I had already protected myself against this eventuality by partitioning my feelings. I signed the legal papers there and then and put them in the postage paid envelope the lawyers had provided. Then I just sat and stared.

I heard nothing from her for thirteen days. In that time I went to work as usual and came home as usual. I told nobody. The graph continued its downward descent, now more rapidly. I missed my son terribly. I hadn't partitioned this feeling. In my mind, I had given her two weeks to call before I would contact her parents. On the thirteenth evening, the words 'unknown number' appeared on my phone. I remember the call:

"Hi, Andrew."

"Hi."

"You okay?"

"Yeah, you?"

"Really good, thanks."

In the background I could hear excitable chatter. High-pitched laughter and a deep monster-like groan. The high-pitched voice repeated, "No. No. Daddy. Daddy. Daddy, no. No!"

"Is that Ben?"

"Yeah. He's just playing with…" The pause meant everything. "…with. He's just playing."

At that point there was nowhere further for the graph to fall.

"Can I speak to him?"

"Wait a second." There was some noise and her voice became muffled, but I could still hear her. The conversation I overheard went like this:

"Ben, Daddy is on the phone."

"Daddy, here."

"No, your other daddy."

"No! Daddy here."

"Come and speak to him, Ben."

"No!"

"Ben!"

"No. Want this daddy here."

I hung up the telephone.

It was then that I took the tablets.

Carly is sobbing. I am touched by her ability to express her emotions in this way. My mental programming means that I find the empathy stuff quite hard.

"You took the tablets?" she says.

"Yeah, not sure why I did that," I say glibly.

"Jesus. I didn't expect that, Andrew."

"I know. Fucking stupid, eh?"

She skilfully dodges my rhetorical question.

"And where's Ben now?"

"I don't know," I say. I'm embarrassed.

She looks puzzled.

"After the tablets, I moved back in with my parents. It was a pretty dark time, y'know."

She nods. She has stopped crying.

"Work were good. They gave me as long as I wanted. Said it was a shock. I didn't speak to anyone for months. Refused to see anyone. The usual…"

She strokes the back of my hand.

"The house was sold. Most of my stuff went. I just signed whatever my dad told me to. Took me a bit of time to get going again."

Her face encourages me to keep talking.

"After things improved, I tried to get in touch with Ben. But I didn't have her number, and her parents suggested it was better for Ben not to have me as a 'distraction'."

"A distraction?" she spits. She sits upright.

"Yeah. I think so. My head was all over the place. I believed them. I truly believed it was better for Ben."

"When was that?"

"About five years ago."

"You've not seen him since then?"

"Nope."

"You need to, Andrew." She stresses the word 'need'. She looks serious.

"I know," I say.

And I mean it.

chapter thirty-five

I wake at five a.m. on Saturday morning, exactly three and a half hours after Carly and I hugged and said goodnight.

I am gripped by the exact reason I never get drunk any more. My head throbs, a distressing pulse in each of my temples. This is not just a headache; the pain is all-consuming. It feels like somebody is drilling through my skull. I need the toilet, so I climb out of bed and relieve myself. I lie back down.

Butterflies gather in my chest, flapping at an alarming rate. My heart is beating too rapidly. I try to draw from memory the events of the night before. I cannot recall everything. The butterflies sense my uncertainty and flap more quickly in an attempt to gain my attention. My heart joins in. All the time my head pounds. My brain smashes from side to side and collides with my skull, which in turn increases the pain I feel.

I know I will feel better if I can just get more sleep. I close my eyes and imagine my head is sinking deep into a pillow made of soft, fluffy marshmallow. The pillow encases my entire head and allows me to sink deep inside. Momentarily, it is so comfortable.

My bladder tells me that I will never get back to sleep unless I attend to it again. I climb from the short-lived comfort and return to the bathroom. I squeeze out minuscule amounts of urine and return to bed.

My head pounds.

Boom. Boom.

My heart races.

I try to sleep again. My head. I am in agony. I am desperate. I just want to be asleep. Things will be different once I've slept.

Boom. Boom.

Flap, flap, flap.

I can hear my heart.

(I can actually hear it.)

I imagine myself sinking into sleep. I need the toilet. Again. I have a sharp pain that runs the full width of my body, just beneath my boxer shorts. As if my bladder is stretched to the point of snapping. It feels so full. I need to empty it. I get out of bed once again. A dribble. I get back into bed.

Boom. Boom.

It is the turn of the butterflies to take centre stage. They dart around inside me. I imagine there are hundreds, if not thousands. I can hear their wings. They are relentless. As they swoop inside me they remind me that I have something to worry about. Thoughts dive in time with the butterflies.

I can't remember everything I said to Carly last night.

What will she think of me?

She will hate me now.

I should never have spoken. It would have been safer not to open my mouth.

I try to tell myself that it is just a hangover. That I will be able to deal with things much better later in the day. The butterflies tell me that isn't true. That I've really blown it this time. That I'm worthless. That there is only one thing to do to stop all of this RIGHT NOW.

I open my mouth and pull the pillow over my face. I hold it there for a minute or so until the white cotton is damp, and then I pull the pillow away, sit up and gasp for breath.

I feel pain all over my body. My head. My bladder. My legs. My heart. And still the butterflies go on. Their excited chatter drives me into a thought process of their choice.

They are enjoying my suffering.

I can't stop their control.

I want to hurt myself. Until now I have managed to avoid the temptation of self-harm. I cannot understand why people make tiny little cuts all over themselves to release pain. Small vents to release small amounts of pain. The butterflies inform me that such an action won't help here. Pah, they won't be freed by a couple of little cuts or burns. They inform me that the only way to stop them is to take proper action. The type of action a proper man would take.

I pull the pillow over my ears to stop the sound of their voices, taunting and teasing me. The pillow simply encases their voices and makes them louder. The sound isn't coming from my bedroom; it's coming from within me.

I want them to stop.

They tell me they will.

If I just release them.

They want one action. A swift, deep wound between my ribs. Into my heart. A wound that opens up my insides and frees them. I imagine them racing eagerly from the gash, pushing one another to avoid the blood gushing down my chest. A few will be weighed down in the liquid and drop to the floor.

Plonk.

Plonk.

Plonk.

The rest will race for the outside air and fly freely around my head. Around my room. Until I am no more.

I leave the bed and pull on my pyjamas.

I must go downstairs.

I spend the rest of Saturday locked in a power struggle with the captive butterflies. As the day goes on, the pain in my head begins to subside. I no longer need the toilet. My heart slows a little and the butterflies begin to tire.

I spend fourteen hours alternating between the sofa and the back door. By eight o'clock I get the distinct feeling that I may have triumphed. The butterflies are exhausted. Aside from a handful that lightly flutter, they are now silent. I order Chinese food, watch a film and vow never to drink again.

By ten o'clock I am asleep.

It is Sunday. I have survived.

I wake early again, but this morning I don't mind.

The sun streams in through the bedroom window. Today seems better. For a couple of hours, I lie and read about Tom Luther, a guy I certainly wouldn't want to meet. I get to the point of his capture by the Colorado police authorities and turn the corner of the page to mark my place. To save time, I point the corner to the exact word I will read next time I open the book. This involves folding the page almost in half. I kick off the duvet, immediately releasing billions of tiny grey particles into the air. For a moment I am captivated as they twist and fall in the sun's rays. I make a mental note to dust my bedroom today.

The kitchen is also brightly lit and the floor tiles have been warmed by the early morning sun. I suddenly feel thankful that my house is positioned as it is. I run the tap until the water is cold and fill up a glass. I gulp it down too quickly, splashing it down my chin and onto my t-shirt. I wipe my shirt and then cup my hands under the tap and throw water onto my face. It is ice-cold and feels like tiny pins hitting my face. It feels good.

I go out into the garden and sit on a chair that has been there since Friday. The air feels good around me. I close my eyes and see red veins through my eyelids. I hear a sound and open them again. The blackbird has arrived and is sitting no more than ten feet away from me, perched in his usual position on the gate. He looks directly at me. I stare back at him. I feel there is an air of understanding. He moves his head from side to side, taking in different angles of me. I do the same and for a moment we are synchronised.

"What do you want today?" I say.

He moves his head to the right. His feathers swallow in the

sunlight and remind me of an oil slick. He seems to want to tell me something.

He opens his beak wide and sounds a loud, long chirp.

He then turns his ringed eye toward me and blinks.

He bends his legs slightly and pushes himself off into the sky. Although I don't know it at the time, I'll never see him again.

I spend Sunday cleaning. I play loud music and the drum beat drives me from room to room. I start upstairs and work my way through the house. I sing at the top of my voice. From time to time, I grab random objects (a vase, the hoover extension) and sing into them.

I realise that I probably haven't cleaned the house properly for three or four months. I do hoover each week, and of course I wipe the kitchen surfaces, but the rest...well, it doesn't get done. I don't really see the need. There is only ever me here. The mess is mine. The hair in the shower plug is mine. The dead skin that creates the dust came from me. I don't see a problem.

Regardless of my thoughts about cleaning in general, today just seemed like a day to put that extra effort in. Don't ask me why. By six o'clock every room is cleaned to the best of my ability. I won't lie to you and use the word 'spotless'. It isn't.

I know that I polished around things instead of moving them.

I know that beneath the sofa is a whole host of magazines

and various grey dust-and-hair tumbleweeds.

I know that I have thrown things into the spare room that have no real place anywhere else in the house. I can't see them. I closed the door.

Clouds have begun to gather outside as I finally move the kitchen chairs back to where they belong. I pick up the tartan picnic blanket and knock off a few filters that have clung heroically to the underside. I fold up the blanket and lay it just inside the back door. I then get on my hands and knees and begin to pick up the cigarette ends one by one, dropping them into a large, unused plant pot. Initially, I amuse myself by holding imaginary funerals for each unnamed soldier that I collect. This wears thin quite quickly, and instead I spend my time counting each one in an attempt to stop my mind drifting to unwanted thoughts. I realise that today is just the beginning of a much longer journey.

It takes me two and a quarter hours to realise that exactly four thousand eight hundred and eleven unfortunates lost their lives on the battlefield. I counted every single one. I tip the plant pot into the black bin for the third time, and stand back to admire my garden. The difference is uninspiring. The right-hand side of my garden now reminds me of a penalty area on the football fields, where I used to play with my friends when I was younger. The memory prompts me to set a reminder on my phone to return Ian's calls this week.

I close the back door and make a sandwich, which I eat

whilst my bath is running. As you know, I rarely take a bath, due to the time lost in doing so. A shower brings about the same result in a twentieth of the time. I suspect that I have been drawn into taking a bath by the fact that I have cleaned it today. The shiny chrome taps have lured me in.

I finish my sandwich and, as I head for the stairs, I notice a piece of white paper sticking through the letterbox. I grab it and carry it up to the bathroom. The bath looks enticing. I poured in some bubble bath I received one Christmas, and when I arrive foam is escaping onto the bathroom carpet. I switch off the taps and remove a sock. I dip my toe into the water and remove it quickly. It's far too hot. There is no room for cold water, so I plunge my arm to the bottom and hook my nail under the black rubber plug. The water is released and whilst it gurgles I undress.

I sit on the toilet naked and empty my bladder. I can reach the taps from here and I set the cold tap running. I unfold the paper and read:

Hi, Andrew.
Sorry I've not been over – busy!
Just a note to say thanks for Friday. Loved it! You're
probably the strongest person I've ever met.
Speak soon,
Carly x

Her handwriting reflects her personality perfectly; beautiful cursive strokes that stretch openly all the way across the note. Her words fit perfectly into the rectangle that I am holding. I put the note on the floor.

I plunge my arm back into the water and insert the plug. After flushing the toilet, I climb into a lukewarm bath.

I remember why I usually never take baths.

Half an hour later, I am in bed. I lie and think about the week ahead, cheered by the fact that my time in the office will be shortened by the conference on Thursday. I open my book and unfold the corner, eager to make sure that Tom Luther gets what he deserves in the end.

chapter thirty-six

My office is near empty when I arrive this morning. Martin and Elaine are the only ones behind their desks. My heart sinks. The events of the weekend have left me thoughtful and I was hoping to take a few days' annual leave. About a year ago, the company introduced the concept of 'duvet days'. I think this was an attempt to let the staff know that the company was forward thinking and 'cool'. The idea is simple. Staff are allowed to take two days' annual leave without giving (the usual) one weeks' notice. The theory is that you wake up in the morning, cannot be bothered to go to work and decide to spend the day in the company of your duvet. I suspect somebody in the higher echelons read about duvet days in Steve Jobs' or Jordan Belfort's biographies and decided to introduce it here. The only stipulations are that you must take the days consecutively and you are required to come into the office on the first day to personally clear it with your manager. The latter rule kind of defeats the object of the whole thing, unless you take your duvet with you on your commute to work. The lack of personnel in my department today means the chance of taking a few holiday days at short notice is less than zero. Regardless, I put on a smile.

"Morning both," I say, as I walk the length of the office.

"Morning. Good weekend?" Martin says. He looks straight back at his computer screen. He is gripping a stapler in his right hand. I don't think he is expecting an answer, but I give him one all the same.

"Yeah, great. You?"

He wasn't. I get no reply.

"Morning, Elaine," I repeat as I pass her desk.

"Oh, er, morning," she grunts, pretending she didn't hear my first greeting. "Good to see you're on time."

I bite my tongue. I am surprised that I haven't developed a lisp by now.

"Yep," I say happily.

"Don't get too comfy. Nick wants to see you as soon as you arrive."

I can tell she is enjoying what appears to be my forthcoming demise. She lifts her arm and scratches just below her armpit. Wiry black hairs spill out from beneath her short sleeve. I turn away and telephone Nick.

"Come in, Andrew," Janet says. I have been waiting in corridor outside the room she has just emerged from for the last twenty minutes.

"Thanks," I say.

I follow her into the room and sit on the same chair I sat on last time I was here. She introduces Mark again to me as if he were a stranger. I don't have the energy to correct her. Nick nods from across the table and mouths "Andrew" to me. I think he expected my name to make a sound, but it didn't. Janet shuffles some papers until they are straight and then places them down in front of her. Mark watches her and then does the same.

"So..." Janet says, "this is just an update really as to our investigation."

I pull my chair forward and lean in to listen.

Nick looks down.

"Mark will record our discussions and then at the end of this meeting we'll prepare some meeting notes for you to agree. These will then be placed on your file. You'll note that Nick is in attendance in place of Alan. This is simply due to Alan's imminent departure. Okay?"

I don't react. Mark begins his frantic scribble. He is pushing down far too hard on his pen – it's likely these notes will be imprinted on the entirety of his pad.

"So, we've interviewed all the staff in the department about the incident, and although those discussions will remain confidential, we can tell you that a similar theme ran through all the interviews."

"Okay," I say, opting for laconic replies as a strategy to push the pressure across the table.

She continues: "All the staff members have reported hearing a noise from the room where the multi-functional device is kept. A noise, followed by a scream."

"Right."

"Do you have anything to say about that, Andrew?"

"Not at the moment."

"Would you say that it was a fair summary, Andrew?" Nick

asks.

"Yes. Sounds fair."

Mark tears the first sheet from his pad and tosses it down. I cannot think what he has managed to fill the first sheet with; it's not as though his handwriting is particularly large. He begins writing again immediately.

"Okay," says Janet. She turns. "Mark, have you got a note of Andrew's response?"

Of course he fucking has.

"We have also interviewed the victim in this matter twice," she continues. "Elaine is obviously extremely distressed about your outburst and is fearful of being in the same room as you."

"Right."

I look at each of them in turn. I want them to know that I am considering everything that Janet is saying. I would not want them to get the impression that I was being flippant. I'm not.

"Do you have anything to say about that, Andrew?"

I'm silent for a moment.

"I do, yes."

Mark looks up from his pad and eyes me over the top of his glasses. Nick pulls his chair in.

"And what is it?"

"I have to say that I think the whole incident has been completely blown out of proportion. It was a simple accident."

For a moment, I'm afraid the friction from Mark's pen may start a small fire.

"That's not really what our investiga–"

"Sorry to interrupt, Janet, but the only thing that has come from your investigation is the fact that nobody saw the accident."

"Incident," Mark corrects.

"Accident," I say. "It was an accident and there were no witnesses to it."

Nick nods slowly.

"We do have a report that you..." Janet flicks through her notes and reads, "...purposefully kicked the drawer closed to injure me, er, Elaine, after finding out that he had not got the promotion."

"It's pretty obvious whose statement that is."

"Andrew, as you know we have to take reports of this nature extremely seriously. We cannot have staff – senior staff in this case – being scared or worried about coming to work."

"In all the years I have been here I have never once caused any issue for anybody," I argue.

"Elaine has also reported that since she was promoted your punctuality has left a little to be desired."

At that moment I know that I am fighting a losing battle. There is no possibility that I can turn this situation around. Minds are made up, decisions have been made and now cannot be changed.

"So what happens next?" I say.

"In respect of?"

"The investigation. The meeting. Today."

"Okay." She looks straight at me. "Nick and I need to

discuss the outcome of this stage of the investigation. We will then agree today's meeting notes and submit our report to the directors for consideration and for them to agree any further action."

"And what's the timescale?"

"Mark will email meeting notes to you today. If you could agree them before close of business, that would be good."

Mark nods eagerly.

"And then?"

"We'll submit them to the directors and get something in the diary..." She begins scrolling through her phone. Both Mark and Nick do the same. "...for, say, Thursday?"

"I'm not here on Thursday this week," I say.

"Okay." She scrolls with her thumb. "How about Friday morning?"

"I'm not here then either. I'm at a conference Thursday and Friday."

"Right. Well, it'll have to be early next week. Say, Monday ten a.m.?"

"Yep, fine."

Nick and Mark both agree.

"Well, I think that's all." She glances at Nick and he nods. "Thank you for your time, Andrew."

I push my chair back.

"Oh, just one final thing," Janet says. "In line with company procedures for incidents such as these, we'll be asking you not to come in tomorrow and Wednesday."

"Sorry?"

"You are free to work in the office today as the victim has meetings outside of the office for the rest of the day. Tomorrow and Wednesday please do not come into work."

"You are kidding?" I say.

"Think of it as a couple of days off," adds Nick unhelpfully.

"No, Andrew. I'm not," replies Janet.

"What about Thursday and Friday?"

"You are still employed by the company and I see no reason why you can't attend the conference. Nick?"

"Fine by me."

"Great. Well, thank you again, Andrew, and we'll see you on Monday."

Nick and Janet rise from their chairs. I'm not in the room long enough to see whether they offered their hands to shake.

By the time I get back to my desk, Elaine has indeed gone.

There are two long, shiny patches leading from the edge of her desk to her keyboard, which I assume have come from her arms. They indicate she has very recently left. The room is empty, aside from Jacob, who must have arrived after I left for my meeting. He is on the telephone. I skim-read three new complaint letters which have appeared on my desk. I have an overwhelming urge to write back to each and uphold their complaint regardless of whether it is valid or not. I lean back in my chair and stare at the ceiling until Jacob's call ends.

"Morning, mate," I say.

He wanders over and sits in Elaine's seat.

"Careful, you'll get accused of theft."

"You okay, Andrew?" he says genuinely.

"Yeah, I'm alright. Where is everyone?"

"Holidays. Well, Martin's in a meeting, probably about stationery or something equally thrilling. Elaine left a few minutes ago."

I nod my understanding.

"What did they say?"

"I don't know. Pretty much stitched me up."

I explain to him what happened in the meeting and tell him about being asked not to come into the office. He listens intently, shaking his head throughout. He waits until I've finished before he speaks.

"Makes you wonder whether it's even worth working for a company like this."

"Yeah, suspect I won't be for much longer."

"So what now?"

"Home for two days. Conference for two days. Meeting next Monday."

"It's ridiculous," he says. "There must be something in employment law or –"

I cut him off. I know he is trying to be helpful but I cannot cope with a conversation about a law that neither of us knows anything about.

"Yep, it is ridiculous. I suppose the only bonus is that I have loads to do at home." My voice trails off.

He stands and puts a firm hand on my shoulder. He tells me that if there is anything he can do to help, he will. We both know his statement, though well-intentioned, is hollow.

I am sitting in my car. It is exactly one minute past five. I do not want to drive home. Not yet. I have approved the meeting notes, signing them off as an accurate description of what was discussed. I resisted the temptation to add that I found the whole process a complete whitewash.

Much as I have other dreams in life to pursue, I do not want to lose this job.

Not yet.

I'm not quite ready.

I need the money.

I have someone who is waiting for me.

Someone who needs me to provide for them.

I start the engine and take a deep breath. I stretch my arms and hands and fingers out as far as I can and grab the steering wheel tightly. A quick look in the rear-view mirror and I begin to slowly reverse the car. I push the gear stick into first and as I drive away, I wonder whether I will ever return.

chapter thirty-seven

All of a sudden there is so much to do.

Strangely, I am thankful to be away from work. Usually, the thought of extended time in my own company would be enough to have me panicking within minutes. But now I have an unusual feeling that perhaps these days have an unspoken meaning attached to them. I am not talking about any of that 'fate' nonsense. None of that 'it was meant to be' rubbish that people tell themselves. As you know by now, I don't believe in any of that higher-being stuff. It's a feeling that somehow the conversation with Carly has fallen at just the right time for me. These are my first thoughts when I wake this morning.

I feel completely different. I pat at my face lightly with my right hand. Everything feels the same, yet nothing feels the same. As usual, I mentally scan my body, trying to identify any noteworthy or unexpected problems. My home MRI scan. There is nothing to report. I want to classify today as a Nothing Day™ but I can't. It doesn't feel like one. Neither is it either of the other two types of day. Far from it.

I kick off the duvet and rest my arms by my sides.

My legs are slightly parted and, looking down the bed, I see that I resemble the man you see on the door of a public toilet. I smile and begin mentally preparing a list of the things I have to do today. The vast majority of them are mundane: sorting the

287

spare room, painting, purchasing furniture, purchasing a new carpet. They may be dull, but they have a purpose. They are all small building blocks toward a much higher goal.

I realise that far too much time has slipped away from me. Perhaps now I've been able to let the words out to Carly, some room has been freed up for other thoughts. Maybe there really is a capacity to the number of thoughts we can hold. Perhaps we don't have infinite capacity to hold every thought. Sometimes they get blocked. Like the final hair that blocks the plughole. Nothing can pass until it is removed. Then the water can flow on. It feels good that my conversation with Carly has cleared the bottleneck that has existed for so long.

The sun streams through the window, casting a rectangle of light on the opposite wall. It looks like a doorway to a bright new world. As I stare at it, I ponder how I am going to approach the telephone conversation with my ex-wife. There is a little flutter in my chest, which soon disappears when I label its purpose. Before I can speak to my ex-wife I need to actually find out where she and my son are. It has been such a long time. I lift my phone and scroll through the numbers. I find her parents' home number. I take a deep breath.

My ex-wife's parents are nice enough people. I am sure that we had a more than acceptable relationship for the years I was around them.

Her mother is small and pudgy – a stay-at-home-and-bake type with a short, bowl haircut. From almost the first time we met, she would greet me at the door with a large smile.

Invariably, she would be wearing large oven gloves and she'd pull me close and hug me tightly, leaving a residue of dough and flour on the back of my shirt. On the rare days she wasn't baking, she would instead greet me by holding my face and looking directly into my eyes. "How are you?" she'd ask cheerily. "No really, Andrew. How are you?" Whether she was as happy as she consistently portrayed I have no idea. I personally don't think it is possible. Nevertheless, her perpetual smile was infectious. She was a pleasure to be around, especially as she smelled of cinnamon and hot sugar.

Her father, a tall, thin estate agent, took a little longer to warm to me. His staid, and at times aloof, demeanour was completely at odds with his wife's nature. I didn't see this as a reflection on me. I got the distinct impression that he was cautious with everybody. He is the type who only feels relaxed when entirely confident that he is with allies.

Over the years we became a close enough unit. Christmases together. One or two holidays in cottages around the north of England. You know the type of thing. Close enough that they sent a card and visited at least three times in the few months following the tablets. Of course, I didn't agree to see them.

I hope that they remember these times as I press the button to make the call.

The phone rings out.

And again.

And again.

And then it clicks, and there is a voice.

"Good morning," it sings. I recognise it instantly.

"Hello, er, Sandra?" I don't know why I turned this sentence into a question. I know the answer already.

"Speaking."

"Hi, Sandra. This is Andrew."

The line is silent. I imagine a wire rack filled with fresh scones falling in slow motion toward her kitchen floor.

"Andrew? Is that really you?" There is urgency in her voice.

"Yes. It's been some time."

"My God. How are you? Listen, let me just –"

I hear the scraping of a chair. She is breathing heavily.

"Sorry," she says, "I wanted to sit down. Sorry. How are you?"

"I'm alright," I say, "I'm alright. How are you? And Paul?"

"We're very well, thank you." Her voice is breaking. "Sorry. It's just so long since we heard anything from you."

"I know. I'm sorry."

Neither of us speaks for a few moments. It's awkward.

"Listen, I'm ringing to see whether you can give me a contact number for –"

"My daughter, I assume?" Her tone has quickly changed. She reminds me of a schoolteacher.

"Yes. And Ben."

"God, Andrew. After all this time you just ring out of the blue and think you can…well, I don't know."

"I'm sorry." I pause. "How is Ben?"

"He's really well, thank you. Doing really well."

We talk for a few more minutes. Each question and answer ends with an uncomfortable silence. She says that my ex-wife appreciates the financial support that my father has given over the years. She also tells me that she won't give me a contact number; instead, she will ring my ex-wife to see whether it is alright. I say that I understand. She promises me that she will ring me back and takes down my number. I say goodbye.

"Andrew," she says, her voice softening, "it's lovely to hear you sounding so well."

"Thank you," I say and the phone clicks down at the other end.

I don't recall any day I have previously lived beginning the way today has. I have achieved something before I have even left my bed. It feels good. It also feels good to know that I have a number of somethings to do today. This is different to anything I remember. I mentally scan my body and the results come back exactly the same as before. No unexpected problems or issues. I am ready for the day ahead. I cannot wait. This is a new type of day.

A Something Day™.

A day with a purpose.

I watch the sun's reflection on the wall and allow myself to imagine what may be on the other side.

I would usually be able to tell you exactly how many black bags of rubbish I have filled this morning. But today I am too wrapped up in my own thoughts to even bother to count. I wonder whether my theory of the brain's finite capacity could actually be true.

The best I can do is tell you that throughout the morning and into the early afternoon I have emptied the entire contents of the spare room. This will be the last of three journeys to the local tip. I am keen not to make any more, so I fill the car until I am unsure whether it will move. I hold the final bag in my left hand and stretch to reach the boot door with my right. As I do, a couple of bags begin to tip toward me. I manage to force the last bag into them and pull down the boot door just in time. A few items escape and scatter onto the road. I bend down to collect them.

I return to the house with two compilation CDs (without cases), an Irvine Welsh book and a small plastic toy. I believe their escape from the car has meaning. Something is telling me they shouldn't be discarded. What that something is, I don't know. I'm funny like that.

I lock the front door and walk to my car. The bags are pushed tightly against the side and rear windows. They resemble the contorted black faces of people desperately trying to find a way to escape. I will set them all free when I reach the tip.

Today I have rediscovered that the spare room has a light-green carpet. It is filthy with several dark stains that serve to secure the carpet's fate. Once I have painted the room, the carpet will be reunited with the black bags.

On my way back from the tip I decide to call in on my parents. I am visiting earlier than my usual Tuesday slot, and when I arrive I find that my mother isn't at home. My father therefore isn't in the garden. I feel a slight pang in my chest as I realise that my mother will be unhappy to have missed me. Later, this will lead to several calls as she tries to understand the reason that I arrived whilst she was out without telling her. I disregard the feeling. I don't have time for it today.

My father greets me at the front door and we hug. He wants to know why I'm not at work. I tell him I have a couple of days' holiday. "That's not like you," he says.

As we stand in the hall, I tell him about my earlier phone call. He is visibly shocked. Suddenly, he holds his chest and struggles to breathe. I help him sit down on the stairs. The step is too low for him and his knees point up toward the coving. I kneel alongside him and ask him if he needs anything.

He gasps again.

I can hear jets of air coming down his nose and then stopping abruptly.

Then silence.

I get to my feet and hurry into the kitchen to get a glass of water. I'm not entirely sure why. I figure I must have seen it on television. I return to the hall and kneel in front of him.

"Here, have some water," I say.

He takes the glass from me. His hand is shaking as he lifts it toward his mouth. He takes a drink. Water runs the length of glass and drips down onto his grey trousers. I watch a dark circle grow on his thigh. He can't swallow the liquid and he makes gurgling sounds. I take the glass from him and put it on the floor.

"Dad?" I say.

He turns to me and smiles. The water falls from the corner of his mouth and runs down his chin onto his neck. I pat him on the back and he tries to breathe again. He coughs, and then pulls a huge breath into the vacuum of his lungs. He pushes a small breath out, and then repeats the process. His body is collecting air. He sucks in another mouthful and pushes out a long breath through pursed lips. It whistles as it passes through. He breathes again, long and deep.

"Dad? Are you okay?"

"Yes," he says quietly, "I'm fine."

He runs his hands from his groin to his knees.

"Ooh," he says and turns to me. He looks confused and reminds me of a person who has been hypnotised returning to normality. His pupils dilate and he tries to focus on me. He smiles at me. I manage a brief smile before my face returns to a frown.

"What was that, Dad?"

"Oh, nothing," he says. He grips my hand; his is still shaking.

"Has this happened before?"

"Only once or twice," he says.

I get the feeling he is trying to protect me.

"Have you been to the doctors about it?"

"Yes."

"What did they say?"

"It's just shortness of breath. Nothing serious."

"Did they give you anything for it?"

"Just aspirin."

He tells me where the tablets are and I go and collect them for him. He pops them into his mouth and washes them down with water. I notice his hand has stopped shaking.

"Thank you, Andrew," he says, passing me the glass. He fixes his eyes on mine. "Listen. Don't tell your mother about today, will you?"

"She doesn't know about this?"

"I don't want to worry her. Let me speak to her."

I am left with the feeling that he won't.

I get my dad settled in his usual place on the sofa and go into the kitchen to make him a cup of tea. When I return, the pinkness in his cheeks has returned and he is smiling. We talk for an hour, uninterrupted, about the telephone call. He asks whether I am sure that I can deal with seeing my son – "y'know, upstairs". He taps his temple when he says this and I realise immediately what he is referring to. I reassure him and tell him that I feel I have had some kind of awakening. I immediately regret using the word. But it's too late; it has already come out. I go on to tell him that the time has come for me to make changes in my life. He eyes me suspiciously. He and my mother don't use words like 'awakening' and they come from a generation that views change with distinct wariness. I am convinced that my father has related the word to something inherently evil. I would bet my life that he now expects me to join some kind of religious hippie cult. I can tell from the look on his face that every word I speak is giving him more and more cause for concern. He is armed with the ammunition to conclude that 'upstairs' in my head has been burgled and the thieves have utterly destroyed the place. I quickly change the subject. It gives me great ironic pleasure to tell him that I've spent the entire day clearing out the spare room at home.

I tell him a little bit about Carly and he nods approvingly. I answer his brief questions about her age, background, job etc. and he mutters something about me "needing a pal to share my time with".

He finishes his tea and gets up to use the toilet. Whilst he is away I slide my phone from my pocket to check for missed calls. There are none. It is perhaps too early to expect a response. My father returns and I stand before he can get comfortable again.

"Right, I'm heading off," I say.

"Already?" he says, looking at his watch; then: "Oh! Is that the time?"

"Yep. I've got stuff to do."

"Won't you wait for your mother to come home? She'll be back in half an hour."

"I've really not got the time."

"Oh, okay. She'll be sorry to have missed you, you know."

I have edged to the front door. I post a finger into my trainer and pull it on. It's quicker than undoing the shoelaces. The tongue digs into the top of my foot. I look up at my father from the floor whilst I pull on the other.

"You'll have to apologise for me not seeing her."

"Yes."

"You can update her anyway, can't you?"

"Yes," he says, his brow furrowing. I wonder whether he'll remember. I stand and hug him. I feel his hands on my t-shirt, his strength gone. We part.

"You will tell Mum about your breathing, won't you?"

"Of course," he says.

He smiles unconvincingly.

I put the bin out and spend the rest of the evening preparing the spare room for the next morning. And intermittently worrying about my father.

chapter thirty-eight

I lay down the roller for the final time today. It makes its own way down the tray and immerses itself into the remainder of the paint in the reservoir at the end. A runaway steamroller finally ending its journey in a river of white treacle.

I lie on my back in the centre of the green carpet and stare at the room. The glare of the late-evening sun reflects into my eyes. Directly in front of me, near the window, it is difficult to make out where the wall finishes and the ceiling begins. The room is transformed. It has taken the best part of ten hours and three coats to cover the yellowed wallpaper beneath. For once in my life I have done the job correctly. I haven't cut any corners. I've filled holes, glued straying wallpaper back into place and sanded the woodwork down. I am especially pleased that the small cracks that littered the ceiling show no sign of returning. At least for now.

Apart from breaks for Coke and cigarettes (which, you'll be pleased to know, I deposited directly in the plant pot by the back door) I have worked solidly on decorating this room. I walk over to the windowsill and collect my watch. It's just after six. I check my phone for the umpteenth time today. Still no missed calls. I have decided that should I not have heard anything by tomorrow evening I will ring Sandra again. I am not expecting any calls from my mother as I managed to speak to her exactly thirty-one minutes after I left yesterday. We spoke and I explained the incident with my father to her. I know that he asked me not to, but I am quickly learning that sometimes I should just act and do what I think is right. She didn't sound as worried as I expected and I got the feeling there was something she wasn't telling me. She did, however, promise to take action. I wonder for a second whether she finished him off in the night.

I place my phone and watch on the carpet and begin sanding the windowsill. It is the same colour as the two fingers I hold my cigarette in. Random patches of wet paint cover my hands and as I sand, yellow flecks of gloss chip off and stick to them.

I hear a knock on the door downstairs. I sigh, but in all honesty I am ready for a break. I put down the sandpaper and rub my hands against an old Bon Jovi t-shirt that I have been using as a rag.

I open the door. It's Carly. She immediately giggles.

"Nice look," she says.

I look in the oval mirror in the hall. My face and hair are covered in a spray of white paint. A large piece of dried white paint sits like a mole in the crevasse where my nose meets my cheek.

"I've been painting," I say, dead-pan.

"No way!" She smiles.

"Come on in," I say, sweeping my arm in an arc and allowing her to pass.

We walk through the lounge into the kitchen. I pick up my cigarettes and head for the back door.

We sit outside on the ground, our backs leaning against the wall of the house, staring down the garden. She comments on the lack of cigarette ends on the ground. I pass it off as something I had been meaning to do for ages. She laughs and turns to me. I look at her. Our faces are no more than six inches apart. I notice that she looks more beautiful than any other time that I have seen her. In the interests of my new-found honesty, I want to tell her that. But I'm scared to. Freckles have developed beneath each of her eyes, forming two caramel-coloured half-circles. Her eyes look like perfect blue glass. The freckles continue down her nose and drift to nothing across her cheeks. I notice she isn't wearing make-up. She hasn't had to paint this beauty on; it is natural. I can feel warmth coming from her. Her lips look softer than anything I've ever seen. I have to stop myself from reaching out and touching them with my finger. She speaks:

"So…" she says. The word is long and flows through the air. We are so close that I feel I could breathe in and suck the word from her mouth into mine. And swallow it. To keep inside me forever. I wait for the sound to disappear. Before I can speak she continues: "How are you?"

"I'm good," I say. "You?"

I have a flutter in my chest. It feels nice.

"Really good," she says.

"Good."

The sentences are short and I feel that they are leading to something much bigger.

"What are you painting?"

"Spare room." I want to continue the theme of brief responses.

"Okay. Why?"

"Needed doing." I look into her eyes, trying to mentally project to her what I am feeling inside.

"Are you okay?" she says, sitting up and craning her head so she is facing me. The distance between us has tripled in less than a second.

"Fine, why?"

"I dunno. You just seem different."

She crosses her legs and sits opposite me. The moment has gone.

"No, not at all."

"So, the spare room –"

"I spoke to my Ben's grandma," I blurt out.

"What?"

"I called and asked to get in touch."

"Really? That's amazing."

She leans in to hug me. I shuffle forwards slightly so I can reach across her knees. I hold her for a second longer than she holds me. Her hair smells like freshly washed laundry. I rest back against the wall and light a cigarette.

I tell her about the day after the night I spoke to her.

I tell her that the relationship she shares with Abby has inspired me.

I tell her how gutted and profoundly ashamed I am about the years that have slipped by.

I tell her that I feel different; that getting the words out has made me hear them for the first time. That speaking out loud has allowed me to accept the existence of the fear inside. And now it has been uncovered, it's time to take it on. I am under no illusions that I can change my life with a click of my fingers. But at least I've raised my hand in readiness.

I realise that the journey I am about to make will not be easy. I expect many setbacks and I have no idea what the outcome will be, but because of Carly – no, because of myself – I now feel ready. As I tell her this, she blinks back tears.

"What's the matter?" I say.

"I'm just happy."

"Why?"

"With what you've told me. You're so strong."

"Nah." I shrug.

"You are. As for inspiration, I wrote you that note, didn't I? You've inspired me, you know."

"Yeah, how?"

She tells me that all she has done since we last saw one another is think. She tells me that thoughts have dipped and swirled like a kite through her head since Friday. She tells me that she has deconstructed every word I said to her that night. I interrupt her and ask how she can possibly remember my every word. She laughs and the freckles seem to jump from her nose as she throws her head back. She says that she drinks more than I do; she is skilled in storing information whilst inebriated. She tells me that she hasn't been able to sleep

302

properly. Thoughts that she has locked away for years have recently crept out in the night, sliding under the doors in her mind. Appearing unexpectedly. They have frightened her.

I wonder aloud whether in the short time she has known me she has become cursed with my thoughts. Perhaps it's dangerous being around me. Perhaps my racing thoughts are contagious. I worry about the worst pandemic the world's ever seen. She assures me that she hasn't become cursed – the thoughts she has been fighting with have been there for years. It is only from hearing my story that she has allowed herself to properly deal with the reality of what her thoughts represent. They've been dormant; ignored for years. Like my spare room.

When she finishes speaking, I go and get us both a can of Coke. I sit back down and she sits alongside me again. Our arms are touching.

"So, you come to any conclusions?" I say.

"I don't know. Actually, yeah, I think I have."

I turn to her. She continues to look directly ahead.

"I think I'd better prepare myself for plenty more bin days on this street."

I look puzzled. She doesn't see.

"What does that mean?"

"I think I'll be here a while." She turns to me. "Can't see it working with me and James."

"Really, why?"

"I think that too long has passed, y'know. We've been doing this for too long. We're just terrified to break the habit. It's time to move on."

"Yeah, maybe," I say.

We are both quiet. I stare at the sky. It is entirely clear. Its blueness is consistent in all directions. A solid powder-blue. It is like being inside the eggshell that surrounds everyone on this planet. Aside from the intermittent sound of birds chattering, it is entirely peaceful. I am expecting small cracks to appear at any moment, because just on the other side of the shell – in the vast, infinite blackness – I know that the meteor I have been expecting is heading directly toward me. I tell Carly that I don't mean to be rude but I really have to finish the spare room. I don't want it on my to-do list. As we reach the front door, she asks whether I need a hand. I thank her for the offer but tell her I only have a bit of sanding and glossing to do. She said she doesn't mind.

I see my opportunity and ask whether she'll bring my bin in as well. She does.

We then take it in turns to sand the windowsill whilst the other sits and watches. We also take it in turns to choose music. We both sing loudly. Each time I rest I check my phone. Nothing. Carly insists on painting the windowsill herself.

My shoulders and back are beginning to hurt, so I let her. I lay on my side on the stained green carpet, my head resting on my hand. I watch her sing and paint.

And I am convinced I see the intensity of the little red heart above the house on her skin increase.

chapter thirty-nine

I am sure that when packing for a conference most people have some kind of business luggage. In fact, I know this to be the case (pardon the pun) because I've seen my fellow delegates appear in the hotel reception at the same time as I do, and generally they have luggage that befits their position in whatever company they are representing. They have a small black leather case with a long silver handle that they use to pull the case behind them. Over their shoulder they carry a matching suit bag. Inside, a spare suit and shirt or two, folded in half.

At the check-in desk, they will pull out another essential item. The matching leather document holder. Their accommodation confirmation email is safely stowed inside. There is also a handy sleeve in which they store their company credit cards. If you look carefully, you can see their initials etched in gold on the side of each item. I know this is true because I have spent hours watching these people. I am absolutely sure that a fourth and final matching item – the cosmetic bag – is tucked deeply away somewhere in their case.

I open the back door of my car and throw in my rucksack. I hang my spare shirt behind the driver's seat.

A third consecutive Something Day™.

I could get used to this.

It will take around five hours to drive south to the hotel where the conference is being held. This means a lot of time alone with myself. Depending on the type of day I had awoken to, this may have been enough to make me sick with anxiety. Or for me to hope that I would be involved in a collision of massive proportions. One where they clean bits of me off the motorway for days.

This morning, though, I have woken again with the feeling that there is something waiting for me. Something worth opening my eyes for. I have made a small list of things I need to do on the journey. I have also made a compilation of songs, which will save me from being sucked into some tedious radio phone-in.

I drive singing and smoking for the first hour before referring to my list for the first time.

I press the telephone button on the touch screen in front of me and, using the small grey knob, scroll through my contacts list. It is one contact longer than it was this time yesterday. Carly has been added. She has made me promise I will ring to say I have arrived at the hotel safely. She texted me this morning to remind me and to wish me a safe journey. I thanked her and told her I would drive carefully.

I find the number I'm after and push in the knob. The car is filled with a short hiss and then I hear the blast of the dialling tone. I turn the volume down.

"Hello?"

"Ian? It's Andrew."

"Hiya, mate." His voice is quiet. I turn the volume back up.

"You okay, mate?" I ask.

"Yeah, you?" (The first word of his sentence is evidently a lie.)

"I'm good, thanks. What's up? You sound terrible."

He begins to breathe more deeply.

"I'm okay. Well..."

"What's happened, Ian?" I'm worried. I've never heard Ian sound like this before. He is usually self-assured. Resolute. Strong. I am immediately ashamed by the length of time it has taken for me to contact him.

"It's Anäis," he says. "She's left me."

"Jesus," I say.

"She's gone, with the kids."

"When did this happen?"

"I dunno, three weeks ago." He sniffs. "Left a note."

"Fuck. I'm so sorry I didn't get back to you sooner."

"Don't worry."

"And what's happened since? You spoken to her?"

"Yeah. She's got someone else, mate. She's in France."

"With the kids?"

"Yeah."

We talk for another half an hour. I am worried. The way Ian talks scares me. He doesn't feel that there is any point now. His voice is barely a whisper. Like he is struggling to push words out. Like he is struggling even to breathe. He says he has had enough. I am convinced that he has.

Threats of suicide are just so throwaway, so disposable nowadays. Social media kids threaten it on a daily basis. They colloquially throw it around simply as a means to grab attention from their friends or followers or whatever they are called. Don't get me wrong, some of them really are suffering, they really do need help. The rest of their peers don't help with their free and easy use of the word. Those who need someone to hear them get lost in text static.

I'm from a generation where we don't say it unless we mean it. Ian says it. And I know he wouldn't say it to me, especially me, unless he meant it.

"Listen, mate," I say firmly, "you know everything about my life. I can promise you right now that nothing is ever as bad as it seems."

I am as shocked as you are to hear myself say this. Ian is silent.

"Ian? You still there?"

"Yeah," he whispers.

"Listen to me. I'm going to fly over, okay? I can be there on Saturday."

"It's okay. There's no need."

"Ian. I'm coming. I'll sort a flight when I get to this conference and I'll be there Saturday morning, first thing. Maybe even tomorrow night."

"It's fine, Andrew. Honestly."

"I'm coming over whatever you say, okay? You promise that you'll meet me at the airport?"

He begins sobbing again.

"I will," he says.

"No. I mean it. You promise me you'll be there?"

"Yeah, I will. Promise –"

"'Cos I don't want to waste money on a flight..." I joke.

He manages a laugh through the tears and sniffs.

"I'm not made of money, y'know."

"I know."

"Listen, I'll text you in a few hours with the flight details, okay?"

"Cheers, Andrew. Really appreciate it."

"No problem. See you soon, mate."

"You will."

I drive for another hour in complete silence. Out of all the people I know Ian always appeared to have the warmest glow coming from his windows. Always. I used to model my life on the way that he lived his. He seemed to take each step so easily.

Girlfriend.

Job.

House.

Wife.

Better job.

Child.

Bigger house.

Child.

Better job.

Bigger house.

I followed each step he took. I tried to take his strides, replicate his pattern. I envied how easy he found it all. I was playing a dangerous game. I blindly followed each step of the way wondering why I wasn't as happy as he appeared to be.

Ultimately, I couldn't do it.

I failed.

I've already told you about the place that took me to a near death sentence, commuted to life in prison. Where I remained until I was unexpectedly released on licence, at least for the time being, a few days ago.

The last cigarette has dried out my mouth. I need a drink. I drive for a few more miles and pull into the motorway services.

chapter forty

I arrive in Starbucks. I intended to grab a coffee and continue my journey to the hotel. This is what I would usually do. Race to the destination. Get settled. But now I've arrived here I just feel so tired. So drained. There is no rush to get to the conference. I decide that I will follow the advice of the motorway signs and 'take a break'.

I order a flat white coffee and a cookie and pay the cashier. As I put my wallet into my trouser pocket, I am bundled to the side by an overweight woman who wants a better look at the slices of cake. I am instantly reminded of Elaine. The woman bends down, almost pushing her face against the curved glass counter. Both her hands are on the glass, helping her to keep balance. She seems to be trying to smell the pastries. I can see down her vest, so I avert my eyes and stare at the rows of white and green cardboard cups instead.

Fortunately, my coffee arrives quickly and I grab my cookie from the counter and leave.

I find a place by the window overlooking the car park. In the distance I can see cars whizzing north in the direction I have come from. A waitress cleans the table around me and removes a discarded newspaper. I stare out into the distance and am suddenly struck by the thought that this is likely the last time I will ever represent my company.

A very real sadness descends on me. I have committed nearly

a decade to this company. I can honestly say that I have given my everything. I am sure that I'll find another job. Maybe even change direction altogether. It is the nature of my leaving that saddens me. I contemplate the events of the last few weeks. One moment I was arriving at work hopeful of a promotion, and then, within a day, I was effectively ejected. One human destroying another. I ponder just how fragile each and every human being's world is. How quickly any path in life can be extinguished.

In a heartbeat.

It's done.

It's over.

Find a new life.

I sip my coffee and watch the cars. I stare for so long that they begin to blur in front of me. They become long ribbons of colour. I wonder what is happening in the lives of every single individual in every single car. The only thing that I can be sure they share in common is that at this moment they are all going in the same direction. I wonder how many of the people will have their world extinguished today.

I break the cookie in my hands and feed small fragments into my mouth. It tastes good. The taste of the biscuit and small chunks of chocolate remind me how lucky I am. One of the fortunate people. Yes, my life is about to change significantly. I consider that when I return to the office first thing on Monday morning, Elaine will be waiting. She will be keen to tell me that I have to attend a meeting immediately. Her face will be an excitable red and she will be wearing a smug look, knowing that I am walking into a corporate death. I feed another piece of cookie into my mouth and wonder how unhappy Elaine must be in her personal life to take enjoyment from my destruction. I cannot comprehend it. Then, I will be called into that bland grey room with those same three people who, after half an hour of following company protocol, will ask me never to return to my workplace.

But this won't destroy me. It will, at best, disrupt me. The sun breaks from the clouds and sends a huge shaft of light onto the motorway. The reflection of the metallic ribbon temporarily blinds me. I place my hand above my eyes to shield them. As I stare into the distance, the cars become dark silhouettes crawling over the edge of the horizon. I consider that there will be people within those cars who will have to deal with trauma and tragedy incomparable to my insignificant predicament.

A man will receive a call to say his child has died in an accident.

A woman will find out that she has terminal cancer.

Another will find out that her mother or father has passed away.

These are the real problems. These are the very fabric that defines the fragility of life. The other matters that crop up on a daily basis are just part of living. They are there to be dealt with. They are there to help us in some way keep moving. To remove any inertia.

I finish my coffee.

313

Before I continue my journey, I visit the toilets and whilst at the urinal I try to guess which of the four men on the advertising poster in front of me are impotent. I suspect it's the tough-looking construction worker. Sadly, the poster doesn't reveal this.

I return to my car, start the engine and pull forwards. I pass a petrol station before reaching a long slip road that leads back onto the motorway. As I reach the top, I see the seemingly endless stream of cars going the same way as I am.

I have no doubt that, similar to their compatriots heading north, the people heading south will have to deal with far more problems than I currently have.

I light a cigarette and remind myself again how lucky I am to be alive.

chapter forty-one

I continue my journey toward the hotel. Before I began transforming the spare room, I stored several numbers in my phone that I noted down from internet research. It was in my mind to make the best use of the time I have whilst driving, to plan the future. I ring the first. The female receptionist at the university answers.

"Could you put me through to the admissions department?" I ask.

She answers affirmatively and I hear three long tones before a second female voice answers.

I explain to the lady that I am hoping to enrol on a course. She asks for my name, address and email. She asks whether it's okay to call me Andrew and I say that it is. She talks me through the process and explains a little bit about the university and the courses offered. She has been trained extremely well, as she can answer almost all of my questions about the course and the modules that I would need to sit. She also explains the costs and the funding needed to take the course.

"I suppose I should have mentioned this at the beginning..." I say, suddenly realising that I may be automatically disqualified from enrolling on what seems to be the perfect course.

"Yes?" she says patiently.

"I don't have any qualifications aside from A levels."

My heart jumps as I wait for her response. A tiny feeling of fear, but excitable fear. Like waiting to find out whether you've convinced the man you are tall enough to ride on the roller coaster.

"Oh." She says. "Can I assume that you are over twenty-one, Andrew?"

"How rude," I answer.

The line is silent.

"I'm just kidding – yes, I am. I'm well over twenty-one."

"Right!" she says, sounding relieved. She goes on to explain that due to my previous qualifications along with having worked for the years I have, she can't foresee any issues in my getting on the course.

"Fantastic," I say. My stomach flips again. It feels really nice.

The lady promises to send me out the various application forms and the course prospectus in the next few days. I thank her. For once I am actually looking forward to the post arriving. Something interesting in the pile of bills and invitations to apply for credit cards with extortionately high interest rates. I light a cigarette and smoke it in silence. The bluish smoke dances for a moment around my head before being sucked through the open gap at the top of the window.

I telephone the next number and have a similar conversation. This university doesn't offer criminology, but does have a number of interesting psychology courses. Again, I am assured that the relevant information will be sent to me.

I work through the four numbers I have stored, and when

I finish the final conversation, I pull my knees together and scream loudly. I'm excited. Change will be good for me.

The rest of the journey drags and the optimistic sunshine is covered by a grey blanket as I get closer to my destination. The headlights of the approaching cars shine brightly as the sky stirs itself like a giant candy floss machine. Cloudbursts threaten ominously overhead. Everywhere but inside the car is grey.

I begin to think of the events of the last month – you know, to the time you and I first met. Something has definitely changed for me. I'm not sure at this moment exactly what that is. I'm concerned that you may think the things I've told you are not true. I can assure you that they are. I promised that I would tell you everything with total honesty. I've kept my half of the bargain.

You may find it difficult to believe my life has changed over such a short period of time. We both know that life can change forever in a heartbeat, never to be the same again. A matter of weeks therefore shouldn't be such a leap of faith.

I am sure that my path would have led to a wholly different destination had I not chosen to be honest. I don't like to think where that may be.

I find Polar Bear Club on my iPhone and sing loudly as I follow the endless rectangles toward my destination.

317

I turn the music right down. I tend to do this when I am in unfamiliar surroundings; it is an unnecessary distraction.

I am relieved to be away from the tedium of the motorway as I weave through narrow country roads toward my destination. I pass through a small market town. I am surprised that at this time it is already deserted. The conference is at a new venue this year and my satnav tells me I am now only a mile or so away. I light a cigarette as a reward to myself for successfully getting this far. I indicate left and wait for a space in the oncoming traffic.

I join the dual carriageway which is separated by a perfectly cut green hedge. It runs like a large Mohican down the centre of the road. Within a few hundred yards, I am instructed to turn right through a break in the hedge. As I wait to cross the traffic, I notice the hotel standing proudly at the top of a hill. In front of it are vast, lush gardens which fall steeply away as they reach the edge of the road. The hotel reminds me of a stately home. It is likely the former home of some seventeenth-century dignitary or politician.

A gap appears and I turn into a thin sand-coloured track, then immediately pass over a small humped stone bridge. As I cross, I see water that wasn't visible from the main road running beneath me. It's not quite a river, but a little large for a stream. A huge temporary sign has been erected alongside the track. In massive green letters it states: 'THEB Insurance welcomes guests to the conference.'

The track widens and continues to climb toward the hotel. About halfway up, I pull to the side to allow a white van to pass. The man waves; I wave back.

As I reach the top, the track opens into a large area in front of the hotel. A stone fountain sits in the middle, surrounded by hedging and numerous topiaries clipped into fantastic twisting shapes. The sand track becomes cobbles which form an enormous turning circle around the fountain. A smartly dressed man in a long black morning jacket and top hat directs me toward the car park off to the left. I find a space easily and collect my belongings from the car.

The fences surrounding the car park are covered in balloons that fight and struggle with one another in the wind. Grey and green balloons alternate, and I notice that each is stamped with the corporate logo of THEB.

Once, I used to get very excited about these events. Aside from the night away from home, which always makes a nice change, the main reason was the level of hospitality shown to each of the delegates. I know that once I get inside the hotel reception I will be swamped by green and grey everywhere. The insurance company will ram these colours down our throats from the moment we arrive until the conference finishes. The first time I attended such a conference, I remember being shocked by the sheer scale of the marketing. Before I even manage to get to the hotel reception to check in, a representative

319

of the insurance company will shower me with grey pens, green pens, pads, post-its, golf tees, mugs, wallets, mints, watches, soft toys, calculators – you name it, each and every one covered with the THEB name and logo. A colleague of mine once came back from an insurance company event with an iPad. I've never been that lucky.

If it rains tomorrow, I'll be provided with a complimentary THEB grey-and-green golfing umbrella. If the sun shines, I'll be given a complimentary grey-and-green cap and visor set. Seriously.

Everything – and I mean everything – from the moment I walk into the hotel will be free.

Unlimited food.

Unlimited drinks.

Unlimited grey.

Unlimited green.

The gravel cracks under my leather soles as I make my way across the car park. I turn the corner in front of the hotel and take a deep breath.

chapter forty-three

The smartly dressed man holds open the giant oak door for me to enter the hotel. He offers to carry my bags for me, but I refuse and thank him. I have never been comfortable with the master and servant relationship. I get the same feeling in a restaurant when a waiter refers to me as 'sir'. It immediately makes me feel that I am being seen as superior. It makes my chest tighten. We are all equal.

Inside the hotel foyer, it is quiet. I have obviously arrived earlier than expected. The lack of activity in the car park is testament to this. The insurance company is clearly not ready for delegates to arrive. Over to my left, I see two men and a woman emptying a number of brown cardboard boxes onto a long table. The smaller of the two men is removing green mugs and lining them up in neat rows at the far end of the table, carefully ensuring that the THEB logo on each faces forwards. The woman is removing grey name badges from a smaller box, rubbing each on her lapel to remove any fingerprints and lining them up in a similarly regimented way to the mugs. The taller man is speaking into his phone.

I make my way over to the long reception desk and put my rucksack down. I lay my spare shirt over the top of it and wait for a staff member to arrive. The foyer is enormous. The ceilings stretch high above me, meeting the walls with intricate gold-painted coving. Ancient-looking tapestries hang from most walls. As I wait, I realise that I am being watched by the taller man. As I turn my head toward him, he immediately takes a profound interest in a tapestry behind me. He is a picture of insurance company perfection. His grey suit is cut to fit him perfectly. He wears a white shirt and a green tie. His cuffs escape his jacket sleeves to display gold cufflinks shaped in the company logo – I have no doubt that they are solid gold. His dark hair is brushed back and has been sprayed so it dare not move. His face is a golden orange colour. Like syrup. I suspect he may have been using the corporate fake tan. He reminds me of a host from an afternoon TV quiz show.

At that moment a pretty blond girl appears behind the desk. Her badge tells me her name is 'Grace'. I inform her mine is Andrew Walker. I give her my credit card and she runs it through the machine on the counter. I tell her that I am attending the conference. She smiles and, in a whispered voice, tells me that the hotel is fully booked and that everyone in the hotel is attending the conference. Her accent reminds me of a Cold War Bond girl. I raise my eyebrows and she giggles. THEB has everyone where they want them. We are all cornered with nowhere to run. The hotel's stately home surroundings are a perfect setting for a murder mystery. This one is slightly different, though; all the delegates are victims. She passes me a form I am required to sign in two places, before she removes the perforated portion and folds it around a plastic room key. Tonight, I will be in room 512.

Grace points me in the direction of the lifts and I thank her.

She smiles again.

As I leave the reception desk I notice two further guests are being welcomed into the hotel. Both are wearing suits and are carrying a selection of matching black leather cases and bags. The quiz show host finishes his call and is instantly upon them. I stand and watch. Within moments their hands are full of branded stationery. Each are given grey calculators. With green buttons. I suspect they are strangers, yet they throw back their heads and laugh like old friends. They take it in turns to toss a sentence-long anecdote for the others to feed on. I overhear them being told that there will be a meet-and-greet-drinks-and-canapés bash in the main bar at six thirty. It is essential that they have registered and collected their name badges prior to that time. Their conversation seems to be coming to a close.

I am keen not to be ambushed by the quiz show host and so I walk quickly toward the lifts passing numerous sofas that run down the centre of the vast room. The sofas are placed back to back. I imagine a giant game of musical chairs. The perimeter of the room is lined with more sofas, positioned in the alcoves. A low coffee table guards each sofa. I reach the lift and press the gold button marked 5. It is circled by a red light and I wait for the doors to open. I check my watch, two hours to go. I will stay in my room until six twenty-nine and fifty seconds.

The less time with these parasites, the better.

And to be honest, I don't really need any stationery.

I leave the lift and head in the direction of my room. The corridors are quite dark and the ceilings are low. At each corner an individually lit sign tells me whether I am going in the right direction. I follow the signs and appear to have reached a dead end, until I push open a small, nondescript door which leads through to another identical-looking corridor. I twist and turn around corners, passing numbered doors which are accessed up (or in some cases, down) three or four stairs.

I continue my journey through yet another random door. Exactly the same corridor presents itself and I wonder whether I am just walking around in circles. The ever-changing door numbers suggest not. I am reminded of The Shining and wonder whether I will meet my fate wandering eternally around a maze.

Finally, the signs tell me I am close and I count down aloud from room 520 as I pass each door. I've arrived. I insert the key card into a silver panel to the right of the door. The panel buzzes and the door promptly clicks open. I walk inside and throw my rucksack on the floor. It collides with a small fridge.

The room is spectacular. The ceilings reach high enough to allow an enormous silver chandelier to hang above the bed. (This is in stark contrast to the height of the corridors, and I wonder for a moment how architecturally that can possibly work.) The chandelier is lit by dozens of bulbs. There are two large sash windows immediately ahead of me. Window seats are hidden behind tasteful maroon netting. I can just see the main road from the window. The bed looks lost, even though three sets of pillows stretch horizontally across its head. A maroon chaise longue has been placed at the end of the bed, no doubt to keep it company. I wander around the room, touching random objects like my mother would at a church jumble sale.

In keeping with the rest of the room, the bathroom is enormous. Ahead is a walk-in shower, complete with three different shower heads, the lowest positioned at a very personal level. A cast-iron bath stands off to my left. It has been painted maroon, its feet silver. Opposite the bath are two sinks. Various free toiletries are lined along them. I will sweep these into my rucksack before I leave.

I kick off my shoes and lie back on the bed, my feet still touching the floor. I push my fingers into my jeans pocket and prise out my phone. There are no messages. I am reminded that I made a deal with myself to wait until seven tonight before ringing Sandra again. And that is another three hours away.

I am uncomfortable, so I stand and empty my pockets onto the desk near the window. Cigarettes, lighter, car keys, wallet, coins, phone. It is no wonder I wasn't comfortable. I collect the hotel information folder and carry it over to the bed. I am killing time. I lie back down, my head on the pillows, and begin to read. I find that the hotel was once home to Isaac D'Israeli, the famous father of the English prime minister many years before. I wonder whether he got as lost as I did trying to find his bedroom.

I am uncomfortable again. I get up and wander around the perimeter of the room, opening the cupboards and drawers.

They are all empty. I sit on the window seat and watch the fountain for a few moments. The padded cushion keeps slipping from the seat, so I stand again. I fill the kettle and start it boiling. I decide that my difficulty in relaxing must be to do with my jeans. I remove them and climb back onto the bed. I am suddenly cold and decide to get under the covers.

For the next hour I am tormented by small bat-like creatures with grey and green reptilian skin. They live inside the enormous chandelier and fly at alarming speeds clockwise around the room. Then, in perfect synchronicity, they all land on top of the huge maroon pelmets above the curtains. From there they watch me with unblinking red eyes. They make no sound. All of a sudden they take flight again, their scutes glimmering in the light. For most of the time all I can see is grey and green blurred trails left in the air like a sparkler. I am fortunate that the sound of my telephone humming on the desk wakes me. I rub my eyes and climb out of bed to get my phone.

I sit on the edge of the bed and swipe the screen. As I do I glance up at the curtains, just to be sure. I have three missed calls, all within the last five minutes. It appears that it was the last call that finally woke me from my unanticipated slumber and rescued me from D'Israeli's Chupacabras.

All the calls are from Carly. I notice the time; the conference registration and welcoming party begins in less than forty minutes. I suddenly experience a hollow feeling in my chest. Then a tiny fluttering, like I have swallowed the bats whilst asleep. I begin to breathe quickly. I am not sure why this feeling has arrived and I consider this sudden change.

Is it the calls from Carly?

Is it that shortly I am to be surrounded by the insurance vampires, attempting to suck business from me?

Is it because I haven't had a call regarding Ben?

Is it my impending change of career?

Is it my father? He was breathing like this. Wasn't he?

I begin to suck in air and force it out. My apparent need for oxygen becomes urgent. My brain needs it – quickly. My heart is pounding. The fluttering increases. I realise that sitting in my boxer shorts staring at my phone is not helping. But I am frozen. I cannot think what to do. I continue to suck in air and blow it back out. I feel like I am breathing in reverse. Like my intakes of breath should be when I breathe out and vice versa. I read somewhere that when this happens I should breathe into a paper bag. I cannot remember the last time I even saw a paper bag. My mind is spinning. I need to take action.

I stand and make my way to the bathroom. I switch on both taps and water cascades down into the bath, making a heavy smacking sound as it hits the porcelain. I unscrew the lid on a tiny bottle of bath foam and empty its contents under the burgeoning waterfall. I discount each one of the reasons as a cause for this sudden fear. My thoughts continue to race and my heartbeat dictates that I must find a meaning for its thudding pattern. But I'm unable to find anything. I'm satisfied with everything I've considered. None of the reasons equate to this feeling.

I collect my phone and lay it on the sink in the bathroom. I remove the remainder of my clothes and leave them in a pile on the floor. I stare at my unremarkable face in the mirror and look deep inside the eyes of the reflection. "Why?" I say out loud. I watch the movement of my mouth as I form the words. I say it again. My lips purse, as though I am blowing an imaginary kiss to myself. Try it; you'll see what I mean. I repeat the word again and again.

I personalise it.

"Why, Andrew?" I repeat.

Over and over.

I'm hopeful that if I say it enough times, my reflection will break the pattern and answer me. As I repeat the mantra I realise that there is no reason for these feelings. They are just part of me. No need to panic. No need to understand them. They are just me. It's time to embrace them. Allow them to be. There is nothing to fear. My heart rate begins to slow. My racing thoughts approach the finish line. I needn't think; that just feeds them. My face visibly lightens in front of me.

And then the phone rings again. It excitably vibrates towards the sink. I grab it before it gets too close to the edge.

"Hello you!" Her voice sounds silky. Flirty.

"Hi there," I say, conscious that I am naked.

"Just ringing to see if you got there safely?" she says.

"Yep, I did."

"What time did you arrive?"

I glance at the clock on the phone. "Hmm. I dunno, a couple of hours ago maybe. I've been asleep."

"Seriously?" She laughs. "Long journey, eh?"

"Sure was."

"I bet it was. Well, I know you'll be busy with your insurance people –"

"Lucky me. Do you wanna swap places?"

She giggles again. "Er, no thanks. I'll leave that to you."

"Thanks."

"I just wanted to make sure you were safe," she says in a near-whisper.

"Thank you. I am."

"Okay. Right, I'm gonna go and let you get on."

"Yeah, I'd better get ready."

"Listen, Andrew, do you fancy going out for something to eat when you get back? You know, like, just me and you."

"Yeah. That'd be great," I say. And it feels like it would.

I don't want to hang up quite yet, so I tell her about Ian, and that my trip will be a little longer than I first anticipated. She sounds genuinely sorry for Ian. We agree I'll call or text to let her know where I am over the next few days. I say goodbye and she says the same. I lay the phone on top of the pile of clothes and step through the bubbles and into the bath.

chapter forty-four

I have to say that in general I love staying in hotels. I would have thought that you are probably the same. Most people I have spoken to agree. There is something quite exciting about pushing open the door to your room for the night. The reason may be that you get to step into your own private universe. Somewhere different from the norm.

Thinking about it, I do stay in hotels quite regularly. Perhaps once a month. This is, after all, the nature of my job. Huge layers of governance are passed down to each and every regulated company in the field where I operate. These are basically the rules of doing business. Massive fines are handed down to those companies that don't follow the rules. Therefore, my company makes sure that staff are sent to conferences and seminars whenever possible, so we have the knowledge to avoid us receiving a fine. I would need twenty hands to be able to count on my fingers the number of times Nick has sent an email to tell us that we could be closed down for not following the rules. Then I'd be out of a job. Which, currently, is pretty ironic.

My love of hotels comes from a genuine interest in each and every person staying in the hotel. I am fascinated by what it is that has brought those people to the same place as me on that same day. I will usually position myself somewhere in the bar where I can see people arrive and, later, leave. There, with a novel in my hand for subterfuge, I'll sit for hours simply watching people. I take in their clothes, their hair, how they walk, sometimes (if I am close enough) how they speak. I watch with wonder and try to imagine who they are, what they do for a living, whether their life has more meaning than mine. I never tire of it, even though I seldom, almost never, find out whether my imagined thoughts are correct.

I watch people as they take calls and wonder who they are speaking to and what they are speaking about. I rarely actually talk to any of them. In fact, I rarely talk to anybody at the hotel except the staff. I'm not one of those people who will just go up and introduce themselves to some stranger. To be able to do this requires a large assumption that anyone would be vaguely interested in speaking to me. I sometimes watch other people do it and wonder where they developed such a strong sense of self-confidence. Or arrogance. It's a thin line.

On an evening in most of the hotels I visit, you will find individuals scattered throughout the bar and lounge. One of them will be me. I will have quickly bored of my private universe and headed downstairs in search of humankind. To ensure there was no apocalypse whilst I was in the bath. My fellow guests will sit at tables where invariably the other three chairs are vacant. You can guarantee that they will have a phone on the table in front of them. Probably their room key as well. Sometimes those essentials will be accompanied by a novel or perhaps a black leather business folder. There will usually be a bottle of Peroni or a clear drink garnished with ice and lemon as well.

In the past, at times of extreme boredom or frustration, I have considered introducing myself to a stranger. I have even worked out the words in my head:

"Hi, I'm Andrew. Do you mind if I sit here?"

I have concluded that it is highly unlikely that I'll receive a negative response to this question. People are generally polite. However, once they've agreed to my question the next line is a little harder. I suspect that they'll expect a reason for my targeting them. That I have something important to say. I haven't yet worked out what that may be. The only times I've seriously considered seeking company is when I've been in one of those moods where I cannot settle on anything. An evening where I've flicked up and down the channels a hundred times on the TV in my room. Or when I've been in the bar and read the same sentence in my novel for the eighth time and still have no idea what the scene unfolding is. At those times I have closed my novel, eyed the room and selected somebody to sit with. Somebody I imagine is my type of person.

You won't be surprised to learn that I have never actually carried this through. I have always stopped myself. I've often asked myself why. I don't think it's because I'm shy. I'm not. Not really. I think it's because I am extremely interested in why the person is there, why our paths crossed; but, conversely, I have no interest in telling them why I am at the hotel. I have no interest in explaining to them my job, where I'm from, my home life. If I wrote an autobiography, I'd call it Why Would

You Want to Know About Me?

And I mean it.

I suppose that this is because I'm not my type of person.

You'll note that I did caveat my love of hotels with the words 'in general'. I'm glad I did too, because today I have no love for this hotel. It's not the place. It's the people. We are all here for the same reason. A hotel full of people who all do the same job that I do every single day. To make things worse, we are all paid-for guests of the grey-and-green parasites that swarm around the room. That appear around each corner. I think you'd agree that this destroys the magic.

The lift doors open. Off to my right, I see the archway that leads to the bar. I take a deep breath and walk towards the table to register for the conference.

chapter forty-five

As I reach the registration table, I realise that I am late. I can see that most of the delegates are already at the bar, holding drinks.

I notice that they are predominantly male. Smartly dressed employees from THEB wearing their corporate colours hover around offering drinks, making introductions, ensuring that everybody joins in. Their aim is simple: to deliver the corporate message to everybody present. Near the bar, a group of men are crowded eagerly around the quiz show host. He is telling a story, though thankfully I am too far away to hear it. They are listening intently. All eagerly waiting to laugh.

I approach the registration desk and am greeted by the badge woman. The desk is near-empty. One or two mugs remain. She asks my name.

"Andrew Walker," I say.

"Right." She runs her finger down a list. Most of the names have been crossed out. She finds me near the bottom. "Oh," she says, "the second today."

I nod. Frankly, I'm not interested.

Her eyes turn to the table. Three badges remain. She picks mine up and passes it to me. It is rectangular and made of brushed chrome. My name is etched into it in green. "If you could pop that on?"

I take the badge and pin it to my shirt. She looks relieved.

"Mug?" she says as an afterthought.

"No, I'm fine, thank you," I reply.

She straightens the remaining two badges on the table.

"You can join the party," she says, nodding toward the crowd.

I thank her and walk in the direction of the bar.

I spend the next half hour on the fringe of the quiz show host's group. I decide this is the best strategy, as he clearly loves to talk, which means I won't have to. My mind drifts in and out of the conversation whilst I take small sips of my Coke. There is suddenly a rapturous crack of laughter, and I open my mouth, pretending to join in. I make no sound. He then begins a story about the largest life insurance policy he ever sold. The members of the crowd jostle for position. I am more than happy to be pushed to the outskirts. I watch them whilst he speaks. Their eyes are directly focused on the quiz show host. They laugh when he does. He reminds me of an evangelist, his followers waiting on his every word. Like children crowded around Santa.

I feel my phone buzz in my shirt pocket and remove it. I don't recognise the number. I march quickly past two or three similar groups, apologising as I knock the elbow of a fellow delegate. I reach the quiet of the reception and take a huge breath. Then I answer.

"Hello?" I say.

"Andrew?"

I recognise the voice. I doubt it'll ever leave me. I walk quickly towards the lifts and sit on one of the many vacant sofas that surround me.

"Hi."

"Hi, Andrew. Mum said you called."

My heart pounds.

"I did, yeah. Thanks for ringing back."

"It's okay."

"How's Ben?"

I hear a sniffle at the other end of the phone. At the same time, I hear loud laughter followed by a huge round of applause. The sound is coming from the bar. I push my finger into my left ear.

"Where are you?" she asks.

I tell her I'm at a conference. Down the vast hall, I see the delegates filing from right to left. One peels off and begins heading in my direction. He seems flustered. As he hurries past me I recognise the character on his tie: Mr Grumpy. I smile – my father used to read the Mr Men books to me as a child. The man notices me staring and suddenly changes direction and disappears behind where I am sitting. The rest follow the quiz show host like an army of ants and disappear through a large dark-oak door into what I assume is the dining room.

"Oh, right," she says.

"So, how is Ben?"

"He's great, thanks. Doing really good. Really good." She sniffs again.

There's no easy way to do this. I have to be brave.

"I'd like to see him."

"Andrew. It's been years."

"I know. I'm sorry. I understand he has another dad. I get that. I get that I haven't been there for him. I get it all –"

"Stop," she says, "stop. You don't get any of it. You haven't been there. You can't just ring after years and say that you 'get everything'. You don't 'get' anything."

I am silent. She is, of course, right. I don't get any of it. I haven't been there through anything. I don't even know how tall he is. How long his hair is.

I can hear her breathing.

"You're right," I finally say. "I just want a chance, that's all. I won't let him down ever again. I –"

"He hasn't," she interrupts. Her words are resolute.

"Sorry?"

"He hasn't…" She pauses. "…got another dad. We broke up."

"Right."

"A couple of years ago. Not seen him since." I sense regret in her voice. I imagine she is shaking her head as the words drift from her mouth.

"Oh. I didn't know. Sorry." I'm not entirely sure why I am apologising but it seems an apt thing to do.

"It's okay."

I feel the conversation heading nowhere. I have to bring it back.

"I want to see him. I want to be there for him."

Tears run down my cheeks.

"It's been so long, Andrew."

"I know. I know. I need him, though. I need to be there for him. I need –"

"How are you, Andrew?"

My eyebrows wrinkle.

"Sorry?"

"How are you? Personally? You know…" She pauses to let me complete the sentence. I do.

"The tablets? That's behind me. A dark time. Really dark."

"I have to think about Ben. There's only me, y'know. And Mum and Dad. I need to do what's best for Ben."

"I know. I understand. Will you at least think about it? Maybe we could meet up and talk about it? Or something?"

"I'll think about it. I've got your number now. I just need some time, okay?"

"Yeah, of course."

I don't know how else to respond.

"This has come out of nowhere, Andrew."

"I know. I'm so sorry."

"I'll call you," she says, "after the weekend."

"Okay. Thanks."

"It's okay," she forces out through her sobs.

I sit back on the sofa and hold the phone in both hands. I just stare. My butterflies return and dance joyfully inside me. I know why they are here. They are here to celebrate excited anticipation. They bring back a memory from when I was a child. They are the butterflies that came in the week leading up to my birthday; when I was woken in the dead of the night to go to the airport; on the night before Christmas.

I realise that they have always been with me.

They are part of me.

It's up to me to define their intentions.

I get up and go outside.

I need to smoke.

chapter forty-six

I remove a cigarette from the packet as I walk through the hotel entrance. I take out my lighter and place the cigarette in my mouth. I have second thoughts; it doesn't seem right lighting it in front of the main door. I don't know whether my choice comes from respect for the history of the building or the sight of the smartly dressed man standing in the moonlight, his arms clasped behind his back. He nods as I pass him, touching the edge of his top hat with his white gloves.

The light from the huge windows illuminates the cobbles. As I pass I look inside. The delegates are sitting around huge circular tables. Some have adjusted their chairs so they can see the speaker at the front. He is standing behind a lectern, speaking into a microphone. A giant THEB logo is projected onto the wall behind him.

I round the corner and stand near my car. I light my cigarette and suck in the smoke. I want to tell somebody about the call. I consider calling my parents, but decide that it would be better to tell them once I know when (whether?) I can see Ben. I text Carly and tell her I've spoken to Ben's mum, and that I think it was a positive call. That I am hopeful. Her response is instantaneous. She can't wait to hear more, and she sends one kiss. I tell her I'll call her tomorrow and send one back.

I finish my cigarette and flick the end into the night sky. It somersaults like a broken firework and lands on the bonnet of a white Porsche.

I return to the hotel and make my way across the almost-empty bar. I order a Coke. The bartender informs me again that everything is free. I think he is hinting that maybe I want something stronger than Coke. I thank him and tell him that I am fine.

I turn and notice the flustered man I saw earlier. He is sitting alone at a table by the window. The end of his blue tie perches on the edge of the table. It reminds me of a waterslide. I note that he is wearing a similar badge to mine. In front of him is a half-full glass of lager. I lean against the bar for a moment and watch him. I realise that we are both missing the evening meal. I wonder why he is here. In this bar, at this moment. I know why I am and it's not because of the call. It's because I don't want to be here. Around anybody connected to this apocryphal excuse for a career. Around any of these people.

I smile.

I am escaping this life.

I am starting another.

The man walks a square beer mat across the surface of the table. It makes a knocking sound as he rotates it ninety degrees onto its next edge. It's slightly hypnotic.

Suddenly, I am compelled to speak to him.

He is the only person in this hotel I may have something in common with.

I need to know.

I need to know his story.

I watch him for a little longer until he becomes aware of me. I smile and nod. He nods back and I walk over. I am nervous. I have never done this before. I stand behind one of the chairs, my hand resting on the velour fabric. He places the beer mat down.

"Hi there," he says.

"Hi. Didn't you fancy the meal?" I inflect the 'you' to let him know that it's okay if his answer is affirmative. He is the same as me. We are comrades.

"Nah. Not really."

"Me neither."

The man is a little older than me. He has short brown hair, cropped neatly above his ears. He wears thin-framed silver glasses. He has an untrimmed brown beard, which is gradually being taken over by wiry grey hairs that poke through. Both his elbows are on the table, his cheeks resting on his fists.

"Sit down," he says softly.

"Cheers."

I pull out the chair opposite him.

He offers his hand. "Andrew," he says.

"Me too," I say, pushing my badge out.

He straightens his back and chuckles. He moves his hands to his lap. "Seems we're the same person, Andrew."

I look at his badge. It is the same as mine. Exactly. The same green font displaying 'ANDREW WALKER' across the chrome background.

"No way," I say. "What are the chances?"

"It's a pretty common name," he says, "especially where I'm from."

I realise that he didn't understand my question. My question was literal. What is the actual chance of him having the exact same name as me? Especially on the occasion of me approaching a stranger for the first time in my life? I am momentarily shocked. I think that he sees this in my face as he furrows his brow questioningly.

"Did I say something?" he asks.

"No. Sorry. I was just, just thinking."

"Right," he says.

This could be the most short-lived dialogue in my history, I need to take action. The conversational flame is already flickering in the wind. It could soon be extinguished.

"So," I say, "the meal. Not hungry?"

He leans forward. His eyes dart around the room as he makes sure nobody else is in earshot. "To be honest, I don't want to be here. I couldn't care less about these people. I'm not interested in free drinks and free food." He counts on his fingers as he explains: "Free pens, free pads, free calculators, whatever."

I nod. "I'm the same."

He looks slightly suspicious.

"In what way?"

I lean in. "I don't want to be here either. I can't stand

listening to these people."

"So why come?"

"Work sent me. This is the last one for me. I'm gonna do something else."

"What like?"

"I've got a few ideas. Career change, though. Something completely different."

He agrees with me. He tells me that this is his last conference as well. He tells me that after the weekend he is likely to be sacked. He corrects himself: 'managed out' of the company. He tells me of his new boss, and an incident where he was blamed for purposely injuring her. Apparently, he trapped her arm in the photocopier. He chuckles as he relates this to me.

"You know," he says, "it all sounds so ridiculous when I tell somebody else. Sacked for trapping a colleague in a fucking photocopier."

I laugh. "It's pretty original."

"Yeah. It is."

He tells me that he hasn't yet told his wife or children about the possibility of losing his job, so as not worry them. He has been at the same company for just under ten years and feels he has been badly treated. I ask him about bringing a case for wrongful dismissal. He believes he has a strong case.

"But I reckon instead they'll give me a pay-off," he says. "Maybe three months' salary. I don't care. The sooner I'm out of the industry, the better."

Then he asks: "So what's your story?"

I tell him that I've simply had enough. Of the job.

Of the direction in which my life was leading. In fact, I tell him the story I've been telling you. Kind of. I don't go into details like I have with you. After all, I have only just met him. No, I wanted to tell you everything, because talking worked with Carly and I really don't mind now if you tell everyone you know. But I tell him a little about my home life, about my plans to leave work and study criminology and of course, Ben. I also tell him I feel like I've had some kind of epiphany. He laughs.

"Mid-life crisis, eh?"

"Not at all. I just realised that there's more to life than work..." I show the palms of my upturned hands. "...than this."

He furrows his eyebrows and nods repeatedly. He tells me that he has a small amount in savings that will get his family through the remainder of the year. He is ready to move on now. To do something else with his life. He tells me that he is fascinated by watching people. That he'd love to write a novel and has always wanted to be a college lecturer. He says he is going to pursue both. He declares that the incident is "almost certainly for the best".

I admire his positivity. I am not sure that I would be able to move on as well if I had been pushed. It feels better to be the one making the decision. But we are different people and his resolve impresses me. I tell him of my career plans and he nods approvingly.

We talk for more than an hour, and although we've never met before, I feel strangely close to him. Maybe the connection

345

is simply his name. Or perhaps that we are both changing our lives and taking different directions. Our conversation is interrupted by a large round of applause coming from the dining room across the hall. I turn to look. Moments later, the smartly dressed man pulls back the oak door and hooks it to the wall. Through the door, I can see the delegates getting to their feet. The meal is over and in minutes the bar will be packed with people ready to take advantage of more free drinks. Only a few hours earlier they were strangers and now they will stand arms around one another, back-slapping and laughing – united by wine.

Andrew Walker stands and offers his hand.

"Good to meet you, Andrew," he says. "I'm escaping before they come back."

"I'm with you," I say.

We leave the bar and head toward the lift. I walk quickly, slightly worried that the quiz show host might apprehend us. I worry that I may have to explain my absence from the meal. I feel like a schoolboy playing truant.

When we get to the lift I press button five. Andrew presses two. My stomach flips as I await an imminent hand on my shoulder. Fortunately, the lift is already on the ground floor and the doors open immediately. We both get in. As the doors close, we watch the delegates shuffle and stagger their way across the hallway. They are all clutching grey folders.

"Phew," he says.

We both laugh and as the lift begins its ascent, he removes his tie.

"It was ironic, wasn't it?" I say, nodding at the blue fabric in his hand.

"Of course," he says smiling, "for my own amusement."

I laugh again.

Moments later the doors open.

"Well, it was good meeting you," he says.

I know that he means it.

He holds out his hand and I shake it.

"Yeah, you too."

I mean it.

"Good night and good luck," he says, leaving the lift.

"Yeah, you too. Take care."

As the doors close I watch him post his tie into a gold cylindrical bin. And then he is gone. I stare at the circular buttons as one by one they light up, counting upwards toward my floor.

chapter forty-seven

I am awake early and I lie in bed, staring at the enormous coving that stretches around the room. I feel entirely refreshed. I can't wait for today to begin. Whatever something the day has in store for me, I am ready. The thick duvet crunches as I roll over to retrieve my phone. I have a flight to book.

I turn on the television for background noise. Whilst I search for flights, I am rewarded with the same news loop every five minutes. The same soundbites from politicians; the same story of the displaced people of a war-torn nation; the same goal from Arsenal. I grab my wallet from the bedside table and enter my card details. My flight is confirmed for later this evening. I text Ian. He responds immediately and thanks me. I tell him there is no need, just to be sure to meet me at the airport. He confirms that he will.

I lie in bed and watch the news for another half an hour, then I burst into action. I take a long shower and shove my few belongings into my rucksack. I realise that I am now effectively under house arrest until the conference starts. I do not want to be caught sneaking through reception as the hungover delegates leave the breakfast room. I decide that it is better to wait in my room until the conference actually begins, then I can make my escape.

I have about an hour to wait, and I decide to call Carly. Prior to pressing the green button to connect to her, I spend ten minutes procrastinating and thinking about our previous call. I wonder whether I have misread her invitation to dinner. Perhaps she meant just as friends? I reread her texts and try to recall everything she has said to me over the last day or so. In the end I tell myself out loud to shut up and call her. She doesn't answer and her phone goes to voicemail. I listen to her recorded message long enough to take in every inflection in her voice and then hang up.

My instant panic that everything has changed is quickly dispelled when she rings straight back. She explains that she was just pouring some apple juice for Abby. I breathe a sigh of relief and then instantly regret that it was audible.

I tell her I'll be back in five hours. I need my passport. She asks whether there will be time to call in, "y'know, just to say hi." I tell her that there will. That I'll be home for about half an hour before leaving for the airport. She sounds excited and I imagine her clenching her fists and pulling her arms in tight in front of her chest. Her reaction makes me feel warm inside and I desperately want to see her smile.

I lie on the bed and pass the time watching a show about an idiotic couple who lost their life savings buying a ramshackle property somewhere in Bulgaria. At just after half past nine, I get dressed, brush my teeth and sweep the little bottles of shower gel, shampoo and conditioner into my rucksack. I am ready to leave.

I am thankful that the reception is entirely deserted when I leave the lift. I walk to the desk and wait. Grace arrives and smiles at me. I pass her my key card and she begins to type on her computer. The doors to the conference room are open and I hear a loud round of applause. Then, through a slightly too amplified microphone, I hear:

"Firstly, I'd just like to thank each and every one of you for attending today. It is much appreciated. Before we begin, I'd like to introduce myself."

Grace raises her eyebrows and pulls a face of mock excitement. I smile at her.

She grins. "Nothing to pay, Mr Walker."

"Can I go now?"

"Of course. The conference is –" She points to the open doors.

"Thank you."

"No problem. See you again."

I walk past the conference hall directly to the exit. The smart man is nowhere to be seen, so I push open the heavy door. The sun blasts directly into my face.

I drive over the cobbles and cross onto the sandy road. I look into my rear-view mirror. As the prodigious building shrinks, I feel that my old life is doing the same. The sun streams down onto the car bonnet.

My heart begins to quicken.

And the butterflies awaken and begin to gather in my chest.

I turn on my music. The Hold Steady.

Loud.

Guitars kick in.

The drum beat hammers at the same rate as my heart.

I know that the butterflies are here today to tell me something is happening. Something good.

I like how they feel.

There is so much to do.

So much life to live.

The vocals begin and I sing at the top of my voice.

chapter forty-eight

I don't know it when I leave the hotel, but I will never speak to Andrew Walker again.

I wonder whether he even bothered to attend the conference the next morning.

I wonder whether he did get dismissed on the following Monday. He seemed pretty sure that he would. If he did, I'd be interested to know whether he did leave the industry. Maybe he just settled for the next job that came along. For the sake of his family. That's some sacrifice. I hope not.

Maybe he will be attending the annual conference until the day he retires.

chapter forty-nine

I don't know it when I leave the hotel, but I will never speak to Andrew Walker again.

I wonder whether he even bothered to attend the conference the next morning.

I wonder whether he managed to get into university. He seemed focused. He certainly seemed to know that the time had come for him to change his life. I wonder whether he got to see his little boy. I suspect so. The way he spoke convinced me that he would make up for the time they'd missed together until his dying day. I don't think I've ever met someone so unwavering. So steadfast.

I have no doubt he won't attend the conference next year.

Or any other year.

AUTHOR'S NOTE

A Tiny Feeling of Fear can be read as one novel or two novellas. The left-aligned chapter headings relate to the first Andrew Walker. The right-aligned headings relate to the second Andrew Walker.

ABOUT THE AUTHOR

M Jonathan Lee was born in Yorkshire, England where he still lives to this day.

When not writing, you'll find him standing at the back door thinking.

His first novel, *The Radio* was nationally shortlisted in the Novel Prize 2012. *A Tiny Feeling of Fear* is his third novel.

HIDEAWAY FALL

web: www.hideawayfall.com
twitter: @hideawayfall
facebook: /hideawayfall